FOLLOW YOU DOWN

Michael Bradley
Amberjack Publishing
New York | Idaho

AMBERJACK
PUBLISHING

Amberjack Publishing
1472 E. Iron Eagle Dr.
Eagle, ID 83616
http://amberjackpublishing.com

Publisher's Cataloging-in-Publication data
Names: Bradley, Michael, author.
Title: Follow you down / by Michael Bradley.
Description: New York, NY; Eagle, ID: Amberjack Publishing, 2018.
Identifiers: ISBN 978-1-944995-55-3 | 978-1-944995-56-0 | LCCN 2017948562
Subjects: LCSH Attorneys--Fiction. | New York (N.Y.)--Fiction. | Camps--Fiction. | Bullying--Fiction. | Reunions--Fiction. | Revenge--Fiction. | Thrillers (Fiction) | Suspense fiction. | BISAC FICTION / Thrillers / Psychological
Classification: LCC PS3602 .R34273 F65 2018 | DDC 813.6--dc23

Cover Design: Dane Low

For Brian, John, Keith, Leo, Steve, and Anthony. Thanks for making our long overdue reunion nothing like this one.

CHAPTER ONE

IN HIS TWENTIETH-FLOOR apartment, Neil Brewster was sweating. His disheveled chocolate-brown hair was matted with moisture. Beads of perspiration formed across his broad forehead, one dislodging and racing down the cheek of his tapered face to his chin. It hung for a moment and then plummeted six feet, spattering upon impact with the black treadmill belt.

Through a nearby window, Neil watched the Monday morning sun breach the horizon, casting a faint orange kaleidoscope across the towering steel and glass forest of the Manhattan skyline. It'd be another hour before the streets began to swell with pedestrians. Even in his upscale part of Manhattan, the homeless wouldn't be far behind, sitting on street corners with their hands out. The thought alone disgusted Neil. *They should just get a job like everyone else*, he often thought.

As his gray running shoes pounded on the treadmill, Neil glanced at the display positioned above the forward hand grip. Forty-four minutes. One more to go. His chest heaved with each breath as he maintained a steady pace through the final stretch of his workout.

To the thirty-six-year-old defense attorney, these early morning moments of solitude were sacrosanct. No phone. No discussions. No interruptions. Neil considered it his Mecca, his quantum of solace. Even his fiancée knew better than to enter the room while he was working out. It had happened once. It never happened again.

The daily workout characterized the intensity with which he lived every day of his life. From eager Harvard Law School graduate to the most sought after defense attorney in New York, his forceful nature had helped accelerate his career, skyrocketing him to eminence among his fellow attorneys and making him the bane of every prosecutor in the city.

As the display passed forty-five minutes, the treadmill slowed to a cool-down cycle. As his pace slowed from a full-on run to a fast jog, Neil permitted his mind to finally begin processing the day ahead of him and, most importantly, the case on which he was currently working.

He knew it'd be easy to sow doubt about the bloodied baseball in the minds of the jury. The police could only tie it back to his client, Rodney Sinclair, because it was found nearby when he was arrested. It was circumstantial at best. The two witnesses claiming to have seen the New York State senator's son beat the homeless man to death should be easy to break during cross examination. Especially if his legal aides had been successful in digging up some dirt over the weekend. It was the eight ounces of cocaine found in the trunk of Sinclair's BMW that would be tricky. Neil hadn't quite determined his angle on that yet, but he knew he would. He always did.

When he crossed the hall from the exercise room to

the bathroom, he paused for a moment to glance into his bedroom. Sheila was still asleep, laying huddled beneath the beige silk sheets, her long auburn hair flowing down the pillow onto the bed. He was tempted, for a moment, to slip beneath the sheets for an early morning grope but decided against it. Smiling, he moved on toward the bathroom.

In the shower, Neil allowed the near-scalding water to flow over his trim physique. As he scrubbed his chest and arms with a washcloth, he continued to contemplate the details of the Sinclair case. Lost in his thoughts, he wasn't aware that Sheila had slipped in behind him until he felt her arms wrap around him and her breasts press into his back. Neil smiled. "You're awake."

Sheila kissed his earlobe. "When I heard the water, I just couldn't resist." Even in the steamy shower, her breath against his skin was warm and arousing. Her hands reached up to caress his chest, causing him to draw in a deep breath.

He turned to face her, watching the water cascade through her hair, down her firm breasts, and over her smooth legs. With her eyes half-closed, her lips parted in anticipation. Wrapping his arms around her slim body, he gripped her butt in a tight grasp, pulling her toward him, and kissed her hard on the lips. Neil felt her lean backward into the cold tile wall, pulling him with her. As her nails raked down his back, he knew he'd have to disappoint her. When their lips parted, Sheila's mouth formed an exaggerated pout, as if she already knew what he was going to say.

Reaching up, Neil touched her cheek. "It's Monday morning. I don't have the time."

"You always say that."

"It happens to be true."

She smiled. "I'm beginning to wonder if you're just using me for weekend sex."

"Not just weekends."

Sheila laughed and leaned forward, giving him a brief kiss on the lips. "At least it's great sex."

Stepping out of the shower, she reached for a towel and began to dry herself. His eyes locked onto the curves of her sleek body, admiring its soft skin and shapely form. It hadn't been easy for him to turn her down moments before, but sex was just sex. He could get that anywhere if he wanted. It was his well-cultivated reputation as an attorney that made him who he was. Neil smiled as she leaned over to dry her legs, making him pause at the sight of her voluptuous ass.

"I'm one goddamn lucky bastard."

"What was that?"

"I said I'm lucky."

Still bent over, she glanced back at him, smiling. "You could've been just now."

He laughed, grabbing the bottle of shampoo from the small shower shelf. He poured a generous amount into his hand and began to lather his hair.

"How's Rodney's case coming along?" she asked.

"Good so far, as long as he doesn't say something stupid."

"Rodney isn't the brightest of the Sinclair family."

He dipped his head under the shower head to rinse away the shampoo. "You know him?"

"Rodney's family has a summer home near ours in the Hamptons. Daddy's known the senator for years. Do you think he did it?"

Neil's mind harkened back to his first meeting with Rodney Sinclair. His pale complexion and the bags beneath his client's eyes had told him all he needed to know. Hearing his client's side of the story only solidified his opinion. Guilty as sin. But Neil didn't care. He wasn't being paid to care, only to get his client off. He turned the water off in the shower. "Of course he did it."

Stepping out of the shower, he grabbed a towel and began to dry his hair. Sheila slung her towel over her shoulder, gave him a teasing wiggle of her ass, and then left the room.

WHEN he entered the bedroom, Neil found Sheila curled up beneath the bed sheets once again. Crossing to the tall ebony dresser, he pulled gray bikini briefs from the top drawer. As he bent to pull them up his legs, a long sensual purr came from the bed.

He said, "No catcalls allowed."

"Oh, it's okay for you but not for me?"

Neil smiled. "Of course."

He moved to the closet, pulling out a white silk shirt. As he worked the buttons up the front, he glanced at his fiancée. She was leaning on one elbow, watching him dress.

She said, "I'm going with Gina today to pick out the bridesmaids' dresses. Do you have any preferences?"

"Something with a low neckline."

"Jerk. You just want to see their cleavage."

"My dear, yours are the only tits I want to see from now on."

She flopped back into the pillows. "Liar."

His only response was a smile. Theirs had never been a relationship based on love. Neither of them had any expectation of that. A sense of mutual attraction and reciprocal benefit was the only thing that kept them together. He had never completely figured out what Sheila really got out of their relationship. He'd always assumed she was there for the sex. Neil, for his part, had his eye on the wedding gift promised by Sheila's father: a senior partnership in Waldstein, Conner, and Strauss.

Reaching back into the closet, Neil pulled out the black slacks of an Armani suit. Sliding his legs into the trousers elicited a whistle from Sheila. After fixing a half-Windsor knot in his silk tie, Neil crossed to the bed and, leaning close to his fiancée, kissed her hard and long on the lips. He felt her hand touch his shoulder and glide down the front of his shirt, making Neil wish even more that he didn't have to leave. When their lips parted, he reached for his suit coat.

"Sorry. I've got to go."

As he stepped out of the bedroom, he heard, "Tell Daddy I said hello."

IN the kitchen, Neil placed a K-Cup—Caramel Vanilla Cream—into the Keurig and slid a mug underneath. As he waited for his coffee in silence, his eyes traced the random design in the gray granite countertop. He'd handpicked the granite slab himself three years prior when he was preparing to move in. It was a nice complement to the restaurant-grade, stainless-steel appliances and handmade walnut cabinets he'd specially ordered from an Amish furniture maker. Running his finger along the edge of one of the cabinet doors, he found a faint layer of dust on the tip. He'd have to reiterate to Maria what he meant when he said everything must be spotless. He paid his maid well and expected far better from her. Maybe he'd threaten again to report her to Immigration. That always made her shape up.

With his mug in hand, he leaned against the sink,

enjoying the morning's first sip of coffee. His eyes roamed the kitchen, falling upon the French-door refrigerator, and more specifically, a folded card hanging on the door from a red magnetic clip. The invitation had arrived ten days earlier in the mail, and it had intrigued him ever since. From across the room, he read the embossed words "You're Invited." The fancy silver script stood in contrast to the black front flap of the card.

When the invitation had arrived, it brought with it a flood of memories from Neil's childhood, many of which made him smile. The names listed within the card were ones that he hadn't heard in over eighteen years. Despite the fond memories, Sheila had seemed more excited about the card's arrival than he had.

"It sounds like fun," she had said, reading the card over breakfast. "You gonna go?"

Without looking up from the New York Times financial section, Neil shook his head. "I don't do reunions."

"Why not? They're your friends."

"Were. They were my friends. I haven't spoken to any of them in . . ." He paused to do a calculation in his head, "At least eighteen years."

"This would be a good time to get reacquainted."

The newspaper crinkled louder than it should have when he turned the page. His patience was thinning. "Sheila, I've no interest in getting reacquainted. No need to look back on the wistful days of my youth."

"Don't you ever wonder what everyone's up to?"

"No. Not in the least. I couldn't care less what my friends are doing right now." Sighing, he set the newspaper down, peering across the table at her. "I've got better things to do with my time than watch a bunch of sad losers try to reclaim the glories of their youth." He'd tried to keep the irritation out of his voice, but no such luck.

Sheila huffed in frustration. "Sometimes you can be such a prick."

Her words still echoed in his mind as he sipped his coffee. Despite his remarks to Sheila two weeks prior, Neil had held onto the invitation, leaving it hanging on the refrigerator where he saw it every morning. Although he had no intention of going, the invitation intrigued him, almost haunting him. The very idea of a reunion with old friends flew in the face of every philosophy he had ever lived by. He never looked back at his past and never kept in touch with anyone who could no longer provide value. Casting off irrelevant acquaintances had become routine, and his life was littered with the discarded relationships of friends, allies, and even enemies.

The invitation should have gone in the trash the day it arrived, but something had held him back. Taking another sip from his mug, Neil traced the silver lettering with his eyes, wondering what hold it had on him, wondering why he couldn't let it go.

CHAPTER TWO

Standing in his Manhattan corner office, Neil gazed out of the floor-to-ceiling window upon the cityscape thirty floors below him. His hands were buried deep in the pockets of his trousers as he rocked back and forth on the heels of his patent leather shoes. His eyes scanned the skyline, inspecting the windows of the buildings within his immediate view. He caught sight of an over-weight man two floors down in a window of the building across the street. The man's shirt sleeves were rolled up and his hair slicked back over a balding head. Like Neil, the man appeared to be admiring the scenery beyond his own window. When their eyes met, the man across the way smiled, giving Neil a quick wave of his hand. Neil, in response, returned a cynical smile, and then gave him the finger.

"Jackass," he said.

Where many might find his office view to be awe-in-spiring, Neil found it to be empowering. Looking down on people from such a lofty height wasn't just a metaphor. Standing before his window, he was a potentate surveying his kingdom from a high tower. Somewhere amidst that forest of glass, steel, and concrete were millions of lowly citizens working to support that kingdom, keeping the potentates like himself fat, happy, and rich.

"There are three kinds of people in this city," he'd once said to a reporter from the New York Times. "The filthy rich, who won't give you the time of day unless your net worth is followed by at least eight zeros. There are those of a similar intellectual and financial status as myself. Not too many of them around. And finally, there's everyone else. The riff-raff. The laborers. The middle class and below."

When the reporter seemed to be at a loss for words, Neil added, "In case you're wondering, you're in that last group."

The law offices of Waldstein, Conner, and Strauss occupied five floors of the office building, twenty-six through thirty. Neil's office was the most spacious, save those occupied by the firm's three senior partners. Two of the four walls were glass, providing him with an unobstructed view of Central Park and Manhattan's Upper East Side. Floor-to-ceiling bookshelves along the opposite wall were overrun with heavy bound volumes of legal reference books. His own expensive tastes were evident in the small Jackson Pollock hanging from the wall. It was one of the artist's lesser known pieces, but Neil had still paid a small fortune for it.

At the faint rap on his office door, he gave a slight turn of his head and said, "Come."

Hearing the door open, Neil returned his gaze to the view beyond his window. A sweet fragrance wafted into the office with its wearer, telling him all he needed to know. Chanel No. 5. He knew without looking who had just entered. Closing his eyes, Neil inhaled deeply, allowing the floral bouquet to invade his olfactory senses and elicit the hidden desires he harbored for the new arrival.

Dressed in a navy business suit, Jenni crossed the office with the grace of royalty. With her flowing blonde hair falling carelessly onto her shoulders, the twenty-six-year-old secretary flashed him a broad smile. She set a steaming mug on his mahogany desk. "Your coffee, Mr. Brewster."

His eyes traced the curves of her hips, then roamed up her body. "Ah, my morning vision of loveliness."

"Two sugars and two creams. Just as you like."

"Jenni, are you sure I can't persuade you to run off to the tropics with me?" He smiled. "We could make love on the beach every night."

Jenni tilted her head to the side, feigning embarrassment. "Now, Mr. Brewster. What would Miss Waldstein say?"

"Nothing. She'd never know."

Neil crossed to the desk, picked up his coffee, and took a slow long sip. Watching her over the edge of the mug, he admired the blazing blue of her eyes. He was certain she must wear colored contacts. No one could have eyes that blue. The color reminded him of his birthstone, sapphire. Sheila had gifted him a pair of cufflinks with brilliant sapphires embedded in gold for his last birthday, but Jenni's eyes put those to shame. Setting the mug back down, he leaned against the desk, folding his arms.

"Just between us, Jenni. If I'd met you first . . ."

"You'd still have chosen Ms. Waldstein."

Neil laughed. "Perhaps you're right." He tapped the desk with his finger. "If you won't run away with me, how about a quickie here on the desk?"

Some would call his comments sexual harassment, but he knew Jenni would never complain. She was paid well enough to tolerate his occasional inappropriate behavior. She'd be hard pressed to find an equivalent salary anywhere else. Besides, she seemed to enjoy their little tete-a-tetes. And who knew? Maybe one day she'd give in to his advances.

As she touched his shoulder, Jenni gave him a mischievous grin. "You're a naughty boy, Mr. Brewster."

"You can call me Neil, you know."

She turned toward the door. "I know, Mr. Brewster."

With his eyes swaying in accord with Jenni's departing hips, Neil gave a soft whistle, causing her to stop just long enough to wag her index finger at him. When she pulled the door closed behind her, Neil began laughing out loud. Grabbing his mug from the desktop, Neil returned to the window.

WHEN he entered the conference room, Neil's three legal aides were already seated around the oval table, awaiting his arrival. Kaitlyn Stranton looked up as he crossed the threshold, sliding the tortoiseshell reading glasses from her round face.

"Good morning, sir." The laptop resting on the table before her cast a whitish glow on her tanned skin. She'd changed her hairstyle over the weekend, Neil noticed. The charcoal hair was now close cropped and parted over her left eye. *Makes her look like a man,* he thought.

Jamie Peters, who was sitting across the table from Kaitlyn, pushed his laptop closed and rested his hands on top. Neil had only ever found one way to adequately describe Jamie—Ichabod Crane from *The Legend of Sleepy Hollow.* That seemed to say it all.

Emily Ross, the oldest of his three aides, didn't even look up when Neil entered. Her fingers continued to tap with a fervor on her laptop keyboard. Her molasses-colored hair, which she had pulled back into a ponytail, was streaked with gray. The gold medallion around her neck was accented with an oval-shaped piece of turquoise. Neil thought it, as well as the matching earrings, were gaudy as hell.

"Nice necklace," he said, hoping his sarcasm wasn't too subtle.

Rounding to the table's far end, Neil folded his arms, looking back down at his three aides. They were supposedly the best in the firm, but Neil sometimes wondered. These three, by far, had lasted the longest. There had been a time when Neil went through legal aides about every three to four months. On at least two occasions, he'd sent a crying aide running from the office, never to return. These three were pushing a year, with Emily Ross having the most seniority.

"I'm assuming you all worked through the weekend. Tell me it was fruitful."

Jamie was the first to speak up. "Harriet McCartney—the witness who claimed to have seen our client tossing the baseball bat into the trunk of his car—she's got a rap sheet a mile long."

"Tell me more, Peters."

"All petty crimes, along with a little prostitution, too. Turns out that street corner where she claims to have seen everything is the same corner where she's been picked up several times by the cops for soliciting sex."

"I like it. Nothing pisses off a jury of women more than a low-class hooker. Ross, make a note that we'll have to stack the jury with women when we go in for selection." Smiling, Neil added, "Your overtime wasn't completely in vain, Peters."

Jamie grinned, leaned back in his chair, and pushed away from the conference table. With the flurry of movement, Neil caught sight of Jamie's feet, and his smile quickly faded to a frown. From under Jamie's dark pinstripe trousers peeked red canvas high-top sneakers. A misstep during a rainstorm the previous week had resulted in the ruin of Jamie's patent leather shoes. His only pair, according to Jamie. The next day marked the first, and Neil had hoped, last appearance of the red sneakers adorning his feet.

"Peters, what happened this weekend?"

Jamie looked at Neil, puzzled. "Huh?"

"Your feet. Why are those damn things still on your feet?"

Neil wondered if it'd been just involuntary instinct that caused Jamie to slide his feet back under the table out of sight. Neil leaned forward, placing both hands flat on the table. "I gave you one day with those goddamn sneakers. One day. That was being generous. And today you show up wearing those damn things again! Did I not make myself clear on Friday? What part of 'do not wear those things here again' did you not understand?"

Unlike his fellow lawyers, Neil had never been in favor of casual attire in the office. He paused for a moment, just for effect. "Do you not make enough money to afford a new pair of shoes? I'm sure I could find at least a dozen other monkeys who would happily wear a diaper, if I asked them to, just to get your job. You see where I'm coming from? Don't push your luck with me."

Jamie had slouched down in his seat while Emily and Kaitlyn watched in silence. With his head bowed, the young legal aide avoided looking his boss in the eye. Opening his mouth to unleash further denunciation,

Neil was interrupted by a buzz from the office intercom centered on the table. Pressing the green button, Neil gave a terse "What?"

Jenni's husky voice filtered into the room through the speaker. "Mr. Brewster, there's a call for you."

"Who is it?"

"He wouldn't say. But he says it's important."

Neil paused for a moment. "I'll take it in my office."

Heading toward the conference-room door, Neil halted, spun around, and glared at Jamie Peters. "Leave now. Get new shoes. Come back."

PUSHING the door to his office closed, Neil crossed to his desk, dropping into the leather office chair behind it. He reached for the phone on his desk and brought the receiver to his ear.

"Neil Brewster."

"Neil? Is that really you? Holy shit! You sound different!"

The voice held a twinge of familiarity, but Neil couldn't place it. "Who is this?"

"I didn't think your secretary would put me through. Damn, she sounds hot!"

Neil didn't have time to play games. "Who's speaking?"

"You don't recognize my voice? Hell, no reason you would. It's been eighteen years! It's Steve O'Reilly!"

The name invoked visions of a simpler time and a simpler life, of playing baseball in the field behind his development, getting covered in dried leaves while playing football on an autumn afternoon, and racing bicycles down Wilberforce Drive.

A smile crossed Neil's face. "Steve? What the hell are you doing?"

"Trying to find out if you're coming to the reunion."

The invitation hanging on his refrigerator flashed to the forefront of his mind. He recalled its arrival, inviting him to a reunion at Camp Tenskwatawa, an old summer camp in the woodlands of southern New Jersey. The camp had been the furthest thing from his mind for over eighteen years. But the Saturday after the invitation had arrived, Neil found himself digging through a stack of old boxes in the back corner of a closet, dragging one particular box into the living room. Sitting on the floor, he spent the next few hours pulling out old photographs and mementos, and reliving the "good ole days." One stack of Polaroids, held together with a deteriorating rubber band, had fused together over time and could only be salvaged by carefully peeling each photo off the stack with a slow, precise hand.

Neil's parents had given him the Polaroid camera for his fifteenth birthday, and he'd taken it every summer, along with a backpack full of film. As he dug through the Polaroids, he found posed shots of old friends, candid scenes from around camp, and even the occasional nude photos of a few girl counselors. He'd gotten a good chuckle out of those, recalling how he could charm them into showing a little skin for the camera. Then everything went back into the box, and the invitation went up on the refrigerator, unanswered.

"Did you get the invite?" Steve asked.

"Yeah, I got it. I'm not sure if I'm going to make it."

"You're kidding! Neil, it won't be the same without you."

Hearing the disappointment in Steve's voice, Neil leaned back in his chair, considering what to say next. It'd be easy to lie to his friend, saying that he was simply too busy with this upcoming case to take off for a three-day-weekend. It wouldn't have been that far from the truth. But it wasn't the whole truth. Camp Tenskwatawa had been a part of Neil's life that he'd left behind, along with the rest of his childhood. Moving on to bigger and better things was all he'd ever been concerned about.

"Look, Steve. I don't really feel like going back to camp, especially to see a bunch of people that I didn't like then, and surely don't like now."

"What are you talking about?"

"You know what I mean. Dwelling on the past is for people who can't aspire to greater things. I don't need to get together with fifty or sixty losers for a weekend of reminiscing."

Steve began to laugh. "You never change. Neil, that's the beauty of this reunion. There's only gonna be five of us. Just Los Cinco Amigos. That's it! Just you, me, Rob, Jeremy, and Patrick. Like John Belushi said in *The Blues Brothers*, 'we're getting the band back together.'"

CHAPTER THREE

THE DEWALT CORDLESS drill went silent, causing Sammy Wilcox to glance down toward her father. He was kneeling on the floor across the room, facing away from her. She watched him set the black and yellow drill down near a small pile of wood shavings that had accumulated on the pine wood floor. A frown crossed her face when her father's hands trembled. His bald head and round face were coated in perspiration. *He's overexerted himself again,* she thought. She'd told her father that he didn't need to help, but he'd insisted. She'd tried to convince him to stay downstairs and relax in front of the television, but he was having none of that. As she tilted her head, a few strands of auburn hair fell in front of her face. She brushed them back in place with her hand and climbed off the step stool on which she'd been standing.

"Dad, are you okay?"

As she crossed the room, her father shifted his knees and sat down on the floor, stretching his legs out before him.

"Yeah, Samantha. Just need a breather."

Sammy cringed. No matter how hard she tried, she'd never been able to get her father to call her anything other than Samantha. After thirty-four years, she'd given up on trying to correct him, but it didn't mean she had to like it.

Kneeling beside him, she touched his shoulder, giving it a comforting rub. Her father was breathing heavily, his wheezing worse than usual. She worried that he wouldn't live to see this through. They'd been making these plans for a long time, and she didn't want to end up going through it alone.

"Relax, Dad. We've got plenty of time."

She rose to her feet and crossed to the nearby dresser. Watching her father suffer with his cancer was getting more difficult each day, and she felt her emotions welling up again. She had to find something to distract herself before she broke down and cried. Her hands picked up the old clock, and holding it in her palm, she turned the small knob on the back. When she'd finished winding the clock, she turned it over and stared at the face. The hour and minute hands stood still while the red second hand raced around and around. What was the old saying, "time heals all wounds"? There was one wound time hadn't healed, leaving her with no choice but to take matters into her own hands. But it wouldn't be healing. It'd be justice. The threat of tears abated. There'd be plenty of time to cry after . . .

"Samantha?"

Her father's voice sounded soft and weak. Turning, she set the clock back on the dresser. He was gazing up at her, his eyes holding her in a lackluster stare. She wrestled with the tears forming in her eyes, hoping he didn't notice.

"What is it, Dad?"

He held out his hand. "Can you give me the hook?"

"Sure."

She crossed to the twin bed along the far wall, grabbing a large steel hook that had been resting on the pale blue comforter. Placing the hook into her father's hand, she saw his mouth crack a faint smile. Sammy didn't see her father smile very often anymore. It'd been eighteen years since she'd seen him truly happy, and since the cancer diagnosis six months ago, he'd gone from being apathetic to darkly despondent.

Her father's hands quivered as he tried to insert the threaded end of the hook into the hole he'd just drilled in the wall. Sammy could only watch him struggle for a moment before she leaned over his shoulder and steadied his hand. With the hook inserted into the hole, Sammy stepped back, allowing her father to screw the hook into the wall. With slow turns of his wrist, her father turned the hook around, sinking it into the wall stud behind the pine wood paneling. Grabbing another hook from the bed, Sammy stepped back up onto the step stool, inserting it into the hole she'd made earlier in the ceiling.

"Are you sure these can hold the weight?" she asked.

"As long as they're in the stud. Biggest ones they had at Home Depot."

With her hook secured in the ceiling, Sammy returned to her father's side. He'd stopped working again and was staring, unmoving, at the hook in the wall. These moments of immobility had been occurring more and more frequently over the past few weeks.

"Dad?"

"I'm sorry, Samantha. I don't think I can go through with this."

She sat down next to him. "Why not? We've both wanted this for so long."

"I know. But it's not going to fix anything. He'll still be gone."

This wasn't what Sammy wanted to hear. Their plans had progressed so far that it would be almost impossible to stop now. Besides, she didn't want to stop. She, more than anything, wanted to see things through to the end.

"Dad, I need you to help me with this. I don't want to do this alone."

Closing his eyes, her father shook his head. "What's it gonna achieve?"

"Closure. It'll give us closure."

"Closure? We should've had that eighteen years ago. Now . . ." His voice faded for a moment. "Now it's just rubbing salt in the wound."

Sammy rubbed her eyes with her fingers, frustrated by her father's sudden reluctance. "We've been talking about this for years. You wanted this as much as I did. You can't back out on me now. Not after all that I've done to arrange things." She placed her hand on his shoulder. "It'll be worth it. Trust me."

He turned his head away from her, avoiding eye contact. She didn't want to pressure him, but she wanted him to understand that she needed him. She was prepared to go through it alone, but Sammy preferred to have her father by her side.

"Do the ends justify the means?" he asked suddenly.

"In this case, yes."

He turned to look at her. "Are you sure, Samantha? Are you sure?"

CHAPTER FOUR

"Los Cinco Amigos? Damn, that's a name I haven't heard in a long time," Neil said.

Steve let out hearty laugh. "Yep. Remember who branded us with that moniker?"

"Miss Fleming."

"Yeah, what an odious little witch!"

Neil closed his eyes, smiling at the memory. "The polyester queen herself."

"She did love her plastic clothes."

"Three years of Spanish and all I remember is how she rolled the 'r's every time she said 'Señor Brewster.' I hated that bitch."

Another loud laugh came through the phone. "We all did."

"It's just the five of us?"

"Yep. We've got the whole camp to ourselves for three days. No one else but Los Cinco Amigos!"

Picking up his mobile phone from the desk, he noted

the date. The third week of March meant that Camp Tenskwatawa would soon be ramping up for the summer-camp season. "How'd you pull that off?"

"Oh, you probably didn't hear. The camp closed down two years ago—money issues. My company bought the whole place up."

"Your company?"

"Well, the company I work for. Tyndale Real Estate Group. We're going to clear out the camp, the forest—just about everything—and put up a high-end gated community surrounding Lake Friendship," Steve said. "Starting price, seven hundred and fifty grand. Big ass houses, loaded with all the amenities. We're dumping a few million into this project, figuring it'll pay out big."

"Hmmm. What do you do at Tyndale?"

"CFO. Been there nine years. Truth be told, you might as well just call me the head accountant. We might be a multimillion-dollar real estate developer, but I've only got a staff of three other accountants under me."

Neil laughed. "Steve, that still doesn't explain how we've got the whole place to ourselves."

"We start demolition in June. Before it's all gone, I thought it would be nice to have one last weekend there. I bent the CEO's ear a bit, and he gave me the okay. It's as simple as that."

"Who else has agreed to come?"

"Everyone's RSVPed except you," Steve said. "You're the one holdout that can make or break a perfect weekend. Are you coming?"

Neil spun around in his chair until he could see out his office window across Central Park. The mid-morning sun was high in the cloudless blue sky, much the same way it had been the weekend after he'd received the invitation in the mail. He recalled Sheila's inquisitiveness about Camp Tenskwatawa; it had been a topic he'd never brought up with her before. His past was something he didn't talk about. Not with her, not with anyone.

While they had been taking an afternoon stroll through Central Park, he remembered her suddenly asking, "What's Camp Tens . . . Tenwatata?"

He corrected her. "Tenskwatawa. It was a summer camp where I worked in high school."

"You had a job in high school?"

A young woman jogged past them, tight spandex shorts embracing her round, pert buttocks. Neil's eyes narrowed and, as if by instinct, followed the woman as she jogged away from them. The corners of his mouth twitched into a brief salacious smile. "Why's it so surprising that I'd have a job in high school?"

"Why would you? It's not like you needed to work for money."

Neil smiled. Like Sheila, he'd grown up with the proverbial silver spoon in his mouth. His father had been highly respected cardiovascular surgeon and his mother a high-priced corporate lawyer. Unable to shower their only son with attention because of their busy schedules, they showed their love in more material ways.

"I didn't . . . My friends and I didn't do it for the money," he said. "It was something to keep us occupied during the summers. It got us away from our parents."

"But a summer camp in the woods? Couldn't you go to your parents' beach house?"

"We wanted something different. Something fun."

Sheila furrowed her brow in disgust. "Fun? You call that fun? What did you do all summer?"

"We were counsellors. They'd ship in a bunch of little brats each week, and we'd do things with them. Hiking, canoeing, arts and crafts."

"Again, you call that fun?"

He smiled, knowing that he couldn't tell her everything that he and his friends did during those summers. She wouldn't approve of the pranks and practical jokes they'd pulled. He was certain she didn't want to hear about some of the more wanton activities that happened between the boy and girl counselors when the younger kids weren't around.

After her questions, he'd finally removed the invitation from the refrigerator and thrown it away.

"Neil! You still there?"

Steve's voice calling through the phone snapped him back to the present. Neil shook his head and smiled. He'd completely blanked out for a moment, missing whatever it was that Steve had said.

"What? What'd you say?"

"Were you even listening to me?"

Neil let out a soft laugh. "Sorry, I was just thinking about the past."

"Stop thinking about it, and tell me if you're coming."

"I don't know, Steve. I've got this big case coming up . . ."

"Don't give me that bullshit! Courts aren't in session on the weekends." Neil noted a momentary change in Steve's voice. Not disappointment, as Neil would have expected, but more like indignation and belligerence.

Making excuses, Neil said, "I've got a shitload of prep to do before the trial."

"Neil, you've got to be there! We all want to see you."

Neil leaned back in his chair, closing his eyes. "What the hell are we going to do for three days?"

"Drink, hike, shoot some hoops. Hell, maybe Jeremy can get his hands on some weed and we can get high. It doesn't really matter. It's the five of us, back together again."

Opening his eyes, Neil gazed across at the potted fern in the far corner. The branches reached toward the office ceiling. For a moment, Neil became lost among the leaves, feeling like he was back in the Pine Barrens that surrounded Camp Tenskwatawa. Memories washed over him, and he found himself standing on the sandy shore of Lake Friendship and hiking through the tall pine and cedar trees. He was young again, young and mischievous. And his friends were there as well. There was Jeremy Kirscher, the foul-mouthed brawn of the group. Rob Ellington, the sweet talker, who could talk his way out of any situation. Patrick Sizemore, the young Casanova for whom the girls always swooned. And then there was Steve, Neil's childhood best friend.

Smiling, Neil said, "Okay, Steve. I'm in. I'll be there."

"Awesome! Neil, this'll be a weekend to remember!"

CHAPTER FIVE

As THE SILVER Mercedes cleared the Holland Tunnel, Neil squinted into the setting sun, a fiery crimson sky in the horizon. Weaving through traffic, the "Welcome to Jersey City" sign became a blur as he sped down I-78. The cool April wind whipped at his hair, and all the tension in his shoulders melted away as mile upon mile of New Jersey interstate vanished behind him.

Two weeks had passed since he'd agreed to join his old friends on their reunion, and Neil would be the first to admit that he'd forgotten about it almost as soon as he'd hung up the phone with Steve O'Reilly. With a high-profile trial looming in the next few weeks, he'd been pressed for time as he developed his strategy, reviewed case notes, and prepared his opening argument.

Neil's legal aides had been busy with research and "dirt digging," and he was feeling confident that he could discredit all the witnesses that the prosecutor was planning to introduce. He knew that the evidence against his client was mostly circumstantial without witnesses. If there was one thing he was good at, it was sowing doubt into circumstantial evidence. He'd have the jury eating out of his hand.

As the weekend approached, Neil was feeling unusually weary. A quick break was what he needed. The case would be an easy win, he was certain of that. A short respite would sharpen his mind for the upcoming jury selection, scheduled to start the Wednesday after he'd return.

On his way out of the city, Neil stopped to buy a sleeping bag, hiking boots, and liquor, putting him on the road later than he'd anticipated. Now free of the confines of the city, he could make up for lost time. As the asphalt passed beneath his tires, Neil put on a CD he'd found among the old Polaroids. As the first chords of "Follow You Down" erupted from the speakers, he turned up the volume, tapping his fingers on the steering wheel to the beat. The Gin Blossoms' song had been an anthem of sorts for him and his friends. The words had struck a chord with them, forming, what Neil now considered, a naive and juvenile idea of what friendship was.

He and his friends had had a foolish notion that nothing could ever separate them, that they'd meet at some bar every week until the day they died. They used to say that they'd follow each other down to the pits of hell, which had been where they all figured they'd end up anyway. With the music resounding, Neil pressed the Mercedes to twenty miles over the speed limit and laughed aloud.

It's going to be a helluva weekend, he thought.

HE'D been on the road for two hours, the sun having

long since disappeared beneath the horizon. As he turned off the dark interstate, the headlights of the Mercedes cut a swath through the darkness. As he passed through Mansfield, he caught sight of the Wawa convenience store on the corner. It was the same one that he remembered passing every summer on his way to Camp Tenskwatawa.

Another half mile further down the road, he passed a small shopping center on the right—another landmark from his childhood. The K-Mart had since closed, and a Dollar Store was there now, along with a Chinese restaurant and an auto parts store. An unfamiliar sense of nostalgia washed over him, leaving him with a mixed feeling of delight and uneasiness. Being nostalgic wasn't something Neil Brewster did or particularly enjoyed.

Unconsciously, his foot lessened its pressure on the accelerator, and he looked from left to right, trying to identify what had changed over the past eighteen years. So much was different, yet so much was still the same. After Mansfield came Springfield, and then Vincentown, both small towns that one could speed through and barely notice. Most of the towns along this stretch of road in New Jersey were the same way, sparsely populated and, to Neil, uninteresting. For a city boy from New York, this wasn't just rural, it was desolate.

As the Mercedes sped into a traffic circle, Neil caught sight of a dilapidated building on the far side. The windows were boarded up and the sign had fallen from the roof. He felt a faint pang in his heart, remembering the small donut shop that had once occupied the ramshackle structure. *Route 70 Donuts*, it was called, with a giant donut on the roof beckoning him every time he'd passed it. He recalled the neon sign in the window reading "Hot Donuts." It was always lit when they were baking donuts. Smiling, he remembered how he could pull a hot donut straight off the conveyor belt.

The distance between street lights increased, and eventually they disappeared altogether. Both sides of the road closed in with enormous walls of dense foliage and tall pine trees stretching up into the night sky. With dense darkness consuming the road, the Mercedes's headlights were swallowed by the gloom, forcing Neil to back off the accelerator even more.

As he rounded a bend in the road, a pair of pinpoint glimmers ahead caught Neil's eye, forcing his foot to jump from the accelerator to the brake. The tires squealed and the acrid smell of their protest against the sudden deceleration penetrated his nose. He stared into the eyes of a white-tail deer; its grayish-brown coat glistening in the beams of the headlights. Man and animal stared into each other's eyes for a few moments. Then, with a huff and a loud grunt, the deer ambled off toward the road's edge, disappearing from sight. Neil heard its hooves crushing the underbrush.

Sitting in his car, surrounded by darkness, Neil felt the cool forest breeze blow through his hair, and he caught the distinctive aroma of pine needles. For close to a decade, he'd confined himself to a forest of steel and glass, never venturing out from beyond its walls. The only animals he dealt with anymore were human, and more times than not, they were the worst kind. Suddenly bursting into laughter, he lifted his foot from the brake and accelerated into the dark.

After another seven miles dimly illuminated only by his headlights, a modest cabin that he thought he'd never see again emerged from a clearing, lights burning bright in the downstairs windows. He eased the Mercedes into the narrow driveway. A porch surrounded three sides of the rustic structure, the railings were made from long, round timbers. The front door was flanked on each side by a pair of double windows, and above it was the single window for the second floor. The roof pitched on a steep slope, which, as he recalled, gave the rooms on the second floor a sloped ceiling.

Situated about a mile from the camp's main entrance, the caretaker's cabin hadn't changed much. It looked more weatherworn than Neil remembered, but it had remained mostly the same. A white Ford Focus was parked to the right of the cabin. Someone was home. No telling who lived there now. Reaching to put the car into reverse, his hand froze as the cabin's front door opened. She stepped out on the porch, staring at his car, peering as if trying to figure out who was behind the wheel. The overhead porch light shone down on her, allowing Neil to see her features clearly. He took a long deep breath, staring in awe at how little she'd changed. After eighteen years, there she was staring into his headlights. He couldn't believe it was her.

SUMMER, 1995

Neil leaned against the outer wall of the recreation hall, arms folded and a frown on his face. He wasn't completely sold yet on whether this had been a good idea. Spending the summer babysitting a bunch of bratty kids didn't sound like his idea of fun, but the picture that Patrick had painted of horny girls in tight shorts and minimal adult supervision had been enough to pique his interest.

The sixteen-year-old boy's eyes roamed across the crowd of teenagers, looking at them with an air of contempt. His gaze ran the length of the hall, from the vast stone fireplace on the far wall to the three rows of picnic tables running its length. Everything—from the balcony railing above them to the stairs and stair rails—had been made from heavily varnished pine timbers, giving the hall a distinctive bucolic atmosphere.

The rustic banquet was a camp tradition, kicking off the new camp season. The evening was a chance for counselors—new and returning—to meet, or in some cases, get reacquainted before the young campers arrived the next week. He scanned the young faces, particularly those of the girls, making mental notes of which ones to try and score with over the summer.

Jeremy Kirscher jabbed an elbow into Neil's side and nodded across the room. Shifting his gaze, he caught sight of his friend, Patrick Sizemore, leaning in close to one of the new girl counselors. His friend's wavy brown hair was brushed to the right, falling over his eye. Patrick had a baby face with which girls were always infatuated.

"Always the fuckin' Casanova," said Jeremy.

Neil gave his friend a half-smile. "Don't forget to stop cursing when the kids get here."

"What? You my fuckin' mom now?"

Neil laughed. Jeremy had always had a foul mouth, which had gotten him in trouble more than a few times in school. He used his litany of curse words as if they were everyday verbs, adverbs, adjectives, and even nouns. "Just saying. I don't want you kicked out on the first day."

"Yeah, Brewster, whatever. Where's O'Reilly?"

Neil gestured toward the door along the far wall. "I saw him slip out with a hot blonde about fifteen minutes ago."

"Which hot blonde?"

"The short one with the big fun bags."

"Damn. Wanted to lay my head on her pillows myself."

Neil laughed. "You snooze, you lose."

His gaze turned back to the crowd in time to see a heavyset man, wearing tan cargo shorts and a pale blue Camp Tenskwatawa t-shirt, walk past with a swift step, he'd greeted them when they arrived. The camp caretaker, Charlie Wilcox. A hammer hanging from a low-slung tool belt jangled loudly as he went by.

"Must be heading to the buffet," Neil said, smirking. "Go, Chucky. Go."

Returning his eyes to the crowd, Neil caught sight of Rob Ellington mingling among the throng of teenagers. Rob, back straight and hands deep in his pockets, looked more like a high school senior than a sophomore. He'd often reminded Neil of Eddie Haskell from *Leave It to Beaver*. "Yes, sir" and "no, sir" were phrases that Rob had down to a science, and he could make it sound so innocent that no one ever believed him capable of doing wrong.

"I'm telling ya, he's banging his stepmother," Jeremy whispered.

Recalling the last time he'd been at Rob's house, Neil laughed at the thought of the thin strings that Mrs. Ellington called a bikini. "Wouldn't you? You've seen the stuff she wears—or doesn't wear—when we're at Rob's house."

"She flashed me once, did I tell you that?"

Neil glanced at his friend. "No."

"Popped them right out of her blouse." He provided a crude demonstration with his hands. "Like it was perfectly normal. Then claimed it was an accident. If I lived in that house, I'd end up going blind."

Neil snickered, then he turned his attention back to the festivities.

"Who's that?" said Jeremy, gesturing to the opposite side of the hall. "He doesn't look old enough to be a counselor."

Neil's eyes followed his friend's gaze, catching sight of a petite figure darting through the crowd. A blur of short auburn hair and a lavender t-shirt weaved around chatting teenagers. He followed the figure as it skirted up to the refreshments table and grabbed a Coke.

Neil smiled. "You're such an ass. That's Samantha

Wilcox, Chucky's kid."

"That's a girl?"

Neil watched as she made her way back across the hall, soda can in hand. "Yeah, ass wipe. Chucky introduced her earlier, don't you remember? She's fourteen, lives in that cabin of his. Said we'd see her roaming around."

Jeremy shrugged his shoulders and grunted. Neil's eyes lingered on the young girl. With her bob haircut, he could see why Jeremy had mistaken Samantha for a boy. She was far from being Neil's type. Underdeveloped and too young. But there was something about her that made his gaze loiter for a moment longer.

As he drew his eyes back to party, Neil watched a tall, lanky teenager move through the crowd whose head, egg-shaped with big round eyes, gave him the look of permanent surprise. Attired in beige shorts, pale blue Camp Tenskwatawa t-shirt, and a bright red baseball cap, Neil thought the kid looked like the poster boy for a camp counselor.

Jeremy leaned his broad shoulders toward him and whispered, "I'm dying for a joint."

The scrawny teenage boy he'd been watching drifted toward them, smiling and looking a little too enthusiastic for Neil's tastes.

"Hi, I'm Chris Bateman." His high-pitched voice cracked when he spoke and had a faint whine which Neil instantly despised. The boy extended his hand toward Neil. "It's my second year. Are you new?"

With the boy's arrival, Neil noticed a pungent, sour odor, just overwhelming enough to force him to restrain his gag reflex. Glancing at Jeremy, he saw, from his friend's scrunched up nose, that the boy's body odor hadn't gone unnoticed. Grasping the boy's hand, Neil was almost repulsed by the sweaty palm pressed against his. The boy's weak grasp shook a little too vigorously for Neil's tastes. He gave a nod and a half-hearted smile. "I'm Neil." Gesturing to his right, he added, "That's Jeremy."

Neil's friend nodded to Chris, and then turned his attention back to the crowd. The boy seemed oblivious to the fact that neither Neil nor Jeremy were interested in socializing.

"Welcome to Camp Tenskwatawa! Where are you from?"

"Princeton." Neil's answer was short and to the point, and he hoped that it would be enough to make the boy go away. But it wasn't.

Chris turned to Jeremy. "And how about you?"

"He's from Princeton too," Neil said before his friend could reply. Jeremy, too often, tended to say the first thing that came to mind without thinking. Knowing that Jeremy had little patience for someone like Chris Bateman, he thought the less his friend spoke the better.

The lanky boy smiled. "If you've got questions about anything related to the camp—and I mean anything—just ask." With that, Bateman moved away, heading toward a small cluster of nearby teenagers.

"Whatever you say, Stinky Bateman," Neil muttered under his breath, just loud enough for Jeremy to hear.

Laughing, Jeremy nudged Neil's ribs with his elbow. "He's gonna be fun to fuck with."

Keeping his eyes on the departing boy, Neil wondered if Chris Bateman was as weak and half-witted as he appeared. What would it take to wipe that stupid smile off his face? *It might be fun to see,* he thought.

CHAPTER SIX

SAMMY CARRIED THE box down the stairs and set it next to four other identical ones. She slipped a black Sharpie from her jeans pocket and scrawled the words *Upstairs Bathroom* on the side. Glancing toward the living room window, she wondered when it'd become dark outside. She'd been so busy packing that she hadn't realized how much time had passed. It must have been three hours since Steve O'Reilly had left.

He'd stopped by on his way to the camp—to "check up on her," he'd said. She was happy for the company. With her father gone, the cabin had become a lonely, desolate place. While sorting through her father's things, Sammy had found herself, more than once, overcome with emotion and breaking down in tears. This was much harder than she thought it would be. She welcomed the distraction of Steve's visit, even if it was only for fifteen minutes.

They'd sat at the small kitchen table, chatting over

coffee, the conversation being mostly superficial and guarded. She didn't know Steve well enough to share her more intimate thoughts and feelings.

"You sure you still want to go through with this?" Steve had asked her just before leaving. "No one'll blame you if you want out."

Sammy shook her head. "No, I'm good. I have to do this. For Dad."

She crossed to the front door, pulled it open, and stared out across the darkened forest. The incessant chirp of the crickets filled the cool April evening air. She glanced at her watch, wondering if he'd driven past the cabin, straight to camp. There was no reason why he would've stopped at the caretaker's cabin, but she'd planned for that contingency just in case.

Stepping back inside, she pushed the door closed and crossed the living room toward the kitchen. A bottle of Johnnie Walker stood on the kitchen counter along with two glass tumblers. She filled one with two fingers of whiskey, and then swallowed it in one gulp. She hated whiskey, but he loved it, therefore she'd been learning to tolerate the taste. At least she could now drink it without retching.

Back in the living room, she drew open the top drawer of an antique roll-top desk. It was empty except for an eight-by-ten picture laying face down in the center. Lifting it out of the drawer, Sammy turned the frame over, her wistful gaze looking at the photo on the other side. The twenty-year-old photo invoked a tear, which fell down her cheek, dropping onto the corner of the frame itself. She remembered the day it was taken. Her father had hired a professional photographer to come to the cabin to take the family portrait. It was first one they'd had taken since her mother died, and it would be the last. Sammy had been dressed in her best jeans and an oatmeal-colored blouse. Her father—in a gray polo—and her half brother—wearing a paisley long-sleeve Oxford—both looked handsome, making her proud to be the "woman" of the house even though she had been only twelve at the time. They sat on the cabin's front porch stairs, her father and half brother sitting in front and Sammy behind and above them, looking over their shoulders.

Finding that she couldn't take her eyes away from the photograph, she had almost missed the flash of light through the windows from outside. Dropping the frame back into the drawer, she crossed to the living room window, peering out from around the blinds. All she saw was a pair of blazing headlights illuminating the cabin. Could it be him?

She opened the cabin's front door and squinted against the intense glare. Lifting her hand to her eyes, she tried to get a better look at the car behind the lights. She heard a car door open and the sound of a foot crunching on the driveway pebbles. A tall silhouette stepped out and moved toward her.

Sammy met the silhouette in the middle of the driveway. She was surprised to feel her heart race. He looked even more handsome than she remembered. His dark hair was a bit windswept but still looked immaculate. The face, although older, still had that sexy charm that she'd fallen for eighteen years ago.

He's not allowed to look this good, she thought. *It's not fair.*

"It really is you," she managed to say.

He smiled, taking a step closer to her. "Sammy, how are you?"

When he said her name, she stopped breathing momentarily. It wasn't supposed to be like this. She was supposed to be in control. She shouldn't have had that whiskey.

"Steve said you were coming, but I just can't believe you're here."

He smiled and held out his arms. "In the flesh."

Since they had started speaking, he had been closing the gap between them until they were now inches apart. An infusion of conflicting emotions seethed within her. She raged against herself for the underlying sense of desire she was feeling toward him. For her body to respond this way was a betrayal of all that she'd become over the past eighteen years. *Get a hold of yourself,* she thought.

Taking a deep breath cleared her head. The cool evening air, with its faint fragrance of pine and cedar, calmed the cadence of her heart. Without warning, she stepped forward and embraced him, burying her face into his shoulder. His arms wrapped around her, pulling her in closer. Deep within his arms, she closed her eyes, forcing herself to think of her father and half brother. The enflamed desire began to dwindle, and she breathed a sigh of relief. She couldn't lose control like that again.

As they parted, she said, "Come on in."

Sammy turned toward the cabin, walking slowly, making sure to accentuate the swaying of her hips. She felt his eyes following as she climbed the porch steps. He hadn't moved by the time she reached the cabin door. She turned and leaned against the door frame, making sure that her figure was silhouetted by the light from within the cabin. "Are you coming?"

He laughed. "That's a loaded question. Let me just turn off the Merc."

She smiled as she watched him dart back to the car. *Got him. Hook, line, and sinker,* she thought.

CHAPTER SEVEN

Neil was surprised at how little the cabin had changed. He'd only been in there once before. But that night had been so memorable that even the cabin's smallest detail had been etched into his memory. Tongue-and-groove pine boards—stained a golden honey—ran up horizontally across the walls, the knots and tree rings forming unique random patterns throughout the cabin. The same dusty ceiling fan hung down from the high sloping ceiling of the large living room. An open staircase led to a loft with two small bedrooms.

"Can I get you something to drink?" Sammy asked.

"Whiskey?"

"Is Johnnie Walker okay?"

He nodded and watched her cross to the kitchen, passing through an archway at the opposite end of the room. The beige appliances, alongside the pine cabinets, looked awkward and outdated. A small round table provided meager seating for four. Nothing had changed.

"Coming right up," she said from within the kitchen.

While she fixed the drinks, he wandered around the living room, taking in the surroundings. There was a distinctive "unlived in" feel to the room. Dragging his finger across the surface of one of the two mission-style end tables flanking the sofa resulted in a thick layer of dust on the tip. A similar layer of dust was visible on the thirty-two-inch flat-screen TV and the cabinet on which it sat. Even the brown microfiber chair sent a cloud of particles into the air when he gave the cushion a light pat.

Glancing toward the stairs, he noticed a pile of cardboard boxes stacked against the wall. The faint fragrance of jasmine lingered in the air. Neil had first caught the scent when she'd embraced him outside. The embrace. That'd been unexpected. But then Sammy even being here had been unexpected. *Could make for an interesting twist to the weekend,* he thought.

The bedroom. That was the room he remembered the most. He pictured it all like it was yesterday. The twin bed. The floral pattern on the comforter. Dozens of stuffed animals sitting against the headboard. Sammy—sixteen at the time—moaning and gasping beneath him as they made love for the first, and only, time.

He'd been eighteen during that last summer at Camp Tenskwatawa, and Sammy had blossomed from a teenage tomboy into a desirable young woman over the previous winter, so much so that he'd barely recognized her at first. Once he saw her, however, Neil knew he had to have her, spending the rest of the summer thinking, scheming, and plotting how to get her to sleep with him. The summer of '97 became a whirlwind of flirting, innuendo, and clandestine make-out sessions in the woods. To his dismay and frustration, making out was as far as Sammy had been willing to go for most of the summer. Whenever his hands wandered too far, she'd push him away, give him a coquettish smile, and tell him "not yet."

Her smile. That was what always sent his teenage hormones into a lustful rage. With an air of mischievous teasing, Sammy had been an expert at leading him on with just a smile, giving him, again and again, a false hope that she was about to fulfill his salacious desire, only to crush that hope every time. Yet, with a tenacity that bordered on the obsessive, he persisted in his attempts to persuade the girl to give in to his amorous intentions.

As Sammy returned carrying two tumblers filled with three fingers of whiskey, he gestured to the boxes. "Are you moving?"

She handed him a glass. "Sort of. Haven't lived here for years. Dad passed away recently. I'm just now getting around to cleaning out the house." Raising her glass, she added, "To old friends."

"And old lovers."

She smiled, bringing the tumbler to her lips. It was one of those smiles. Flirtatious and mischievous. He'd seen that smile so often that, for a moment, he felt like they were teenagers again and he was proposing an illicit rendezvous for later that night.

"I'm sorry to hear about your dad." Looking around, he added, "I can't believe he still lived here."

Sammy lowered herself onto the faded green plaid sofa and crossed her legs. His eyes roamed over the smooth tanned skin of her thigh. She gestured for him to sit beside her, and he did without hesitation.

"The camp was his life. He'd worked here for almost twenty-five years," she said. "When the camp closed two years ago, the owners asked if he would stay on as care-taker, to keep the place from falling to pieces. They thought it'd open again in a few years."

"What happened?"

"It was an unsuitable business model. The owners tried to keep things going as long as they could." Her eyes became pensive and nostalgic. "But costs kept rising and the kids stopped coming. For a while, there'd been some talk about closing for a year or two, to give enough time to reinvent the camp into something new and exciting. But it all fell flat. Eventually, they sold out. Dad was going to remain until the paperwork was completed, but he didn't make it."

He caught a glimpse of sadness in her hazel eyes, but it only lasted a moment. Reaching across, she placed her hand on his knee, giving it a gentle rub. Her light touch was electric, surprising and arousing him simultaneously.

"What's Neil Brewster up to these days?"

Leaning back into the sofa, he said, "I'm a defense attorney up in New York. I work in a big firm, got a corner office. Got a senior partnership at the firm in the works."

"Impressive." She smiled at him. "Let's see if I can remember . . . was it Yale?"

"Harvard."

Sammy laughed and took another sip from her whiskey. "I knew it had to be Ivy League. Married?"

"Nope."

He didn't technically lie to her, just withheld certain information. He didn't see the need to tell her about Sheila in the same way that he wouldn't be telling his fiancée about Sammy. The two were mutually exclusive, and the less they each knew about the other the better. He justified his omission with a simple thought, *who would know?*

"Really? That's surprising. A rich lawyer with your looks? I'd have thought someone would have snatched you up a long time ago," she said.

He shrugged his shoulders. "My focus has been on my career. No time for serious romance."

"Serious romance? So, you love 'em and leave 'em then."

"You could say that." Laughing, he added, "Enough about me. What about you? What about Sammy Wilcox?"

"It's Sammy Piper now."

He glanced at her left hand to confirm what he'd noticed earlier, no ring. "Divorced?"

She gestured with her tumbler. "You're good. The marriage lasted four years. We both had too much baggage. Ended amicably though."

"What are you doing now?"

"A nurse. Work over in Philly. I've got a nice apartment downtown. Walk to work every day."

"No one in your life?"

She shook her head. "Just a little Chihuahua named Snoopadoo."

Try as he may, Neil couldn't stop himself from laughing. "Snoopadoo?"

"Don't make fun of my dog!" She backhanded him on the shoulder.

"No, of course not." He made a half-hearted attempt to fight back the laughter. "I'm sure . . . Snoopadoo is a lovely dog."

"Bastard!" She reached for his empty whiskey glass. "You want another?"

"Absolutely."

Sammy took his glass and walked into the kitchen, leaving him on his own for a moment. As he listened to the sound of her fixing more drinks, his mind wandered back through the years to their last night together. A smile danced on his lips as the memories fueled the reemergence of his childhood desires.

Sammy returned from the kitchen with two refilled tumblers of whiskey, handing one to him as she lowered herself again onto the sofa. She flashed him another of those smiles and gazed at him through half-open eyes. He wondered if she knew the effect that had on him.

"Steve O'Reilly stopped by earlier today," she said over the edge of her glass.

"Yeah? What'd he want?"

Sammy sipped some whiskey. "Just to say hello, to see how I was doing."

Neil gulped at his whiskey, swallowing hard. He'd hoped to keep her to himself. But if Steve knew she was here, then it was a good bet that his other friends probably knew as well. It might complicate things. To his surprise, a streak of jealousy surfaced for a moment, aimed toward his friends, and mostly at Steve O'Reilly. It was the same jealousy he often experienced when he felt his territory was being threatened. Sammy was his territory, and he wasn't about to share. One way or another, he was determined to charm his way back into Sammy's bed, and neither Steve nor his other friends were going to get in the way. The jealousy subsided moments later, however, as Neil realized how ridiculous it'd been. He couldn't help but laugh.

"What?" she asked.

"It's nothing. How do you know Steve?"

Leaning back into the cushions of the sofa, she replied, "Oh, he's just an acquaintance. He stopped by to see Dad a few times while negotiating the sale of the camp. Steve came to the memorial service for Dad when I spread his ashes out over the lake."

"Was your Dad upset when they sold the camp?"

She was looking at Neil, but her eyes seemed to look past him. The sadness he'd seen earlier reappeared, and she hesitated before answering. "Working at this camp was hard on Dad. The past several years, he just wasn't happy at all. There was no joy in it for him anymore. He'd get up every morning, go through the usual routine, and that was it. By the time they sold the camp, he was already a broken man."

Wondering if he should feel guilty, Neil remembered how hard he and his friends had ridden Charlie Wilcox. From letting the air out of the tires of the caretaker's golf cart to shooting out the lights around the camp with a BB gun, they had looked for every opportunity to raise hell around camp. He'd always thought it just harmless fun, but Neil had never considered the impact his actions might have on others. But as he sat there, he felt nothing. No sense of remorse, no sense of condemnation. To feel guilt would mean that he was sorry for his actions. He wasn't. They'd just been a bunch of teenagers having a little fun. If Charlie Wilcox couldn't deal with it, that was his problem.

Gesturing around the room, he said, "The place hasn't changed a bit; it's just as I remember it."

"Dad never was much of an interior decorator." Smiling, Sammy added, "If I remember, you were only in here once."

It was the first time she'd referenced their final night together since he'd arrived. The night she'd finally given him what he'd wanted all summer long. Sammy smiled at him, as if waiting for him to make the next move. Neil was reminded of fencing practice when he was in Harvard, of thrusting and parrying to gain advantage over one's opponent. She had just thrust, now it was time for him to parry.

"It could've been more than once."

"I was waiting until I turned sixteen."

He smiled. "Age didn't mean anything to me."

"It did to me."

"Do you still keep a shitload of stuffed animals on your bed?"

She laughed, and then her smile turned mischievous as she looked at him through narrowed eyes. "If you come back tomorrow night, maybe you'll find out."

"Tomorrow?"

She rose from the sofa, took the tumbler from his hand, and said, "How about around eleven? I'll have a fresh bottle of whiskey waiting."

Her lips formed a smile that tempted and tantalized, but Neil found her eyes to be cold, creating an image of incompatibility that intrigued him. The mysterious vision of contradictions was an enticing paradox, throwing fuel upon his desire to have her.

"You should go. Your friends will be waiting," she said, leading him to the front door. They stood in the open doorway, and she wrapped her arms around Neil's neck, pressing her lips against his ear. "I've been waiting eighteen years, don't disappoint me."

CHAPTER EIGHT

THE WHISKEY HE'D shared with Sammy was still warm in his stomach as Neil turned his Mercedes onto the unpaved road, the headlights sweeping across the camp's entrance. A hundred yards further down from the caretaker's cabin, the rustic sign still stood. Thick pine branches formed the letters of the camp's name. He remembered the story told to the campers on their first day about the camp's namesake: a Native American religious and political leader from the Shawnee tribe. The tale was full of grand adventures, creating an image of a peaceful, wise tribal leader, designed to instill in the young campers a sense of awe and wonder. It was all about providing a role model for the campers to follow during their week-long "journey" at Camp Tenskwatawa.

Neil knew it was all bullshit. He'd looked it up once and found that, far from being a pacifist leader, Tenskwatawa had declared that the settlers were children of the Evil Spirit and led his tribe in the Midwest into battle against them. So much for awe and wonder.

The tires dug into the soft white sand of the Pine Barrens, and the Mercedes shot forward into the camp. The forest around him seemed impenetrable with its thick underbrush, but he couldn't tell if it was really that dense or just his eyes playing tricks in the darkness. The headlights revealed a narrow roadway leading deeper into the camp, tall pine trees lining either side. To the right, the forest opened to briefly reveal a side road leading to the camp's recreation hall. As he passed, he caught a glimpse of a single white floodlight illuminating the white sand of the clearing in front of the building, but the blinding light made it impossible for him to see the structure from which it hung. It was the same floodlight that he remembered shooting out with a BB gun he'd smuggled into camp, forcing Charlie Wilcox to replace to the bulb again and again.

Continuing forward, the forest opened into a considerable clearing, white sand covering it from end to end. The Camp Tenskwatawa parking lot. When the camp was still open, the rule had been that no cars were allowed beyond the parking lot. The camp administrators and the caretaker had golf carts for getting around the camp. But everyone else arriving at the camp was required to leave their cars in the parking lot and walk the rest of the way.

Drifting the car to the right and then to the left, Neil swept the open space with his headlights. Three cars were parked at the far side of the clearing: a Lexus RX, a BMW 3 Series sedan, and a Ford F150. He laughed, wondering who had the pickup truck. *Probably Jeremy,* he thought.

Near the three parked cars, there was another sandy road leading further into the camp. A wooden post stood on either side of the opening, and at one time, a rusting chain had stretched across the opening to act as a barrier.

The chain was gone, so Neil took that to mean he could go on in.

He navigated further into the camp, slowing as the ruts and potholes jolted the suspension of the Mercedes. Steve O'Reilly had said they'd be staying in Sequoia Lodge. Although he'd never spent any time in it, Neil remembered it well from his days as a counselor. Sequoia Lodge had been used for housing the cooking staff. It was larger than most of the other cabins used by the campers and counselors. Located across from the canoe launch down by the lake, Sequoia Lodge was not only centrally positioned for quick access to all the camp had to offer, but it was situated near one of the four bathhouses in the camp, making, as Steve'd said, "midnight runs to take a piss easy."

The wooden structure soon came into view, revealing a dark colored Chevy Tahoe parked against the cabin's side wall. From over the roof of the cabin, Neil saw smoke and fiery orange embers drifting into the tree tops; someone had a fire going. Pulling the Mercedes behind the Tahoe, he switched off the engine. As he climbed out, a tall, slim silhouette stepped around the side of the cabin and stood motionless for a moment.

"Where've you been?"

Steve hadn't changed all that much. He was still tall and thin, but his jet-black hair had receded up his forehead a bit and grayed near his temples. A yellow polo hung untucked over the top of his faded blue jeans.

"You never said I had to be here at a specific time, asshole."

They both burst out in laughter as Steve stepped around the Mercedes and extended his hand. "It's great to see you."

The firm handshake quickly turned into a friendly

embrace, and Neil's doubts about the weekend vanished. He'd always hated looking back at the past. He couldn't change it, so why dwell on it? He passed on his high-school reunions, having no desire to watch people waltz around in a desperate attempt to appear more successful than they actually were. When the woman coordinating his ten-year reunion had called him to see if he'd attend, Neil told her that he "didn't need any sycophantic adoration" from his classmates, and, as far as he was concerned, they "could all rot in hell." He assumed that he wouldn't be invited to the twenty-fifth.

This, however, was different. Neil and his four friends had been more than classmates, more than just high-school friends. They'd seen each other at their best and their worst. The five of them had known each other's deepest secrets and greatest triumphs. They'd been tight, and, despite the years that had passed, he was certain that there was no need to exaggerate their pasts and accomplishments. There was no need to impress, no need to lie.

"Leave your stuff for now," said Steve. "We'll help you unpack later. We've got a fire going, and the others are waiting."

Steve led him around to the front of the Sequoia Lodge and into a small clearing, brightly lit by a roaring campfire confined within a ring of large stones. The white-orange flames surged skyward, standing almost three feet in the air. Smoke and burning embers shot into the tree tops, looking like drifting fireflies amidst the darkened sky. Neil flinched, the intense heat biting at his face. He was certain his cheeks were lobster red, but he soon grew accustomed to the torridity, finding that it helped curb the lingering spring chill in the air.

"He's finally here!" Steve said.

Three shadowy silhouettes emerged from the darkened

fringes of the clearing, stepping into the flames' fiery illumination. Jeremy slapped his palm against Neil's, gripping his hand firmly and squeezing until it hurt. "You old son of a bitch, how are you?" His baritone voice was deeper than Neil remembered.

A broad smile crossed Neil's face. "Couldn't be better! Damn, it's good to see you all!"

Jeremy Kirscher was still built like a football linebacker, and with a shaved head, he reminded Neil of Mr. Clean on steroids. Jeremy's bulging biceps stretched the fabric of a black t-shirt, and gray camouflage shorts covered his muscular legs to just below the knees.

Rob was next to step forward and shake his hand. "It's about time. We'd all but given up on you."

Neil laughed, holding out his arms in a sweeping gesture. "You should know me better than that. I'm never rushed."

As a teenager, Rob Ellington had been a bit on the husky side, but now he stood in the flickering fire light, trim and fit with a full head of shoulder-length blond hair. Gone was the wholesome, clean-cut image from his childhood, replaced by a shaggy tuft of hair on his chin, faded blue jeans with ripped knees, and a tattoo of a snake winding its way down his left arm from underneath the rolled-up sleeve of a plaid flannel shirt.

The last to approach, Patrick took hold of Neil's hand, and then turned a hearty handshake into a quick embrace. His hands rapped hard on Neil's back, and when they parted, Patrick smiled. "This weekend wouldn't have been the same without you."

Patrick Sizemore hadn't changed at all. The young Casanova had held onto his youthful looks. Patrick's well-groomed dark hair was brushed back from his forehead, and the skin on his narrow face was taut and smooth. Neil caught the light from the blazing campfire reflected in his friend's dark eyes, making them look as if they were on fire themselves. Blue jeans and a white t-shirt covered his trim frame as he stood with his arms folded in front of him. Gazing at Patrick through the glare of the flames left Neil with the sense of staring straight into the past.

"Did you have any trouble finding the place?" Steve asked.

Neil shook his head. "No. It all came back to me on the way down, like I was just here yesterday. Same small towns, same dark forest."

"Brewster's Donuts is closed. I saw that coming in," said Patrick.

He'd forgotten that, because of his affinity for the place, everyone in camp had taken to calling the donut shop at the Rt. 70 circle Brewster's Donuts. "I know! I was heartbroken when I went by this evening."

"Someone get this man a beer!" said Rob.

Jeremy stepped to the other side of the campfire and returned moments later carrying an ice-cold bottle of Corona, complete with a slice of lime jammed into the neck. Placing the bottle to his lips, Neil tilted his head back, swallowing a large gulp. When he lowered his head again, his four companions all held bottles in their hands; Steve and Jeremy, like Neil, had Coronas, Patrick held a Coors Light, and Rob's fingers were wrapped around the neck of a Bud Light.

Standing by the warm fire, holding a cold bottle of beer, Neil felt more relaxed than he had in a very long time. Eighteen years had been far too long. These four guys had been his best friends. As he stood by the campfire with them, he understood what it was that he'd been missing all these years. The friendship. The camaraderie. The comradeship.

Steve lifted his bottle in the air. "Gentlemen, raise your bottles. Here's to old times, old friends, and to one hell of a weekend."

The bottles met with a clink. "To one hell of a weekend!" they all repeated aloud.

After another sip from his Corona, Neil asked, "Whose got the pickup?"

"The F150?" said Rob. "That's mine."

Neil smiled. He'd been wrong.

SUMMER, 1995

NEIL HAD COME up with the idea on Thursday afternoon. He, along with his friends, had spent most of Friday plotting and scheming between their counseling duties. By the time all the young campers had been picked up by their parents on Friday evening, Neil had every detail mapped out. He knew what would happen, how it would happen, and when it would happen. The most difficult part of the plan would be catching the snake.

As the sun rose on Saturday morning, he could tell it would be another scorching day. The humidity was thick and oppressive, causing him to sweat before he'd even slipped out of his bunk. He dressed quietly, making sure not to disturb his cabin's co-counselor sleeping in another bunk across the room. By the time he'd reached the boys' bathhouse, his Smashing Pumpkins t-shirt was drenched with sweat. Patrick was already kneeling beside the wall, holding a white pillowcase which was knotted at the top.

Standing along the back wall of the bathhouse, they

leaned against the whitewashed blocks, trying to stifle their laughter. The anticipation was almost too much to bear. Glancing at his watch, Neil nudged his friend with an elbow. "Not long now."

Saturday being a day off, the other camp counselors usually slept in, enjoying the relative lull between the departure of the previous week's campers and the arrival of the next. Stinky Bateman was habitual almost to a fault. The kid would soon be traipsing across to the bathhouse, a towel hanging from his shoulder and his toiletry bag in his hand.

When he heard the distinctive sound of flip-flops approaching, Neil had to clamp his hand over Patrick's mouth to keep his friend from laughing aloud. He heard the flip-flops enter the bathhouse, the slapping of each flimsy shoe striking the concrete floor echoed from the small vents in the bathhouse wall above their heads. Then came the whistling. Out of tune and off key. Whitney Houston. *It figures,* Neil thought. The hiss of water rushing from the shower head was their cue.

Patrick slipped quietly around the side of the bathhouse, leaving Neil alone, holding a squirming pillowcase. Only gone for a few brief moments, Patrick returned carrying a bundle of clothing and a navy terrycloth towel, which he dropped on the ground at their feet.

"Give me a hand," Neil whispered.

Patrick cupped his hands together, forming a step, giving Neil just enough lift to reach one of the vents along the wall. Pillowcase in hand, he turned the already loosened screws and lifted the vent up, leaving a rectangular breech in the wall. The showers stalls were directly below. Heaving the pillowcase up, he carefully spilled its contents into the opening and then leapt back down to the ground. Patrick grabbed the bundle of clothing, and they dashed off into the forest behind the bathhouse.

Circling through the forest, they emerged beside Oak Lodge, one of the boys' cabins. Keeping his eyes alert, Neil watched Patrick creep onto the cabin's porch and drop the bundle of clothing by the door. Then, he and Patrick scurried through the underbrush to Neil's cabin, Redwood Lodge, finding Steve, Rob, and Jeremy lounging on the porch. He noticed the smug smiles on their faces.

"Everything ready?" Neil asked.

Jeremy nodded, handing him the Polaroid. The porch of Redwood Lodge provided an almost unobscured view of the bathhouse, making it the perfect place to observe the fruits of their morning labor. Clutching the camera, he stood with his friends, waiting to see his plan come together in, what he hoped, would be all its hilarious glory.

First came the whining shout from the bathhouse. "Not funny! Come on, where are my clothes?"

Then he heard the pleading, "Please! Give me my clothes back!"

Finally, the moment Neil was waiting for—the scream. It was a high-pitched scream, like one he'd have expected from a girl. There were no balls behind the scream, just a girlish shrill that rang out from the bathhouse. Raising the camera to his eye, he clicked the shutter the moment he saw movement at the bathhouse door. Stinky Bateman charged across the camp—not a stitch on him—with his flip-flops kicking up sand behind him, screaming at the top of his lungs.

Neil smiled as he snapped another picture, knowing what was coming next. From behind the nearby trees and cabins, other counselors stepped out and began to applaud, girls and boys alike. He laughed, knowing how difficult it must have been for Rob and Jeremy to convince the others to wake up early on their day off.

He continued to click the shutter as Bateman reached Oak Lodge, stumbled onto the porch, and yanked at the door. But the wood wedge he'd instructed Steve to jam in the door earlier held firm. Neil took another Polaroid as Stinky Bateman tugged and banged on the door. The boy's thin body lurched back and forth, trembling violently as he struggled to enter the cabin. As the other counselors cheered and whistled, Neil watched Bateman cry loudly, the scrawny naked body looking pale and pathetic. Even from his vantage point, he saw the tears streaming down the boy's face. This was the funniest thing he'd seen that whole first summer at camp, and it was only the end of June. He'd run out of film, and was preparing to reload the camera when Bateman got the door open, plunged into the cabin, and slammed it shut behind him.

It took another five minutes before he could contain his laughter enough to speak in more than monosyllabic sentences.

Neil said, "Someone better go get the snake."

CHAPTER NINE

THE CAMPFIRE POPPED and crackled as Jeremy dropped more firewood onto the flames, sending a mass of ash and embers soaring skyward. Neil's eyes followed the burning particles as they faded into the darkness above. He leaned back in the canvas chair, stretching his legs toward the rocks surrounding the glowing inferno before him. He wiped the back of his hand across his moist forehead, sending a bead of sweat plunging into his eye.

"You're a big-shot lawyer now?" asked Rob.

Smiling, Neil replied, "I prefer to be called a defense attorney."

Rob chuckled. "Excuse me. I didn't realize the word lawyer had become so lowbrow."

Glancing across the fire at Patrick, Neil saw the flames reflected in his friend's dark eyes again. This time he found it a little unsettling. Despite the smile that adorned his face, Patrick's eyes seemed esoteric, hiding something behind their shadowy countenance. Neil raised his beer to his lips, taking a quick swallow, and then, looking back at Patrick, found his friend's eyes bright and clear. *Must have just been a trick of the light, a combination of the darkness around us and the flickering fire,* he thought.

"What do you do now, Patrick?" he asked.

"Lobbyist. In Washington." Patrick leaned forward, swirling his beer bottle aimlessly around.

"He wines and dines those pricks on Capitol Hill," said Jeremy.

Neil took another quick sip from his bottle. "One of those pricks was a recent client of mine."

Jeremy laughed. "I guess that tells us what kind of lowlifes you defend."

Ignoring the comment, Neil looked back toward Patrick. "Who do you lobby for?"

"Anyone who'll pay me. My current client is a coalition of pharmaceutical companies."

"You like it?"

"It's got its perks." Patrick gestured toward Jeremy. "Like that jackass says, I wine and dine with the rich and powerful on Capitol Hill. And I do it on someone else's dime."

Neil's eyes darted around the campfire, pausing briefly on each of his friends. "Have you guys kept in touch all these years?"

Steve brought his Corona up to his mouth, draining it in one long gulp. "Not really. The occasional Christmas card. Just enough to know where we each lived." The empty bottle dropped to the sand near Steve's feet. He rose, crossing to the cooler for another. "At least not until I started planning this weekend."

Neil was surprised that no one asked why he'd never kept in touch after high school. Thinking about it, he wasn't sure he could provide an adequate answer if they had. Best to just change the subject. "The camp's been shut down for what, two years?"

Steve nodded. "Just a little over that."

"Is everything still standing?"

"Yeah. Charlie Wilcox kept the place in good shape right up until he died." Steve twisted the top off another bottle of Corona. "The archery range is still there, the boat house too. The canoes still float." He gestured behind himself into the darkness. "There's even a zipline that still works."

"A zipline? Damn, we never had that when we were here. Kids these days get all the good shit," said Jeremy.

Patrick tossed his empty beer bottle into the fire, sending sparks shooting upward. "The zipline is all yours."

"What? Can't handle a little dangerous living?" said Jeremy.

Leaning back, Patrick clasped his hands behind his head. "Does bungee jumping from the Cheat River Bridge in West Virginia count as dangerous living?"

Neil closed his eyes, trying to suppress a shudder. The thought of dangling over the side of a bridge was enough to make him queasy. He swallowed a mouthful of saliva, then opened his eyes again.

Jeremy was still looking at Patrick. "Really?"

"Last summer."

Jeremy laughed. "Damn, sweet!"

The conversation died away, allowing nature to fill the gap left by their silenced voices. The fire crackled before them, the crickets chirped somewhere off in the darkness, and the breeze rustled the tree branches overhead. Neil glanced around the fire, noting the expressions on each of their faces. Steve looked complacent, Patrick seemed deep in thought, and Jeremy was amused. Rob, whose face held a puzzled gaze, broke the silence. "Do you remember that ugly woman who worked in the camp office?"

Jeremy shot him a confused glance. "What?"

Rob touched his nose. "The one with the huge wart on her nose. What was her name?"

"Ms. Schlappi!" Neil said.

"Yeah, that was her!" Rob laughed. "Remember when we pasted her picture on every target in the archery range?"

The uproar echoed through the trees, filling the otherwise empty camp with raucous laughter. Patrick was doubled over in his chair, and Jeremy stomped his foot on the ground in a hysterical fit.

"She was such a bitch!" said Steve, sending them all into more fits of laughter.

Patrick took a deep a breath. "Whose idea was that anyway?"

"Who do you think?" Jeremy pointed across the fire at Neil. "Our fearless leader!"

He felt their eyes turn toward him, watching the broad smiles form on his friends' faces. Neil feigned an innocent look and pressed a hand to his chest as if surprised by the accusation. "I cannot tell a lie. What am I saying? I'm a lawyer. Of course, I can tell a lie." Neil paused for a moment. "You can't prove it was me."

Patrick laughed again. "What about the time we swapped that Disney video for a porn movie?"

"Oh my god! That was hilarious! Movie night was never more exciting," said Steve.

"My god, those kids got an eyeful," said Rob. "No one could get the tape to stop playing fast enough."

"Especially since we stole the batteries from the remote," Neil added.

"What movie was that, Neil?" Jeremy asked.

"Bambi."

Jeremy raised his hand, flipping him the bird. "Not the Disney film, jackass! The porno!"

Neil shrugged his shoulders. "I don't remember."

Rob lifted the lid to the ice cooler near his chair and pulled out another bottle. "You should. Didn't it come from your dad's collection?"

Setting an empty bottle down beside his chair, Neil replied, "It's been over eighteen years. I can't remember shit like that."

"Judy McIntyre," Patrick suddenly blurted out.

Steve gave him a puzzled look. "What?"

"I was trying to remember the name of that counselor from the girls' cabins," Patrick explained. "You know, the one we always went skinny dipping with on the far side of the lake. Judy McIntyre, I think."

Jeremy's lips formed a bawdy grin. "Yeah! I remember her. Blonde. Nice ass. Big tits." He cupped his hands in front of his chest for emphasis.

The name brought a smile to Neil's face as well. Judy, a year younger than he, had been at Camp Tenskwatawa for only one summer, but what a wild summer it had been.

"She was such a slut. I think we all slept with her at one time or another," said Rob.

Jeremy nodded toward Patrick. "Everyone except Patrick."

Patrick's hands shot up, flipping up both middle fingers. "Go to hell."

"Yeah, he was saving himself," Neil said, laughing. "How'd that work out for you?"

Sighing, Patrick folded his arms across his chest. "Just fine, if you must know."

The other three laughed while, for a moment, Patrick glared at Neil. His friend's eyes once again appeared dark and malevolent. His answer to Neil's quip had been abrupt. A tension hung in the balance between them, one that Neil couldn't explain. But as before, it lasted only for a second.

He'd hit a nerve with his wisecrack and should have dropped it then and there. That would've been the decent thing to do. But as always, Neil couldn't just let it go. "Finally got laid, did you?"

Turning his head away, Patrick gazed into the darkness and then, without warning, laughed. But it seemed a bit too contrived, leaving Neil to speculate that his friend wasn't having as much fun as the rest of them. Patrick had always been the odd man out among his friends. Where Neil and the others had known each other prior to high school, Patrick had moved to Princeton just before their freshman year. He'd fallen in easily enough with Neil and his friends, but Patrick lacked that "mutual history" that had truly defined their group.

Jeremy rose from his chair to lay another log on the campfire, while Rob reached into the cooler and pulled out another bottle of Corona. He handed it to Neil. "Have another cold one."

More than an hour had passed since his arrival, and most of it had been spent drinking, laughing, and reminiscing. When he'd left Camp Tenskwatawa, Neil had left everything behind, his four friends included. Moving on to bigger and better things had meant leaving behind any baggage that might get in the way, like his friends. As he twisted the cap off the beer bottle, Neil realized, for the first time in his life, that being a selfish bastard wasn't necessarily all it was cracked up to be.

Placing the bottle to his lips, Neil took a long sip. "Do you guys remember Stinky Bateman?" When no one responded, he added, "Come on, you gotta remember him. That skinny kid. He was a counselor the same time we were. Damn, we gave him hell every summer."

The memories caused Neil to laugh. He hadn't been kidding when he said that they'd given Stinky Bateman hell every summer. There was no one that Neil remembered who they'd tormented more during those three summers. He and his friends had found endless ways to embarrass and humiliate Bateman before the entire camp. If there had been an opportunity to ridicule the boy, Neil had found it and exploited it to the extreme. He'd become the bane of Stinky Bateman's existence for three long summers. If there had ever been a person who received the most contemptible treatment that Neil could dish out, it had been Bateman.

What had surprised Neil was that the boy seemed to just take it all, never exposing him or his friends to the camp owners. Bateman simply allowed it to continue day in and day out. At the time, Neil figured that the kid just wasn't very smart. Maybe he thought he had no choice but to endure the ongoing harassment. Whatever the reason, Bateman had remained tight-lipped for three summers.

"Remember when we dragged him from his cabin late one night? Taped his mouth shut and hogtied him?" Neil asked, attempting to jog their memories. "Then we tossed him in a canoe and rowed him out into the middle of the lake. We left him floating there until morning, hands and feet tied, mouth gagged!"

Glancing around at his companions, Neil couldn't understand their silence and the solemn looks on their faces. "Or what about the time we shot arrows at him when he was supposed to be cleaning up the archery range? He went hightailing it out of there! I'm surprised we never got kicked out for that."

He chuckled at the memories, expecting to hear additional voices joining in, but the only sound came from the crackling campfire. His laughter died away. He glanced at his companions, noticing the grim looks on their faces, each avoiding eye contact. Patrick rose from his chair, walking away from the fire with his head down.

"What the hell's going on?" he asked. "Why the long faces?"

"I guess you didn't hear," said Steve.

"Hear what?"

Steve bowed his head, rubbing his creased forehead with his fingertips. "That last summer—if you remember—you left the camp two weeks early."

Neil remembered it very well. Before he headed off to Harvard, his parents had sent him on a two-week tour of France and Italy. The timing had worked out in such a way that he had to leave prior to the end of camp season. After his departure, he'd heard nothing further about his friends, or Camp Tenskwatawa. "Yeah, I remember. But what's that got to do—"

Steve interrupted, saying, "It happened the week after you left. They found him, early in the morning. Out along one of the trails. He'd hung himself."

CHAPTER TEN

As a DEFENSE attorney, Neil had grown accustomed to surprises and shocking revelations, learning to take everything in stride with his usual callousness. Not much disturbed him these days, which left him to wonder why he found himself at a loss for words over the news of Stinky Bateman's suicide. No snide remarks. No cynical words of dismissal.

For a moment, Neil felt as if he were on trial. A thick atmosphere of unspoken reprehension surrounded the fire, and he felt as if it were directed at him. But it only lasted a moment.

"Suicide?" Neil said. He paused for a moment, and then asked, "Who found him?"

"Patrick," replied Steve.

Patrick had drawn back toward the fire, returning to his seat. Neil caught sight of his eyes, once again cold and dark. "That must've been a shock," he said.

Patrick nodded, then looked away.

"Wilcox was called over, but he was too broken up to do anything," explained Steve.

Rob added, "They sent all the kids home early that week. The police were called. They ruled it a suicide."

"Did he leave a note?" Neil asked.

"Nothing was found," replied Steve. "No one knew why he did it."

"They allowed the summer's last group of kids to come that following week, but . . ." Rob trailed off. He took a long drink from his Bud Light, and then added, "None of the counselors really put their hearts into it. They were all still too much in shock. Everyone was glad when the summer was over."

"After that, things started going downhill. Several of the younger counselors refused to come back the next summer," Jeremy explained. "Once word got around about the suicide, some parents canceled their kid's reservations altogether. The camp never really recovered. The owners kept it limping along for years, but they never could get things back to where it was before the suicide."

Neil heard a genuine sense of loss in their voices, as if they'd lost a dear friend. He assumed that they must be mourning the loss of the camp—surely it wasn't over Bateman. The camp's closure represented the end of an era, of which they'd all been a part. Even Neil was experiencing a mild whimsical longing for the days of his youth. Grieving for the past he understood. But grieving for Bateman?

As silence fell around the fire, Neil mulled over their words. No note. No way to know why he'd killed himself. It could've been anything. There was nothing to say that his or his friends' actions had anything to do with Bateman's death. If the kid couldn't hack being teased a little, that was his problem. After all, he hadn't even been in the camp when it happened. If anything, Bateman's suicide just proved what Neil had suspected about the boy all along—Bateman was nothing but a coward.

Glancing at his companions again, Neil found an absence of the accusatory stares that he thought he'd seen earlier. Perhaps he'd imagined it, just his mind playing tricks.

"Well, it doesn't really surprise me," Neil said.

"What doesn't?" asked Rob.

"That Stinky Bateman committed suicide. It doesn't surprise me."

Patrick glared across the fire at Neil. "What's that supposed to mean?"

"You know, he was weak, a little pansy," Neil replied.

With sudden abruptness, Patrick rose from his chair, sending it tumbling out from underneath of him. The scowl on his face was brimming with rage, the malicious dark eyes reflecting the glimmering firelight. His fists clenched and unclenched repeatedly while his biceps and triceps twitched and strained against the fabric of his white t-shirt. Steve was on his feet in an instant, placing a restraining hand on Patrick's shoulder. Patrick shrugged it off almost immediately.

"Patrick, take it easy," Steve said.

"A pansy, huh?" growled Patrick.

Without taking his eyes off of Patrick, Neil lifted the beer bottle to his lips, taking a long sip. The calm nature of the action only seemed to enrage Patrick further. With a broad smile crossing his face, Neil found his friend's fury not only amusing but downright funny. It took all of his strength not to laugh. He didn't understand why Patrick was angry, and in all honesty, he didn't care. It amused him to see his friend worked up. It was worth the entertainment value alone. As he stared at Patrick over the white-orange flames, he wondered how much goading it would take to get his friend to take a swing at him.

"Come on, you were there. You know what he was like. Insecure, dim-witted, introverted," Neil said. "No one really liked him, not even the little kids. Bateman was a sniveling little wimp with less brains than I've got in my little finger. If he hadn't offed himself, he'd probably be serving up burgers at McDonald's. That's about the best he'd be able to do."

Patrick remained silent, his indignation manifesting itself as gritting teeth and deep breaths. His trembling, clenched fists gave Neil an unspoken measurement of how close Patrick was to that threshold between inaction and angry reaction. He was too close to let up now.

"Besides, I'm sure Bateman was a little faggot. We all thought that. Don't you remember what I did to him the final week I was in camp? God, that was funny!" He paused for a moment just for effect, and then opened his eyes wide. "Oh, do you think I pushed him over the edge?" Feigning surprise, Neil placed his hand over his mouth. Then he shook his head, giving his best over-the-top impression of someone suddenly realizing the error of his ways. "I should be so ashamed."

To Neil's delight, over the threshold he went.

Patrick took a step forward, exclaiming, "You bastard!"

Jeremy was out of his seat in an instant, as was Rob, both joining Steve to hold Patrick back. Shrugging off their grasps, Patrick tried to push forward, but their hands gripped his shoulders and arms. Neil remained seated, serenely sipped at his Corona, and watched with interest as his companions struggled to hold Patrick at bay. Pushing against their arms, Patrick tried to wrestle free from their grasp. Arms thrashed and shoved in a simultaneous effort to extricate and subdue. Shouts for calm were intertwined with curses as Neil's four companions grappled before him.

"All right! All right!" Patrick said after a few moments. "I'm fine!"

The ruckus subsided as Steve, Jeremy, and Rob cautiously released Patrick from their grasp. Sweat dripped from their faces, and, despite Patrick's assurance, the trio remained guarded, not stepping far from him in case things should turn violent again.

Pointing across the campfire, Patrick said, "You're a goddamn jackass, Brewster. Do you know that?"

Neil smiled. "I think we've all known that for years."

Turning away from the fire, Patrick abruptly strode away into the darkness, his shoulders hunched forward and his head bowed.

"Where are you going?" shouted Jeremy.

"For a walk," replied Patrick without turning around.

Steve asked, "You want a flashlight?"

As Patrick disappeared in the night, he replied, "I don't need a fucking flashlight."

When Patrick had vanished into the darkness, Neil's remaining three companions returned to their seats, each silently watching the flickering fire and lost in their own thoughts. For several minutes, the crackling of the flames was the only sound heard. Neil let out a soft sigh of satisfaction, still recovering from the euphoric rush he'd received watching Patrick lose control. For him, it was better than drugs.

"You couldn't just leave it alone, could you?" Jeremy said.

"Three years ago, I defended a drug addict named Gregory Harrison. Not my usual type of client, but he had friends in high places," said Neil. "The guy beat an old woman to death with her own cane for two-hundred and fifty dollars. All so he could score a little more coke. When I met him the first time, he was still suffering from withdrawal. Nasty son of a bitch. Threw a chair against the wall. Got in my face a dozen times. Probably could've snapped my neck with his bare hands."

"Your point is?" asked Rob.

Neil reached his arms behind his head, clasping his fingers together. "Patrick's little outburst can't hold a candle to Harrison's."

Steve laughed, gestured over his shoulder in the direction that Patrick had walked, and then said, "He doesn't need a fucking flashlight."

Jeremy was the next to laugh. "Serving up burgers at McDonald's? Really?"

Unable to contain himself any longer, Rob burst into laughter. "Patrick's right. You really are a jackass."

As their roaring laughter echoed through the trees, Neil wondered if Patrick could hear it. Most assuredly, it wouldn't help the situation, only serving to anger Patrick even more. But he didn't care. He was having a good time with some old friends, and he wasn't about to stop. Maybe it was the alcohol or just the lateness of the night, but, whatever it was, Neil laughed until his sides hurt. Their raucous chorus rang out from the campfire.

After a few minutes, he caught his breath and said, "Give me one more beer, then I'm off to bed."

As Rob handed across a fresh bottle, he said, "What happened to Harrison? You never said."

Neil twisted the top from the bottle. "That reprobate? I got him off on a technicality."

CHAPTER ELEVEN

NEIL'S HEADACHE PALED in comparison to his shock when he awoke. The first thing he noticed was the resounding noise of nature. The birds chirping and the din of small animals foraging through the underbrush roared in his ears, making him wonder if someone had left the cabin door open. It'd been a long time since Neil had suffered from a hangover this bad. The biting morning chill made him reach over to pull the sleeping bag over himself for warmth. When his fingers touched sand, he knew something wasn't right.

Opening his eyes, Neil first saw above him a canopy of interlocking pine and cedar branches. Glancing around, he found himself laying on the cold ground in a small clearing somewhere in the forest. His white t-shirt and gray shorts were damp with the early morning dew. Sitting up, he startled a trio of small birds that had been standing on a nearby branch. Brown, dried pine needles coated the ground and clung to his clothes when he rose to his feet. Shaking his head, sand and the remains of last autumn's decaying leaves fell from his hair. How had he gotten there?

Despite his proclamation the night before, he remembered not going to bed after one last bottle. It had been his last Corona for the night but far from his last drink. He'd had every intention of calling it a night when his bottle was empty. Before he could make good on his intention, Rob had produced a bottle of eighteen-year-old Highland Park single malt scotch, a brand of which Neil had heard great things but never had the pleasure to try. It had been an opportunity too good for him to pass up. To his pleasure, the scotch went down smoothly with the very first glass, making it impossible to turn down a second. Or a third.

As the campfire dwindled away to ash, they finished the bottle, leaving Neil's head addled and his eyes quickly losing the battle against his need for slumber.

Making his excuses, he headed into Sequoia Lodge with Jeremy and Steve following shortly after, leaving Rob alone to aimlessly poke a stick into the smoldering campfire. The single-room cabin was furnished with four bunkbeds flanking the door along both walls. Streaked with grime, the opaque glass in the square window opposite the door revealed nothing but faint shadows.

Neil barely remembered undressing or climbing into the top bunk. The last thing he recalled was a brief conversation between Steve and Jeremy, debating if someone should wait up for Patrick to return.

"Pat'll be back once he's calmed down," Steve had said.

"He'll be pissed when he finds we drank the scotch without him," said Jeremy.

As his eyes gave in to their heaviness, Neil heard Steve reply, "He'll get over it."

Shivering in the brisk morning air, he stumbled when his heel came down upon a sharp stone. It dug in deep, causing him to yelp and curse. He checked his foot. No blood. Brushing the dirt and pine needles from his arms and legs, he glanced around to get his bearings. The clearing was surrounded by the dense forest of pine and cedar trees. A narrow path covered with white sand was the only safe passage that Neil could find out of the clearing.

He spun around to survey the opposite side of the clearing. Reeling backward suddenly, he stumbled into the underbrush, landing hard among the thick brambles. The thorns of the barbed undergrowth ripped at his skin. Struggling to extricate himself, he rose to his feet, gawking at the tall pine tree before him.

Hanging from the trunk—about five feet from the ground—was a pale blue t-shirt, the Camp Tenskwa-tawa logo emblazoned across the front. Two black-handled hunting knives impaled the t-shirt and stuck it to the tree. Spray-painted across the front of the shirt was a single word, KILLER. The paint was a deep red, almost the shade of dried blood.

He took a cautious step forward, reaching out to touch the hilt of one of the knives. The handle vibrated under his touch. At least he wasn't suffering a hallucination brought on by his hangover. He ran his fingers along the t-shirt's hem, the soft cotton felt smooth between his finger and thumb. Was this some kind of sick joke? Neil caught a slight trembling in his hand and, pulling away from the t-shirt, flexed his fingers. The trembling didn't stop. *Get control of yourself*, he thought. *This has got to be a joke.*

He examined the spray-painted word, tracing the letters with his eyes. It must have been sprayed while it hung from the tree. Narrow streaks of paint had been drawn down the shirt by gravity, drying before reaching the hem, creating drip lines off of each letter. *What the hell is this all about?* he thought.

He gripped one of the knife handles, giving it a quick tug. It held fast in the tree. Reaching up, he wrapped both hands around the handle to give it another pull, but he was interrupted by a distant voice echoing through the forest.

"Neil!"

Steve's call was quickly followed by the deeper baritone voice of Jeremy. "Brewster! Where the hell are you?"

Neil turned around, unsure from which way the voices came. "Over here!"

There was silence for a moment, and then came an echoing response. "Where?"

He sighed, took one more look at the macabre display hanging from the tree, and turned toward the narrow trail leading out of the clearing. He had no idea where he was. He and his friends could spend hours shouting at each other before they would find him. He'd have to find his own way out. Neil took a step forward but paused as something else echoed through the trees. It was so faint that, at first, he wasn't even sure he'd heard it.

"Leave me alone, Neil!"

The distant voice was vaguely familiar, but he couldn't quite place it. He was certain it wasn't any of his friends. None of them sounded that timid and whiny. He listened for it again but heard nothing. Deciding that he must have been mistaken, Neil gave an uneasy shrug of his shoulders and moved forward onto the path out of the clearing.

Treading carefully on his bare feet, he sidestepped twigs and stones as his toes sank into the white sands of the trail. Pausing to shout again, he received the same inquiry in response, this time from Rob. The path twisted and turned through the forest, beginning to slowly widen. Neil called out again, "I'm over here!"

"Over where?" came Steve's reply, this time sounding closer than before.

He pressed on along the widening path until it opened onto a sand-covered road. He knew where he was, or at least had a good idea. Ahead, off to the left, Neil saw the camp's old archery range. That meant that he was on the south side of the lake. If he continued toward the archery range, that would put him in the right direction, eventually ending up back at Sequoia Lodge. He could wait for his friends there.

Neil had only taken a few steps in the direction of the archery range when he heard Steve call out from behind him. "There you are!"

Approaching at a rapid pace along the sandy road, Steve, Rob, and Jeremy quickly closed the distance between them. As Neil watched his friends approach, he thought about the t-shirt and the word scrawled across it. He wanted to believe that the t-shirt was there by coincidence, perhaps left behind by the camp's final group of counselors. But the fabric had been clean and fresh, as if it had just been hung hours before he'd awoken. He wondered what it meant. Was it an accusation? Neil had been called a lot of things in his life, but "killer" had never been one of them.

Giving Neil's appearance a quick appraisal, Jeremy asked, "What happened to you?"

"Fell into some brambles. Did you guys do this?"

His friends shared a perplexed look between themselves, and Steve shrugged his shoulders. "Do what?"

"Dump me out here in the middle of the night."

Rob shook his head in denial. "We thought you got lost coming back from the bathhouse."

Neil peered back at the narrow path from which he'd just emerged, now realizing how secluded it really was. His friends could have spent days searching and may have never stumbled upon it. He gestured toward the path's entrance. "And what's up with that t-shirt back there?"

Another perplexed look passed between his friends. "What t-shirt?" asked Jeremy.

"The one hanging from the tree."

"What are you on about?" asked Rob.

Neil turned, preparing to lead them back down the path. "It's down here." He was about to push through the foliage that obscured the path's entrance when he paused. "Where's Patrick?"

Jeremy nodded in the direction from which they'd come. "He's coming now."

With his gray canvas Nikes flinging sand out behind him, Patrick jogged up, perspiration coating his forehead and his dark hair damp and disheveled.

"You found him!" Patrick said. "Where've you been?"

Rob replied, "He was about to show us."

Neil gestured for his friends to follow. "Come on. This way."

Leading them back down the narrow path, he once again tread cautiously, steering his bare feet clear of stones and twigs strewn across the ground. The gritty white sand, having worked its way between his toes, was rubbing the skin raw. Once or twice, Neil's foot came to rest on the sharp edge of an unseen piece of gravel, causing him to suddenly jerk back in pain. His four companions showed no sympathy for his situation, laughing aloud every time. Perturbed by their jesting, he knew it only served him right. He would've done the same if he'd been in their shoes.

As they entered the clearing where Neil had awoken

earlier, he glanced from tree to tree, looking for the one with the spray-painted t-shirt. He felt his friends' eyes watching him curiously as he spun around in the center of the clearing. The longer his search, the more frantic he became. What must they be thinking of him? He examined every tree bordering the clearing, but found no evidence of the t-shirt or the knives.

"It was on one of these trees. But . . ." he started to say.

"What was?" asked Rob.

Neil darted again from tree to tree, running his hands down the bark, searching for even the slightest indentation as proof of the embedded knives. "I told you, a t-shirt. An old Camp Tenskwatawa t-shirt. You remember, the pale blue ones? It was stuck to the tree with two knives."

Steve tried to suppress a laugh. "Knives?"

"Hunting knives. Black handles and serrated blades," Neil replied, finally realizing the futility of his search. "At least I thought . . ."

"There's nothing here now," said Jeremy.

Neil scowled at his friend. "I can see that."

"What the hell were you doing out here anyway?" Rob asked.

"I don't know. I just woke up out here." His gaze returned to scanning the clearing. "I thought you guys must have . . ." His words trailed off as his eyes caught sight of something. He rushed toward a nearby tree, running his fingers over the trunk. "Here! There's a puncture here on this tree."

Steve stepped forward, examining the bark closely. "It's something, but . . ."

"But what?" said Neil.

"It looks more like the trunk has split with age. Look, it runs down the tree for a couple feet." Steve paused, peeling bark from the tree. "Sorry, Neil. I doubt this is from a knife."

"Come on, let's go back to the cabin," Patrick said. "I want breakfast."

Neil noted the barely disguised condescension in Patrick's voice. His friends began to make their way back down the narrow path, leaving him to give the small clearing one last look. He could've sworn there was something here. He could've sworn.

SUMMER, 1995

As the sun set over Camp Tenskwatawa, Neil lounged on the small porch of Redwood Lodge, staring across at the bathhouse. Every so often, he'd snicker, recalling again the image of Stinky Bateman's mad dash from the bathhouse to his cabin. Throughout the day, the hushed undertones between the teenage camp counselors had been about the morning's incident with the snake, so much so that Stinky had remained in his cabin for most of the day to avoid further embarrassment.

The first few hours of the morning, Neil had watched with interest as Charlie Wilcox and Harvey Brennan, one of the camp supervisors, searched the bathhouse as well as the surrounding area. Presumably looking for snakes. By noon, they'd come up emptyhanded and seemed to chalk the whole event up to nothing more than a freak accident of nature.

Neil hadn't been around when Stinky finally emerged from Oak Lodge, but he'd heard every detail from Steve.

"You should've seen him. Head down, pouting like a baby. He couldn't walk more than a few feet without someone whistling at him."

Now, as the evening shadows fell across the camp, Neil found himself wondering why he was still there. He'd been expecting camp management to call him to account for his actions. He figured that he and his friends would be immediately sent packing with their final paycheck in hand. The morning's escapade couldn't possibly be behavior deemed acceptable in the "finest Camp Tenskwatawa tradition." He laughed as he recalled the lecture about being respectful to fellow counselors from camp orientation. Neil didn't do respectful.

Tossing a snake into the bathhouse while Stinky showered, he knew, would put his job at the camp in jeopardy. Despite the fact that it was only his first summer at camp, he'd decided that the prank was worth risking his job for. Neil had been right. But thus far, there had been no rebuke, no expulsion from camp, not even a slap on the wrist. It left him puzzled.

Jeremy was leaning against the porch railing, rolling a joint between his fingers. Occasionally, he'd glance over his shoulder to see if anyone was looking.

Neil said, "You're gonna get caught."

"What's it matter anyway? We'll probably be out of here before the night's over." Jeremy ran his tongue along the edge of the rolling paper. "They'll figure out it was us before too long."

The flare of a match made Neil glance at his friend. Jeremy drew hard on the joint hanging between his lips. Neil sighed loudly. "Seriously? You're just asking for trouble."

Jeremy shrugged his shoulders, taking another obstinate hit from the joint. "Got to get a couple hits in before more brats arrive."

Folding his arms, Neil frowned and nodded his head. New campers would be arriving early the next afternoon. If he and his friends were getting fired, the supervisors would have to work fast to accommodate the next influx of kids.

The sudden approach of footsteps piqued Neil's attention, and he gave Jeremy a firm stare. "Someone's coming."

"Shit!"

The joint fell to the floor of the porch, and Jeremy pressed firmly on it with his foot. Then he shuffled it forward until it dropped through a crack between the floorboards, disappearing from sight. Neil and Jeremy waved their hands frantically, trying to clear the sweet aroma that lingered in the air.

When Patrick rounded the corner of the cabin and stepped onto the porch, Jeremy cursed loudly. "A waste of a perfectly good joint," he said.

Patrick hiked himself up onto the porch railing, leaning his shoulder against one of the corner porch posts. "I've got news."

Jeremy scowled at Patrick. "You owe me for that joint."

Neil said, "Shut up, Jeremy." He turned toward Patrick. "What d'ya know?"

"I think we're off the hook."

Neil folded his arms. "Go on."

Patrick's grin broadened. "I overheard Brennan and Wilcox talking a few minutes ago. Stinky claimed that he didn't know how the snake got into the shower. Better yet, it doesn't sound like he said anything about us stealing his clothes. I think we're in the clear!"

Neil's eyes narrowed and he turned his back on his friends to stare out into the forest. "Good. We live for another day. We'll have to make sure to repay Stinky's courteousness." He tilted his head back and laughed.

CHAPTER TWELVE

While Jeremy hovered over the Coleman camp stove on the picnic table, Neil sat near the charred remains of the previous evening's campfire. He'd just returned from the bathhouse, his hair still damp from the cold shower he'd taken. His head felt far clearer than it had earlier that morning. The aroma of frying bacon drifted through the air accompanying the sound of it sizzling in the pan, tempting and inciting within him a rampant hunger. He took a sip from the styrofoam cup he was holding, grimaced at the taste, and tossed the cup and its contents into the fire pit. It'd be no coffee for the rest of the weekend. He wasn't about to drink that instant crap.

While Steve and Patrick grabbed their towels and headed off to the bathhouse, Rob lounged with his feet resting on one of the blackened rocks that made up the fire ring. Neil wondered how long it'd be before the chair collapsed under the strain of his friend's attempts to slouch in an almost recumbent position.

"It said 'Killer'?" Rob asked.

Neil nodded. "Yeah, in red spray paint." He'd given his friends a description of what he'd seen hanging from the tree, receiving skeptical glances in return. He couldn't blame them for being dubious. There'd been no trace of the t-shirt or the knives, and the topic was quickly dropped as they returned to Sequoia Lodge.

Rob lifted his feet off the rock, sliding back into his seat, then leaned forward, his hands clasped together between his knees. He laughed. "Sounds like that scotch didn't sit well with you."

Only half-amused by his comment, Neil laughed accordingly. The insinuation was a bit insulting. He was a very capable drinker, and the idea that drinking too much the night before would cause hallucinations was ludicrous. He knew the t-shirt was there. He knew the knives were there. He'd touched them for Christ's sake.

"It doesn't explain how I ended up in the middle of the forest, does it?" he asked, unable to disguise the irritation in his voice.

"Do you sleepwalk?"

"Never."

Rob leaned back into his chair, fingering the tuft of hair on his chin. "You'd be surprised how often a single incident or event can trigger a subconscious behavior. Have you been sleeping okay?"

"What are you, my therapist?"

"Four years of psychology at Princeton," said Rob. Neil's surprise must have shown on his face because his friend added, "I own a bar on South Street in Philadelphia. Four years of listening to lectures and writing papers about phobias, disorders, and all that crap. I just didn't have the energy, or the interest to go any further with it. I couldn't bear to be a respectable psychologist with regular office hours, patient lists, and spending my time listening to other people's problems."

"So you went and got yourself a bar?"

"A highly successful bar for ten years," Rob said. "Jasper's Folly."

Neil didn't quite follow that last remark. "Huh?"

"Jasper's Folly. That's the name of my bar."

Nodding his head, Neil watched his friend lean back into his chair once again, stretching his legs out and placing his heels upon the same rock. As Rob tilted his head back and closed his eyes, Neil was forced, for a moment, to admire his friend's laid-back manner. Every fiber exuded a sense of relaxation, a lack of stress and tension. Rob's breathing was steady, slow, and barely perceptible while his shoulders hung loosely, without any of the tautness that Neil often felt. With the ongoing demands of back-to-back trials, he was constantly plotting his next rebuttal, his next motion, the next subpoena, every item of legal wrangling that he could think of. There was rarely a moment when he wasn't thinking of his latest case. Even while having sex with Sheila, his mind was often preoccupied with whatever case he was working on at the time. She never noticed. He'd always prided himself on being a good multitasker.

Envy streaked through Neil's soul as he watched Rob stretched out by the dead campfire. What must it be like to let go of all concern for one's responsibilities for an hour, a day, or even a weekend?

Neil said, "Who's Jasper?"

Lifting his head up, Rob opened his eyes, gazing through half-closed lids. "Don't know. The place was named that when I bought it."

"It's a nice place. Might be a bit lowbrow for a high-priced lawyer like you," said Jeremy.

Rob raised one eyebrow, then laughed nervously. Jeremy abruptly turned his attention back to the frying bacon, flipping the thin slices in the pan with a stainless-steel spatula. Neil felt the moment of awkwardness hanging in the air between his two friends.

"You been there?" Neil turned in his chair to look across at Jeremy.

Still shuffling the bacon around in the pan, Jeremy replied, "Yeah. Once or twice. When was the last time?" He looked at Rob, as if asking for help. "Was it a couple years ago? That was the last time I was back in Philly."

Rob, without opening his eyes, gave a brief nod. "Yeah, I think so."

"My clients' schedules don't leave me much time for travel. The rich and powerful like their personal trainers to be at their beck and call twenty-four seven." Jeremy's voice changed, taking on an air of condescension. "You never know when they need to drop a few pounds to get into a gown or tux." His deep laugh resonated through the air.

"How'd they take the news that you were abandoning them for the weekend?" asked Rob.

Jeremy laughed. "You know how these Hollywood types can be. One actually offered to pay me to be available by phone."

"So you're on a three-thousand-mile leash?" Neil said.

"No cell service here," said Jeremy. "They weren't happy, but they'll get over it."

Footsteps approaching from the direction of the bathhouse made Neil turn his head, catching sight of Steve and Patrick's return. With his towel draped around his neck, Steve was still rubbing the end of the terry cloth over his damp head. Patrick, shirtless, had his towel carelessly tossed over his right shoulder. His chest was smooth and hairless, just as it had been when they were young, but

Patrick's abs and pecs held far more definition.

"What's so funny?" Steve asked.

Rob replied, "Jeremy was just telling us how his rich, fat clients keep him busy."

Jeremy waved the spatula in the air, pointing it at Rob. "They're not all rich."

"Just fat," Patrick added.

As they laughed, Jeremy removed strips of bacon, dripping with grease, from the frying pan, laying them on a paper-towel covered Dixie plate. With the drippings still sizzling in the pan, Jeremy grabbed two brown eggs from a nearby carton. "How do you want your eggs cooked, Steve? Over easy?"

"Perfect," came the reply.

The sizzle from the frying pan grew louder as Jeremy struck the edge of the pan with an egg, expertly separating the two halves of the shell. Steve disappeared into the cabin while Patrick circled the stone ring, kicking Rob's feet out of the way as he passed. Thrown off balance and almost tumbling out of his chair, Rob quickly righted himself, cursing at Patrick. Neil laughed as he watched his friend settle into the chair across from him. "You been to Rob's bar?"

The briefest of glances passed between Rob and Patrick, but it hadn't been brief enough for Neil to not notice. Patrick shook his head. "No." As Steve returned from Sequoia Lodge, Patrick added, "What about you Steve? You ever been to Rob's shithole bar?"

Rob exclaimed, "Shithole?"

Steve let out a hearty laugh. "Yeah, a couple times."

Neil's eyes followed Steve as he crossed to the picnic table. "What're we doing today?"

"How about a little two-on-two football? Jeremy, you still got that arm of yours?" asked Rob. "You can QB for both sides."

"Might still be able to lob a few around. But I've got my eye on that zipline," Jeremy said as he scooped two eggs out of the pan and set them on a plate. "Here you go, Steve," he added. Grabbing two more eggs, Jeremy cracked them over the pan and asked, "Brewster, how do you want yours?"

"Scrambled."

Steve grabbed the plate, pausing as he glanced at his eggs. "This is what you call over easy?"

"I'm cooking on a camp stove. How did you think they'd turn out?"

Steve laughed, grabbed a plastic fork, and piled three slices of bacon on top of his eggs. Standing by the picnic table, he jabbed at the eggs with his fork, lifting a piece to his mouth. The flimsy plate was balanced on his fingertips, drooping precariously under the weight of Steve's breakfast. Neil wondered how long before it would completely surrender its shape to the wiles of gravity.

"Football? Haven't played in years," said Patrick. "I'm with Jeremy. Let's do the zipline."

"I'm game for either," said Rob. "How 'bout you, Neil?"

"Football." His answer came out more abruptly than he'd intended. He hoped that no one had noticed. He had his reasons for wanting to avoid the zipline, if at all possible.

PATRICK had paced out the end zones and marked them with the four camp chairs they'd brought from the lodge. The sandy clearing where their cars were parked would be more than adequate for a bit of two-on-two football. There'd been, at first, a lot of enthusiasm among Neil's friends toward spending the morning on the zipline.

But to his relief, he'd been able to convince them to forego the zipline for a quick game of football.

With Jeremy acting as quarterback for both teams, they split up—Rob and Neil against Patrick and Steve. Neil flipped a coin, with his team winning the toss. Choosing to be on offense first, he, Rob, and Jeremy huddled for a moment, then lined up for the first play of the game.

Jeremy could still throw the ball straight as an arrow. As for the rest of them . . . Neil would never say it was bad, but it certainly was far from good. Although Jeremy's passes were usually right on target, Neil, more than a few times, found himself able to get his fingers on the ball but unable to haul it in for a catch. He wasn't too concerned about his poor performance as his friends weren't doing much better.

A half hour into the game, they all showed signs of improvement as eighteen years of proverbial rust was worked out of their systems. Catching a long ball, Neil managed to go the distance for a touchdown, with Steve trailing behind him without a prayer of making the tackle.

"That's how you do it!" Neil exclaimed, spiking the ball and breaking into a little dance.

Steve, leaning over with his hands on his knees, said between gasps, "I almost had you."

"Almost doesn't count."

As he caught his breath, Neil looked up the field, catching sight of Jeremy, Rob, and Patrick waiting impatiently for him and Steve to return. His eyes were drawn, however, past them into the forest beyond. Standing deep among the trees was a solitary figure. The distance made it difficult for him to see any details clearly, but the figure was wearing a pale blue shirt and bright red cap. It had been the cap that first caught his eye. Its color stood out from the foliage. The figure stood motionless, as if watching them.

Neil glanced at Steve, who was wiping the sweat from his forehead with his sleeve. "Are we the only ones in the camp?"

"Yep."

Turning his head back toward the figure, Neil said, "Then who is . . ." His words trailed off. The figure was gone.

Steve followed his gaze. "Who's what?"

"There was . . . I could've sworn there was someone watching us."

Looking around, Steve said, "I don't see anyone."

Neil gestured toward the forest. "A red cap. Someone was wearing a bright red cap."

"There's nothing there now." Steve placed his hands on his hips, pausing for a moment. "Red cap? Didn't Bateman used to wear a red cap?"

Neil felt his face grow warm, a momentary wave of anger flashed over him. He glared at his friend.

Steve smiled. "I'm just messing with ya."

"Sometime today!" shouted Patrick from the other end of the clearing.

Steve laughed at Patrick's impatience. "We're coming!" Then he glanced at Neil and added, "Neil's just seeing things again!"

Neil scowled at his friend's remark. Steve returned the scowl with a smirk and then laughed aloud.

"Oh, for Christ's sake!" shouted Patrick from across the field. "He needs to get his head examined."

Neil allowed his irritation to simmer just below the surface. No point in letting them know that they'd struck a nerve. He'd never been able to tolerate being on the receiving end of ridicule, even as a child. The "love thy neighbor" philosophy was one that he'd never been willing to embrace. He'd always preferred "Do unto others before they do unto you."

They continued to play football for another hour, moving the ball up and down the makeshift field with the score remaining relatively even throughout. Despite his best efforts, Neil remained distracted, his eyes always drifting toward the surrounding forest. If the figure with the red cap returned, he wanted to get a good look.

Breaking from the huddle, Neil lined up to Jeremy's right, planning to run a crossing route that, if successful, would put him within easy reach of another touchdown. When the ball snapped, he charged down the field with Steve an arm's length behind. Steve was left stumbling to compensate after Neil made a sudden turn to the right. Glancing over his shoulder, Neil saw Jeremy's hand draw back for the throw. A red blur among the trees captured his gaze. It darted through the forest on the clearing's edge, weaving around the trees and crashing through the underbrush. Distracted, Neil slowed his pace—almost involuntarily—coming to a halt in the middle of the field.

For a moment, the blur came into focus, giving Neil the impression of a thin figure dressed in tan shorts and a pale t-shirt. The same pale blue color as the defaced camp t-shirt he'd seen earlier in the morning. He couldn't see the front of the shirt, couldn't tell if it was the same one.

When the football slammed into his shoulder, Neil was thrown off balance and was sent to the ground. Jeremy had always had a strong throwing arm, and he'd proven throughout the morning that he could still put a great deal of power behind a throw. This one had been the hardest Neil had felt. He rolled onto his side, grabbing at his shoulder in pain. "Damn it!"

"Why'd you stop?" shouted Jeremy from down the

field. "You were wide open!"

As the pain subsided, Neil climbed to his feet, brushing the sand from his hair and clothes and spitting grit from his mouth. "I got distracted."

Scanning the forest, he tried to find the figure with the red hat but saw nothing. His glimpse had been brief, but he would've sworn it was the same figure from earlier. As they walked back up the field, he considered telling Steve what he'd seen but decided against it. Best to keep it to himself.

"Enough with football, let's go hit the zipline," Jeremy said as they approached.

Rob was quick to agree with Jeremy. "Count me in."

Neil felt a knot begin to form in his stomach. He knew this moment was bound to happen at some point during the weekend. His friends had shown far too much enthusiasm the previous night when they learned of the camp's zipline. He knew they'd want to ride it, and he'd have no choice but to go with them. Choosing to simply not participate would mean admitting his fear, and that was not an option.

"I'm all for that," said Patrick.

Steve placed his hand on Neil's shoulder. "What d'ya think, Neil? Want to brave the zipline?"

For a moment, Neil wondered if his friend's question held some underlying subtext, as if Steve knew his secret. He'd worked hard to conceal his fear. With a reputation to uphold, it would have been to his disadvantage if any of his friends knew. He'd hidden it well, even from Sheila. Neil had thrived on exploiting people's weakness for his own amusement—sometimes even for gain. He never wanted to give anyone ammunition that they could use against him.

He faked a casual smile. "Is it safe? The camp's been

closed down for a couple years."

Steve replied, "Yeah. I had one of our engineers give the whole camp a quick once over—at least the stuff we might use."

"I'm not sure how reassuring that is," Neil said, laughing. It sounded lighthearted, but the laugh concealed the underlying anxiety that continued to grow in intensity with each moment. "Experts on ziplines, these engineers of yours?"

Steve replied. "They're good enough. Stop worrying about it."

"Who's worrying? I'm just being cautious." He was lying.

"Steve, you better hope those engineers of yours are right," said Patrick. "Because if the big-shot lawyer gets hurt, he'll probably sue your ass."

"Trust me, it's all good," came Steve's reply. "Everything's ready."

To Neil, the reply seemed more like a pronouncement, and with it the agenda was settled. Whether he liked it or not, they were riding the zipline.

CHAPTER THIRTEEN

Sammy crept through the underbrush, trying to stay away from the main camp trails. The brambles and thickets didn't bother her. She'd always had a knack for being able to scramble through the thickest underbrush without getting a scratch. Most of her childhood had been spent exploring the forest surrounding Camp Tenskwatawa, and she was certain there wasn't an inch of the camp that she hadn't seen at one time or another.

Recalling her childhood brought a smile to her face. Hot summer days running along sandy trails chasing imaginary pixies and fairies came to mind, and, for a moment, she was wistful for the innocent days of her youth. Things had been simpler then, no heartbreak and no pain. If only she could turn back time, turn back the days to before . . .

She froze at the sound of their voices, crouching into the underbrush and remaining still. The main trail around the lake was to her right. They'd be coming along it at any moment. She'd let them pass and then work her way around to the far side of the zipline.

As they drew closer, Sammy heard his voice among the others. His dulcet tones were smooth and pleasant to listen to. She could understand why Neil had been so successful in the courtroom. It'd been his voice she'd first fallen for twenty years ago. For her, it still held some magic.

"Next thing I know, he's jumping out of the witness box and lunging at me," she heard him say.

The other four laughed as he continued to recount his tale. She lifted her head up, just enough to peek over the thick brambles. They were passing close to her, giving her a good look at them. Eighteen years had changed each of them, some more than others. Sammy remembered the last time she'd seen each of them. Five, maybe six months ago. It had been a brief ceremony, if you could call it that. Just a few quick words, and then letting the ashes scatter across the lake in the wind. Five of them standing on the shore of Lake Friendship, silent and morose. Neil was the only one who wasn't there. But then, that had been the plan all along.

Sammy looked at Neil once again, feeling that faint stirring within her. She cursed softly under her breath. *Control yourself, Sammy*, she thought. *Remember who he is.*

Once they passed by, she slipped across the main trail and circled around through the forest until she heard their voices again. Sammy was cautious, moving silently through the forest until she came to the spot she'd scoped out earlier. From her vantage point, she could see almost the entire zipline.

They were standing below the launch platform, which was suspended from the side of a pine tree. The distance from the ground to the platform, her father had once told her, was seventy-five feet. When the camp had been open, the ladder rungs leading up had been painted gray. But time had taken its toll. The paint was peeling off, and splotches of rust had formed on the aged metal underneath. She could just make out the dark steel cable stretching from the platform out into the forest, disappearing into the canopy of branches.

Steve fumbled with the harness. "How does this work?"

Jeremy snatched the harness from his hand. "You got it upside down."

"You've done this before?" Neil asked.

She watched him closely. Neil was fidgety, his feet kept shifting in the sand. Sammy couldn't help but feel a certain amount of sympathy for him. She knew his secret and could only imagine how terrified he must be. Seventy-five feet above the ground didn't sound like much, but for an acrophobe . . .

"Numerous times," Jeremy said, smiling. "It's simple."

Jeremy took a moment to demonstrate how to wear the harness, then asked, "Who's going first?"

Steve folded his arms and looked back at Jeremy. "You go first. Show us newbies how it's done."

Jeremy shrugged. "Works for me!"

Moments later, Jeremy had scaled the ladder to the launching platform and clipped the harness into the zip trolley. Sammy slid lower into the underbrush when she saw him gaze around the forest from his elevated position. She couldn't be certain that he saw her, but his eyes seemed to linger for a few moments in her direction. Then he pushed off from the platform. "Cya, losers!" he shouted.

She watched Jeremy speed off into the trees, his legs flailing wildly. His yells were loud, overshadowing the high-pitched whine of the trolley racing down the cable. It sounded like he was having the time of his life. Glancing across at Neil, she noticed that his forehead was moist. His fear appeared to be getting the better of him. She almost pitied him. Was it really necessary to put him through this? Maybe her father had been right. Maybe this wouldn't bring her closure. Perhaps it would be best if she showed him mercy.

"Awesome!" Jeremy shouted from the far end of the zipline.

Throughout the past eighteen years, mercy had been the furthest thing from Sammy's mind. She'd burned with anger and hatred for the first five, fell into a melancholy haze for the next ten, and, finally, spent the last three years with a focused vigor toward revenge. It made her feel better to think of it as justice, but in the end, she knew it was nothing more than seeking vengeance.

Jeremy came crashing through the underbrush, returning to his friends. She didn't think the smile on his face could get any broader. He held the harness and zip trolley aloft like it was a trophy. She watched him raise his hand in the air, receiving high-fives from Patrick and Steve. Rob, who was leaning against the ladder, just laughed. Then, without warning, Jeremy tossed the harness to Neil, whose hands fumbled to catch it. "Brewster, you're next!" Jeremy said.

Sammy focused her attention on Neil. This could be a telling moment. She saw him smile, but it looked forced. He groped at the harness, unable to get it the right way around. When he did finally manage to get his legs into it, his hands were trembling. Did his friends notice? If they did, they didn't seem to let on. *He must be terrified*, she thought.

When Neil had made snug the harness straps, he moved to the ladder. He paused, his back toward his friends. From her vantage point, Sammy saw something that his friends could not—his face. His eyes clenched closed, as if he were in excruciating pain. His hands clamped on the ladder rungs, his knuckles turned white.

"Neil," said Jeremy.

"What?"

Jeremy stretched his hand forward, holding the zip trolley out before him. "You won't get far without this."

Neil took the zip trolley, and then turned back to the ladder, pausing for a moment longer. Sammy fought the urge to rush headlong from the underbrush to put an end to his torment. Was this fair? Was this right? Every fiber of her being begged her to put a stop to it. Every ounce of compassion cried for her to release him from this torture. But then her hand—almost by instinct—clutched the St. Christopher medal around her neck. The small object between her fingers banished any thought of compassion or mercy from her mind.

"Come on, Neil. We ain't got all day," Rob said.

She watched Neil raise his hand, extend his middle finger, and then grasp one of the ladder rungs. *He hasn't changed*, she thought. *He never will. He deserves everything that's coming.*

His climb was slow and, she was certain, grueling. Hand over hand and foot over foot, he rose up the ladder, the trembling in his arms and legs becoming more pronounced. Every step looked as if it was harder than the last. His face seemed to reveal every agonizing thought. She imagined the litany of questions running through his head. *What if my foot slips? What if I lose my grip? What if? What if? What if?* She wondered how prideful Neil must be to refuse to admit that he was afraid. Her narrowed eyes followed every move of his ascent. *No mercy*, she thought. *No compassion.*

When he reached the platform, Neil pressed his back against the tree with his eyes tightly closed. The platform was nothing more than crisscrossed steel bars, giving her an almost unobstructed view of him as he stood unmoving among the trees. His face looked pale, and, for a moment, she thought he might vomit over the side of the platform. With a slow, deliberate motion, his hand reached upward, touching the steel cable above his head. She watched him slip the trolley over the cable and attach his harness.

"Sometime today, Neil," shouted Patrick.

Sammy found herself again feeling pity for him. Did he realize how pathetic he looked up on that platform? She experienced a moment of compassion, wanting to put an end to his suffering. It'd been a long time since she'd felt anything for him other than animosity. There'd been a time when she felt something akin to love, but those emotions were thought to be dead and buried. Yet, when she'd seen him again last night . . .

With a sudden movement, he pushed off from the tree and sped along the cable. His eyes were open, and a mix of emotion crossed his face—part terror, part exhilaration. His hands clenched the lanyard of his harness while his legs thrashed about in the open air. She smiled, relieved to see that his terror seemed to be subsiding. She cursed under her breath, upset for her moment of empathy. *He must suffer*, she reminded herself. *Just like him, I'll show no mercy.*

The squeal drew her eyes back onto him. The trolley had stopped with an unexpected jolt, leaving Neil rocking back and forth like a pendulum. Sammy figured that he'd traveled about twenty-five feet from the platform. The exhilaration that she'd seen on his face moments ago had vanished, being replaced with utter terror. She watched him bounce and swing from the lanyard's end. His fingers curled around the nylon strap while his head darted from side to side. Sammy lowered herself to conceal her from detection.

It was then that she heard the voices.

CHAPTER FOURTEEN

It took him a few moments to recognize the voices, and only another moment to realize that they came from the same person. There was a childlike innocence in the voice, along with a high-pitched whine that stirred up long forgotten memories. It'd been eighteen years since he'd last heard that voice.

"Neil! Stop it!" echoed through the forest from every direction.

He twisted his head in search of the source but found nothing.

The voice echoed again. "Leave me alone, Neil!"

"Is this a joke?" Neil shouted.

"Stop it, Neil!" was the only reply he received.

The words repeated again and again, overlapping like a dozen people speaking at once. The ghastly montage filled the air around him. There was no way he could escape. Releasing his grip on the lanyard, Neil covered his ears with his hands. He realized his error as he pitched backward, leaving him hanging upside down by a single cord. His arms and legs flailed in desperation, a panicked bid to right himself. His thrashing had sent him into a spin, making him dizzy as the ground twirled below him. He swallowed hard, fighting back the bile that begged to spew forth. The tightening in his chest made every breath an overwhelming effort. And still the voices continued to bombard him.

His hand grasped the lanyard, and he pulled himself upright. His eyes fought to focus on something—anything. Clinging to the nylon lanyard, he pressed his forehead against his clenched fists. He closed his eyes, trying to slow his breathing.

"Damn it! Someone stop it!" Neil shouted.

His hands were tingling, and his blood felt as if it had turned ice cold. His eyes lost the ability to focus. The echoing voices ripped through him, inducing a full-fledged panic attack.

"Neil, stop it! Leave me alone, Neil!" the voice echoed. "Stop it, Neil!"

He could swear it was getting louder, and the words were melding together into an unharmonious chorus straight out of hell. With his heart threatening to shatter his ribcage with its rapid hammering, Neil feared that he might die right there in the air. His lungs burned with each inhale. His head ached, either from the utter terror or the increasingly loud and repetitive words that reverberated in his ears. He didn't know which.

"Neil, stop it!"

"Leave me alone, Neil!"

"Stop it, Neil!"

Over and over the words repeated, getting louder and louder with each repetition. His mind plowed through the scenarios, each as terrifying as the one before. Most ending with a long plummet through the trees to his death. The voices pounded their way into his head, into his psyche, invading every crevice and every cavity not already terrorized by his distance from the ground. His hands trembled violently as they clutched at the lanyard, sending tiny vibrations up into the cable. He opened his eyes, looking up at the trolley above his head. *Why wasn't it moving, damn it?* he thought.

Neil gripped the lanyard and shook it, determined to get himself going. The echoing voices built to a crescendo, louder and louder, more distorted with every second. Squeezing his eyes closed, Neil screamed in a vain attempt to drown out the unending din, desperate to make it stop. He just wanted it to be over.

Then, just as quickly as it had started, it ended. The voices abruptly stopped, and the zip trolley began to move forward. As his momentum picked up, Neil felt the cool wind once again blow against his face. Looking ahead, he saw the landing platform quickly approaching. When he'd pushed himself off earlier, there had been a sense of exhilaration intermingled with his fear. But now, all he felt was pure and unadulterated relief.

The landing platform was a narrow upward slope over which the zipline crossed. As he approached, Neil extended his feet out, slowing himself down as they drug through the dirt. He quickly unhooked the harness from the trolley, dropped to his knees, and spewed his breakfast across the ground, heaving again and again until there was nothing left to come out. The acidic vomit burned his esophagus, leaving a bitter taste in his mouth. Breathing deeply, his nose picked up the sour odor of his own regurgitation, causing him to heave again. This time, there was nothing more to bring up besides a bit of stomach bile. Wiping his chin with his forearm, he stared down at the watery remnants of his congealing breakfast on the dirt below him.

Still trembling, Neil's arms ached as he pushed himself up. Kneeling in the dirt, he tried to work out what had just happened. His first instinct was that it had been a joke, a bit tasteless, but a joke nonetheless.

But it didn't make sense. None of his friends knew that he was afraid of heights. And even if they did, what the hell was up with the voices? He could understand leaving him hanging for a few moments on the zipline, but why bombard him with a voice from the past? He dismissed the idea as soon as he'd thought of it. His friends would never be that cruel, certainly not to him.

Neil tried to think rationally. There had to be a logical explanation. It must have been a mechanical problem. Steve's engineers weren't as sharp as he claimed. Perhaps something got jammed in the wheels of the trolley. That was probably all it was. And the voices? Just his imagination. Already overtaxed by his fear of heights, his imagination must've gone a little wild, causing him to hear things that weren't there. It all made perfect sense. Figuring it out, however, didn't make him feel any better about the ordeal. It'd still been terrifying. Gazing down at the remains of his half-digested breakfast, he sighed, realizing that he'd have to explain this to his friends. Preferably without telling them that he'd been scared shitless.

He heard them drawing closer, crashing through the underbrush, probably coming to see if he was okay. Trying to stand, Neil found that his legs didn't seem to have the strength. He remained on his knees, breathing deeply and feeling his heartbeat finally begin to slow. He closed his eyes, only to snap them back open suddenly—the memories being far too fresh to allow his mind a moment's peace. The moment his eyes were closed, he heard the distant echoes of that voice. They'd been seared into his subconscious. Why would he imagine the voices? Why *his* voice?

"Brewster, what's taking you so . . ." Jeremy started to say as he emerged from the underbrush. "What happened to you?"

Before Neil answered, his three other friends arrived behind Jeremy. Their footsteps stopped abruptly, and, without looking up, he knew that they were gaping at him just like Jeremy. Inhaling deeply, he rose to his feet, slowly at first, still unsure about the stability of his legs. Turning, his eyes met the concerned gazes of his four companions.

Looking down, he mumbled, "Please tell me you guys didn't have anything to do with that."

Rob shrugged his shoulders. "With what? What happened?"

Neil wasn't sure how to explain it. Words, for once in his life, seemed to fail him. The ordeal had exhausted him, both physically and mentally. He felt as if his mind had been shattered into a million pieces, and pulling it back together was like doing a jigsaw puzzle without the picture on the box. The world around him remained a blur, his eyes still struggling to focus. His friends remained patient, quietly waiting as he gathered his thoughts.

Sighing, he began to explain. "It got stuck. The trolley got stuck." Speaking was difficult. His tongue stuck to the roof of his parched mouth. "I couldn't get it moving . . . just hung there."

Jeremy reached over and loosened the harness from around Neil's waist and legs. "Let's get this off you."

As the harness slid down his legs, he continued, "I flipped over . . . was spinning around . . . couldn't move." He paused, glancing at Patrick. The look on his friend's face wasn't one of concern but one of confusion. Patrick's eyes darted between Neil and his friends. With his thoughts and words still coming out in fragments, Neil said, "Something stopped the trolley in the middle of the ride."

"But Neil—" Rob started to say.

"And then the voices . . ." Neil interrupted. "The voices were so loud."

Steve touched his shoulder. "Neil, are you okay?"

Another deep breath helped to clear his mind further. How would he explain this to his friends? They'd want an explanation. There'd be no way to get around it. They must have seen the way he'd panicked on the zipline. He decided there was no option but to tell the truth. "I'm afraid of heights. When the trolley got stuck, I panicked. I, um, must have hallucinated for a moment . . . I thought I heard voices while I was up there."

"Voices?" asked Jeremy.

Neil nodded. "Yeah. I . . . I heard Stinky Bateman's voice. It was coming from everywhere."

Neil caught the glances exchanged between his friends. He could only guess what was probably going through their minds. First, he'd seen a disappearing t-shirt with the word "KILLER" written across it, and now he was hearing voices. The verdict wouldn't have been hard to predict.

Patrick folded his arms and said, "Neil, putting aside the voices for just a moment. You said the trolley got stuck?"

"Yeah." He nodded, gesturing in the direction of the launching platform. "Shortly after I pushed off. I was probably about fifty feet off the ground."

Another glance passed between his friends. Patrick looked at Neil. "We watched your whole ride. From the moment you pushed off almost 'til you landed." He paused.

"We saw you go all the way down the line. You never stopped."

SUMMER, 1996

BORDERING ON OBSESSION, Patrick had insisted on recording almost everything on the Sony HandyCam he'd brought to camp that second summer. Neil thought it was funny at first, but now he wasn't so sure. They'd recorded things that he'd prefer the camp leadership never see. Some of the video footage was innocent enough, but there'd be hell to pay if anyone ever saw the footage they'd recorded from the girls' bathhouse. And he didn't know how Brenda Miller would live down the humiliation if the footage in which she'd played a starring role ever got out. He smiled, remembering how he'd charmed the seventeen-year-old into performing a striptease for the camera. She had the body and the moves, making the ten-minute video the closest that they'd ever come to filming something X-rated. Not that they hadn't tried.

The rain had been falling throughout the day on that mid-July Friday, but the storm was beginning to let up with the approaching sunset. Standing on the porch of

Redwood Lodge, Neil gazed out at the saturated forest, hoping that it wouldn't interfere with the evening escapade he had planned. Patrick stood beside him, video camera in hand, filming the scene. Jeremy, leaning against the porch rail, folded his arms and scowled as the camera lens pointed in his direction.

"Turn that goddamn thing off!" Jeremy said.

Patrick laughed and redirected his focus onto two girl counselors who were passing along the nearby trail. They were huddled together underneath a black umbrella, hurrying along in the direction of the rec hall.

"Hey girls! Give us a smile for the camera!" Patrick shouted.

Stacy, the older of the two girls, waved, and then tilted the umbrella slightly to conceal their faces from view. Neil heard them giggle as they continued past the cabin.

"You're not bringing that thing tonight, are you?" he asked Patrick.

Lowering the camera, Patrick smiled. "Of course. Gotta capture everything for posterity."

Neil frowned. "Just keep those tapes safe. We don't want anyone catching on to the shit we've been doing to Stinky. We could get into a lot of trouble."

"Yeah, whatever," said Patrick, shrugging his shoulders and turning away. "You were happy to have me recording Bateman's squeals when we cornered him in the archery range a couple weeks ago. You've made me replay that at least a dozen times."

"I'll admit that was funny, but I just don't want anyone of importance to see them, that's all."

"As much as I like listening to you two love birds bicker, are we on for tonight?" said Jeremy.

Neil glanced back out across the sodden forest. "I don't see why not. He'll probably get wet anyway."

"What time?" said Patrick.

Running over the plan in his head, Neil calculated the time table for what would be his most audacious prank yet. Stinky Bateman's cabin co-counselor had decided to go home for the weekend, providing them with an opportunity that didn't come along very often— Bateman sleeping in his cabin, alone. It was the sort of thing Neil couldn't pass up. He'd spent two days working out the details, and he'd shared the plan with his friends over lunch earlier in the day. He knew that, if successful, it would probably get them all fired, but, he reasoned, it would be worth it. "Meet me here at midnight."

CHAPTER FIFTEEN

THE COLD SHOWER washed away the odor of vomit that lingered on Neil during the walk back to Sequoia Lodge and helped to push aside any remaining stupor that was keeping him from thinking straight. But it hadn't helped reconcile the differences between his friends' eyewitness statements and his own memory.

The conversation during the walk had left him confused and frustrated. As the cold water from the shower poured over his body, he recalled the dialogue that'd passed between them. Despite everything that they said, he'd been adamant that the zipline had stopped.

"I'm telling you, it got stuck! Maybe a third of the way down the line!" he'd said.

Jeremy had been quick to contradict him. "You were in our sight for almost the entire ride. We would've seen if you got hung up."

"Almost? It must have been when you couldn't see me." He was grasping at straws, but the alternative meant that he might've hallucinated the whole thing in a panicked frenzy over his fear of heights. Neil wasn't ready to accept that.

Steve had been the next to chime in. "Neil, we only lost sight of you during the last few feet. If you got hung up there, you'd only have been ten feet off the ground, if that."

None of what they were saying aligned with his own memories. At least fifty feet, possibly more. That was what he remembered. "I don't believe it!"

"What? You calling us liars?" Rob asked. He stopped walking, turning to face Neil. His face was a mix of concern and irritation.

"No! No! I don't know what I'm saying," Neil replied, and then suddenly asked, "What about the voices? You can't tell me you didn't hear the voices."

The silent stares that Neil observed provided their answer louder than any words could have. They'd heard nothing. Never in his life had he become so distressed over heights to hallucinate disembodied voices. And to experience a complete impairment of his memory? It made no sense. But he had to face the fact that he might have imagined the whole ordeal. It had seemed so real, so terrifying. His friends had no reason to lie to him. If this had been a joke, they'd have delivered the punchline by now.

Finishing his shower, Neil returned to Sequoia Lodge to find Jeremy, Rob, and Steve huddled around the picnic table and Patrick lounging before the campfire circle. The hushed conversation at the table ceased as he approached, and three pairs of eyes turned in his direction, causing him to feel a little sheepish. Patrick was sprawled in a camp chair, his feet resting atop a rock. "They're worried about you," he said, not bothering to open his eyes and look in Neil's direction.

"It's appreciated, but I'm fine," he said. His words didn't seem convincing. Perhaps he'd said them more to convince himself. Either way, it hadn't worked.

"You been afraid of heights for long?" Jeremy asked.

Neil lowered himself onto the picnic table bench. "All my life."

Steve's eyes opened wide. "Really? I never knew."

He shrugged his shoulders. "Never told anyone." Staring down beneath the picnic table, Neil watched a column of ants as they marched across the sandy ground. One thrust of his foot would be all it would take to halt their column in its tracks. They seemed so vulnerable, so exposed. Like the ants in the sand, he felt naked and unprotected.

"Acrophobia," Rob said.

Patrick turned his head toward them and opened his eyes. "What?"

"The fear of heights—acrophobia," Rob explained. "That's what it's called. It belongs to a specific category of phobias called space and motion discomfort."

"Thank you, Dr. Freud," Patrick said, closing his eyes and turning his head away again.

"Neil, what bothers you? All heights? Or just really high ones?" Jeremy asked.

"It's not so much the height that bothers me. It's the falling."

"Falling?" asked Steve.

"Yes, falling. I'm afraid of falling."

"Must make it a bitch to live in New York," Jeremy said.

"Not really. I've been up to the Empire State Building observation deck without any issue," Neil explained. "Even been up to the top of the new World Trade Center building. I'm okay as long as there's something between me and the void. Take away the barriers and the railings, then I'm in trouble." He paused. "Look, can we just change the subject? I don't want to talk about this."

Patrick laughed. "Brewster's gettin' uncomfortable. What's wrong? Can't the hotshot lawyer take a little cross examination?"

He glared across at Patrick. "What's your point?"

Patrick shrugged and smiled. "Nothing. Nothing at all."

DESPITE the fact that Neil's stomach was still queasy from his earlier ordeal, he hungrily partook in lunch with his friends—meatball sandwiches with melted provolone cheese, Rob's special recipe from his bar. With their appetites satiated, Steve suggested that a hike around Lake Friendship would give them a chance to see their old stomping ground. Jeremy, without giving anyone a chance to respond, announced that he thought it was an excellent idea and strode off, his long strides rapidly broadening the distance between himself and the others. It took five minutes for the other four to catch up.

The hike took them around the north side of the lake, down by the boys' cabins. Neil was surprised at how little the old structures had changed in eighteen years. Other than the darkening of the wood slatted walls from age and weather, the small, almost claustrophobic one-room cabins still felt like home when he stepped inside. Bunkbeds, six in all, were pressed against the two side walls, leaving a narrow aisle through which he paced. Dingy glass in the single window opposite the door was grimy, allowing only marginal light through. He brushed aside the thick cobwebs that reached between the bunkbeds. His feet kicked up a dust cloud from the scuffed and dirty floor, leaving the air musty and stifling. He coughed, trying to clear his throat.

Redwood Lodge had been his cabin for three summers. Neil smiled as he traced the letters he'd carved into the door frame. "Brewster was here," it read. It all seemed puerile now. Just his own childish attempt to leave his mark for all eternity. He remembered carving the letters during his first summer at Camp Tenskwatawa. There were plenty more scattered around the camp, some not quite as harmless, but just as puerile.

He moved to the bunk bed closest to the door, sitting down on the lower bunk. The mattress, with its vinyl covering and lumpy padding, sank under his weight, providing little support. Some things never change. A strong musty odor rose from the mattress, reminding him how old it really was. Memories from his childhood washed over him, making it impossible for Neil to not smile.

For three summers, he shared this small cabin with another counselor and a rotating group of ten young boys, a new group arriving each week. Patrick had been his co-counselor during the first summer, and a kid named Jake had been in Redwood Lodge for the second. He remembered the first summer had been a ruckus from start to finish. Being together with Patrick in a single cabin meant there was never a concern about being ratted out by his co-counselor if things got a little out of hand. They could take turns slipping out at night to pull a prank, get into mischief, or meet up with the girl counselors to get laid. The second summer required Neil to tread more cautiously, never sure if Jake would report his nocturnal escapades to the camp owners.

When memories from the third summer surfaced, his smile faded. Raymond, a high-school sophomore, had been his co-counselor. He'd seemed like a nice enough kid and more than willing to turn a blind eye to Neil's extra-curricular activities. But near the end of July, Raymond had abruptly left camp, his father having been diagnosed with cancer. His departure left Redwood Lodge a coun-selor short. The camp rules required two counselors per cabin, forcing the camp owners to quickly shuffle things around to maintain the status quo.

Neil remembered the day clearly, down to the finest detail. He'd returned to Redwood Lodge to find his new co-counselor unrolling a sleeping bag on the bunk across from his. Recalling the pathetically sad eyes that greeted him, he'd swear that his new co-counselor was ready to cry. The irony couldn't have been more perfect. If there had been a God, he couldn't have been more gracious. Neil would spend his remaining three weeks at camp in the same cabin as Stinky Bateman.

Staring across at the empty bunk, Neil could almost list every single thing that he and his friends had done to Bateman over three summers. Stealing Bateman's clothes from the bathhouse while he showered had always been one of his favorites. Watching the scrawny kid run naked through the camp to get back to his cabin just got funnier every time. How many times did they get him with that? Four, maybe five? Then there was the night they ran Bateman's underwear up the flag pole for all to see in the morning. The little bastard had seemed so timid and weak. An easy target. The kid had practically been asking for it just by being there.

He rose from the bunk bed and crossed the cabin to the far corner. Running his hands along the wall near the floor, he felt a long-forgotten indentation in the wood. Using his fingers, Neil pried the board loose, leaving a dark gap in the wall. The cubbyhole between the joists of the cabin wall had become a safe of sorts, where he'd stashed things during his three summers in Redwood Lodge. He was surprised that no one had ever stumbled upon the loose board, and even more surprised to find that the cubbyhole still contained some of his stuff. His fingers wrapped around the rolled-up magazine first. He straightened the decaying, brittle pages, and smiled at the scantily clad woman posing on the cover. Playboy, October 1995. He opened to the center of the magazine and unfolded the faded and crinkled centerfold.

Placing the magazine down, he reached into the cubbyhole once again, drawing out the diary. He'd almost forgotten that it was there. The narrow leather-bound book was covered with dust, and the page edges had yellowed with age. It was tied shut with a brown leather cord that matched the cover. Holding it in his hands, he stared at the diary, remembering the day he'd found it hidden inside Stinky Bateman's mattress.

It'd been the week before Neil left camp, maybe two. He never did read the whole thing, just the last few pages. It was just enough to provide him with the basis for what had become his last bit of tomfoolery before leaving. Opening the book, Neil flipped through the pages, glancing at the clean, carefully written script that looked more like a girl's handwriting than a boy's. The book had only been two-thirds full the last time he'd seen it. His eyes fell upon the last page. The last entry had been written the evening that he'd found the diary. The final words on the page held a long-forgotten puzzle, one that he'd probably never find an answer to. Who was Stinky Bateman meeting with that night?

Reading the words on the page brought back memories of those final days in camp. As his eyes traced the lines of Bateman's girlish scrawl, Neil thought, for a moment, that he heard the kid's voice again.

"Stop it, Neil!"

It was just a faint, distant echo, but he felt as if it were in the room with him. Glancing around the cabin, Neil found nothing but empty bunk beds and musty mattresses. He was alone. It must be his imagination, still stunned by the incident on the zipline. Shoving the diary back into the cubbyhole, Neil placed the board back into place, and then, grasping the remnants of the old Playboy magazine, rose to his feet.

"Whatcha got there?"

The voice from behind him made Neil jump. He spun around to find Steve standing in the doorway. He hadn't heard his friend enter. "You scared me."

Steve laughed. "Sorry. What's that?"

Neil held up the magazine. "An old Playboy from our camp days."

Steve crossed the room, taking the magazine from Neil and flipping through the pages. Stopping on the centerfold, Steve whistled. "Alicia Rickter. Damn. I remember her. Wasn't she on one of the Baywatch shows? The one in Hawaii, I think."

"Yeah. I always thought she looked better without clothes."

Laughing, Steve handed the magazine back to Neil, who rolled it up and started toward the door. Before he stepped out of the cabin, Steve reached over and grasped his arm. "Neil, are you sure you're okay?"

"What? Yeah. Yeah, I'm fine. Why?"

Steve released his hold on Neil's arm and slid his hands into his pockets. "You've just not been yourself."

"Not myself?"

Steve seemed uncomfortable. He shuffled his feet, shifting the dust on the floor. "Yeah, well . . . I've never known you to . . ."

Neil knew where this conversation was going. He couldn't blame Steve for bringing it up, but it didn't make the discussion any easier. A momentary urge arose to lash out at his friend, but Neil decided to suppress it. "Hear things? See things?"

Steve nodded. "Yeah. I've never known you to imagine things that weren't there."

"Is that what you think it was? Just my imagination?"

"Not sure what else it could be."

"I know what I heard, what I saw." Neil folded his arms. It was better than giving in to his other urge: to throw a punch at his friend.

"Look, I'm not saying that you didn't hear those voices." Steve shrugged his shoulders. "I'm just . . . I'm just worried about you, that's all. Can't I be concerned about an old friend?"

Neil looked away for a moment, glancing around the claustrophobic cabin. He hated being on the receiving end of pity. It made him feel weak, placing him in the same category as those he frequently derided. "What's there to be concerned about?"

"Neil, don't give me that bullshit. This is me you're talking to. I've known you longer than the other guys."

"Look, I was just caught off guard with the news about Stinky Bateman. That's all it is." Neil turned his back on his friend. "It's not every day that you hear that someone you knew committed suicide."

"You're not bothered by it?"

Neil turned back toward Steve. "Should I be?"

"You did ride him pretty hard."

"We all did." Neil pointed at Steve. "We were all in this together. Why am I the only one hearing his voice?"

Steve shrugged his shoulder. "I don't know. Guilt?"

"What the hell do I have to be guilty about? I didn't do anything to that kid that he didn't have coming to him."

Steve didn't respond, leaving Neil to wonder what his friend was thinking. All of them had, at one time or another, maligned Bateman. They'd each played their part in three summers' worth of mockery of which Bateman had been the sole recipient. If guilt was to be laid before someone, it should be all of them, not just him. "Do you feel guilty?"

Steve sighed. "I did, at first. But I've had eighteen years to deal with it."

"I've got nothing to deal with. I don't feel guilty. Never have, never will."

They stood quietly for a moment until another voice broke through the silence.

"Yo, Brewster! Where are you?" It was Jeremy, shouting from somewhere outside.

Steve smiled, gesturing toward the door. "Come on. Let's get out of here."

Grasping the remnants of the old Playboy magazine, Neil followed his friend to the door. With his hand on the bar latch, he paused, looking back in at the dingy cabin. Three summers worth of memories seemed to drift among the dust particles, causing him to smile. Good times, he had to admit. They were certainly good times. But just before pulling the door closed, he caught the faint echo of a voice.

"Leave me alone, Neil."

CHAPTER SIXTEEN

When Sammy returned to the cabin, she headed straight for the kitchen, grabbed the bottle of Johnnie Walker, and poured herself a glass. She drank it down in one swallow, and then poured herself another. Over the past few weeks, she'd grown concerned that it'd gotten far too easy to turn to this bottle for consolation. Right now, however, she didn't give a damn. She needed the drink.

She swallowed the whiskey, stared down at the empty glass for a moment, and then threw it across the kitchen. It slammed into the wall, shattering on impact. Falling to her knees, she sobbed uncontrollably. She leaned forward, pounding her fists on the floor as her cries filled the otherwise silent cabin.

She hadn't expected this to be so hard. Hearing Chris's voice again had sent her into an emotional spiral, one that had driven her from her place of concealment near the zipline. She'd stumbled through the forest for a short time, her mind reeling from the memories his voice had invoked. Apparently, eighteen years hadn't been long enough to heal the wounds. Now, all she could do was cry.

Sammy remained huddled on the floor for close to ten minutes. Her eyes had long since dried up, but she felt emotionally drained, unable to persuade herself to stand. When she finally did rise, she crossed to the small closet, pulled out a broom and a dustpan, and swept up the broken glass.

Sitting down at the kitchen table, she aimlessly played with the salt shaker, her mind drifting beyond the room, beyond the cabin. She'd never expected her reunion with Neil Brewster to cause such emotional upheaval. Until the other night, she was certain that she could make it through this weekend without shedding a single tear. The years had hardened her, leaving her cold and unfeeling. Wasn't that how her ex-husband had once described her? Cold and unfeeling. It was probably a true statement. That was why he asked for the divorce. But they'd both entered the marriage with baggage. His had been a porn addiction. Hers had been Neil Brewster.

Sammy set the salt shaker back on the center of the table and leaned back in the chair. Gazing at the ceiling, she recalled her first meeting with Neil. She'd fallen for him the minute she'd met him. While her father spent his days caring for the camp facilities, she had roamed free throughout the camp and the surrounding forest. She'd often mingled with the other campers and counselors. It must have been Neil's first summer. She didn't remember seeing him before. "Dreamy" was the word she'd used back then. Of course, he paid her no heed, leaving her just a fourteen-year-old tomboy with an unrequited crush.

It wasn't until his last summer at camp that he'd finally shown interest in her. Sammy had gone from teenage tomboy to blossoming young woman, catching his eye in the process. Within the first week of the summer of 1997, their camp romance flourished, and she couldn't have been happier. Of course, he wanted to have sex with her. That was clear from the outset. But she'd promised herself to wait until she was sixteen. So she waited. Her promise, however, didn't stop her from enticing him. There was something mischievous about getting Neil hot and bothered, only to deny him gratification.

She'd heard all the stories about his exploits with the other girl counselors, but it didn't bother her. She knew he wanted her just as much as she wanted him. When she was ready, he'd be waiting. By the time Sammy turned sixteen, she'd gone from crush to infatuation to love. The thought invoked a smile. Love. How foolish she'd been back then. What the hell did she know about love? She'd just been a kid, just a young naive kid.

Sammy rose from the table, opened a nearby kitchen drawer, and pulled out a pill bottle—Xanax. She got another tumbler down from the cabinet, half-filling it with whiskey. Popping two pills in her mouth, she washed them down. She'd never told her therapist about this weekend. He'd be furious if he knew what she had planned, seeing it as the absolute collapse of all they'd accomplished over the past five years. She never had the heart to tell him that their sessions had done nothing to help her cope with her feelings. It didn't matter anyway. She wasn't planning to see him ever again.

Sammy crossed into the living room, then walked to the front window. Gazing out across the stone-covered driveway, she thought about his arrival the previous night. Seeing Neil standing in the driveway had stirred up those old forgotten emotions, leaving her with an amalgam of incompatible feelings. The eighteen years of anger and hatred that had fueled her life were in dispute with feelings that she'd not felt for a very long time. She felt betrayed by her own heart.

While she'd been watching him on the zipline, Sammy had struggled to keep herself from putting a halt to her plans. Following through would make her no better than him, right? That argument had crossed her mind many times over the past several weeks, but she'd always just brushed it aside. Now, however, it didn't seem as easy to ignore. Seeing him again seemed to be weakening her resolve.

She climbed the stairs, entering the bedroom at the far end of the cabin. Opening the closet door, she stared down at the coil of thick rope laying on the floor. A faint musty smell lingered in the air. When she'd cut the rope from the old dock by the lake, it'd been submerged for years. The rough fibers had taken two weeks to completely dry out. For years, the thick strands had secured the canoes to the dock, keeping them from drifting into the lake. If everything went according to plan, the rope would soon secure something very different.

Pushing the closet door closed, she turned to gaze around the room. Except for the new hooks in the wall and ceiling, the room looked exactly as it did eighteen years ago. Her father never could bring himself to clean it out. She crossed to the twin bed and sat down on the pale blue comforter. She found herself asking the same question that she always asked while sitting in this room. Why? There was never a satisfactory answer. He'd left no note. No message. Why didn't he ask for help? She'd have done anything to help him if she'd known. If only she'd known . . .

She left the room, crossing to the other bedroom. She peeled off her pale blue t-shirt and laid it on the bed. The floral comforter was faded and fraying along the edges.

She smoothed the wrinkles out of the t-shirt, tracing the letters imprinted on the front. Sammy had found the box of camp t-shirts in the back of her father's closet. He must have been saving them for something. For what, she didn't know. Sliding the tan shorts down her legs, she set them on the bed next to the t-shirt.

Turning to stare into the mirror over the dresser, Sammy wondered if Neil would still want her like he did back then. Her figure had filled out a bit over the years, but she'd worked hard to stay fit. Did she look good enough to entice him to her bed? He'd seemed interested the previous night. Would he come to the cabin like they'd agreed? Her plan depended upon him coming to see her tonight.

Stripping off her bra and panties, Sammy walked to the bathroom, turned on the shower, and stepped inside. As the hot water poured over her, she continued to think about Neil. She'd half-hoped that he'd become bald and fat over eighteen years, but no such luck. If anything, he'd grown more attractive, maturing perfectly with age. His good looks probably came naturally, without a bit of effort. She, on the other hand, struggled every day to maintain some semblance of the body she'd once had with minimal success. *Just typical*, she thought with a huff.

As she lathered shampoo in her hair, she recalled how it'd felt to embrace him again. How warm she'd been within his arms. His deep blue eyes had mesmerized her, and his voice had once again thrilled her to the point of arousal. He'd been everything that she'd fallen in love with years ago. Everything that she'd wanted back then. Everything she wanted now. No matter how much she claimed to hate him, Sammy couldn't deny that she wanted Neil Brewster just as much.

"Damn it."

Her hand touched the St. Christopher medal hanging from her neck. *Remember what this is all for*, she thought.

SUMMER, 1996

KEEPING TO THE shadows, Neil crept through the trees, his friends following close behind. The moonlight struggled to pierce the canopy of tree limbs above him. The rain from earlier in the day had finally stopped, but he still heard water droplets falling from the trees into the foliage covering the forest floor. He made his way from Redwood Lodge across to Cherry Lodge, fifty yards at the most. As he approached the cabin, Neil signaled for his friends to be silent. "Remember, we can't let him scream."

Patrick lifted the HandyCam to his eyes, and a red light above the camera lens blinked, indicating that he'd started recording. Placing his hand on the cabin door, Neil reached for the door handle. The rule in camp was that cabin doors must remain unlocked. He knew Stinky Bateman was a stickler for the rules.

As gently as possible, he pulled down on the door handle and heard the bar on the other side rubbing as it lifted. He heard Jeremy start to snicker and, turning, placed his finger to his lips, trying to shush his friend. Pushing the door open, Neil stepped gingerly into the dark cabin followed by his companions. In the dim light, he saw his quarry on the lower bunk of the nearest bed. The huddled mass of Stinky Bateman was laying soundlessly, his deep breathing barely audible even in the silent cabin.

With his fingers, Neil gave his friends a countdown from three. When he reached one, Jeremy clamped his hands on the young boy's forearms, holding them firmly against the mattress. Steve got a solid grip on Bateman's feet, holding them tightly together, while Rob's hand covered the boy's mouth, ensuring he couldn't cry out. Hovering above Bateman's face, Neil stared into the boy's fear-stricken eyes. He laughed, watching Bateman's terrified struggles. They all knew he stood no chance of freeing himself. "This'll be a lot easier if you don't struggle."

His words only served to cause Bateman to fight more fiercely. The boy twisted his body back and forth, trying to free himself with no success. As Patrick leaned in over his shoulder with the video camera, Neil tore a piece of duct tape from the roll he'd brought. Just as they'd planned, Rob removed his hand from Stinky Bateman's mouth as Neil slapped the duct tape down in place.

Grunts and groans were the only sound the boy made as Rob and Neil wrapped duct tape first around his wrists, then around his ankles. Rising to his feet, Neil looked down at the gagged and bound Bateman, watching him struggle against Jeremy and Steve's grasp. "He's ready. Let's go."

CHAPTER SEVENTEEN

Leaving behind the old boys' cabins, Neil and his friends continued their hike around Lake Friendship, crossing over the old earthen dam that separated the lake from Lower Creek. Standing on the dam, Neil had an unimpeded view across the lake. He glanced down, watching the overflow from the lake wash through the narrow spillway into the creek below. The old creosote-coated timbers forming the walls of the overflow channel were deteriorating, and some had even splintered, lodging themselves in the channel and forming an obstruction over which the water rushed. Moving to the other side of the dam, he saw debris and brownish-white foam congregate where the water flowed out of the chute, giving the otherwise clean creek an unnatural polluted look.

"Remember when Jeremy rode this in a canoe?" asked Rob.

Leaning on the wooden rail above the spillway, Jeremy

laughed. "You thought I wouldn't make it!"

"I thought you'd get us kicked out of here," said Steve.

"If I remember, you didn't exactly make it," Neil added. He pointed down at the chute emptying into Lower Creek. "You sank the canoe coming out of that chute. Damn thing's probably still there."

Jeremy folded his arms over his chest. "I didn't see any of you try it."

Patting Jeremy on the back, Patrick said, "None of us were as stupid as you."

Laughing, Neil and his friends moved across the dam and shortly found themselves standing among the cabins that had once housed the girl campers and counselors. There was little difference between the girls' cabins and the boys': same wood slat walls, same bunk beds, same lumpy mattresses. Rob wandered over to the girls' bathhouse, disappearing behind it. Moments later, Rob poked his head around the side.

"Check this out!" Rob shouted.

Moving behind the bathhouse, Neil found Rob kneeling beside the cinder block wall, his fingers digging at an indentation along the wall's rough surface. After a few moments, an oblong piece of mortar broke away from the wall, revealing a hole in between the joints of the cinder blocks.

It had taken three weeks of careful, meticulous work, Neil remembered, during their first summer at camp. He and his friends had taken turns excavating the already deteriorating mortar joints in the wall. He was surprised that it had never been discovered. There had been more than a few Saturdays where he'd spent the morning with an eye pressed against the cold block wall, watching the girl counselors as they showered.

When Rob and Neil caught up with the other

three, Jeremy, Steve, and Patrick were already making their way around the far side of the lake. The main trail hugged the lake edge tightly, with smaller side trails leading into the forest. White sand coated the surface of the trail, disturbed only by the occasional gnarled tree root. Walking the trail was almost second nature to Neil, leaving him surprised at how familiar it seemed to be.

A short distance from the girls' cabins, Neil and his friends came upon a fork in the trail. The main pathway banked upward to the left, away from the lake, while the other narrower path led down along an isolated sandbar flanked on one side by the lake and on the other by a shallow stream. The path along the sandbar, although more direct, had always been more challenging to navigate because of its inaccessibility. Unlike the main trail, the small island-like path sprouted tall pine trees and thick thorny underbrush along its two sides. The two paths eventually met on the west side of the lake, where a primitive rope bridge crossed the gap between the two trails over the stream. During his time at the camp, the two divergent paths had become a source of competition between Neil and his friends. The race always started at the fork with the goal of seeing who reached the rope bridge first.

Neil smiled, taking pride in the memory of his superiority when traversing the narrow path. He'd gained a reputation for being the fastest at crossing the sand bar. He felt that old thrill return, leaving him to wonder if he still had what it took to accomplish something he'd done as a kid.

"Who wants to race?" he asked.

"You kidding?" Steve said. "You can't get through there."

Neil had to admit that the undergrowth was much

thicker than he remembered. Where he had once been able to see a clearly defined entry point, he could barely find the trail now. If not for the white sand leading into the underbrush, he might have missed it altogether. But it'd probably clear out once he got past the overgrowth. It was worth a try.

"It'll be easy," he said. "Who's with me?"

No one stepped forward to volunteer, at least not at first. His four friends glanced at each other until Patrick finally said, "What the hell, I'll go."

Pointing at his other three friends, Neil smiled. "You three against Patrick and I. Last one to the rope bridge . . ." He paused. Remembering an eighteen-year-old taunt, he added, "The last one there has to give Miss Schlappi a sponge bath." With that, he charged into the thickets with reckless abandon.

As he pushed low hanging branches and thorns out of his way, he heard Patrick shouting after him. "Wait for me!"

Patrick pushed through somewhere behind him, but Neil wasn't about to lose precious seconds to allow his friend to catch up. He had only one goal in mind—reaching the rope bridge before his friends. Brambles clawed at his bare legs, forcing him to admit that Steve's assumption about the path having grown over was more correct than he'd at first thought. The revelation, however, did nothing to deter his forward charge.

The path rose slightly before it dropped suddenly into a water-filled gully. Without even thinking, Neil pushed off with his foot, leaping over the gully. White sand flew out from under his feet as he landed, stumbled forward, and continued with his full-on run. The undergrowth began to thin, and as the path rose and fell, the exhilaration of the competition fueled his momentum. Somewhere behind him, he heard Patrick clambering in pursuit, but, to Neil, it barely registered. The thrill of the race and the desire to win were the only things occupying his attention.

Leaping across another water-filled gully, he landed more gracefully this time and ran on with everything he had. The trees lining either side of the path were a blur, giving him only an occasional glimpse of the lake on his right. Brambles whipped at his legs, causing them to sting, but Neil ignored the discomfort, pressing on as he dropped into another gully, this one not filled with water. As he came up the other side, a pine branch lashed at his face, causing him to stumble. His foot caught an exposed gnarled tree root, sending him crashing to the ground. Rolling in the white sand, he waited for the momentary pain to subside. The gritty particles of sand covered his arms and legs, clinging to his skin. He cursed at his misstep. This might have just cost him the race. Pushing himself up, his eyes drifted out toward the lake.

Neil realized later that if he hadn't fallen he probably never would've seen it. It was the baseball cap's bright red color that had caught his eye first. Resting atop the lake's surface, the cap's black bill was just dipping below the water line. Careful not to tread in the thick mud along the water's edge, Neil inched closer, kneeling to get a better look.

Embroidered silver lettering emblazoned the front of the cap's stiff red peak. He read the words aloud. "Snap-on." In smaller black cursive script underneath was the word "Racing." It had been eighteen years since he'd seen one like it, but the cap was all too familiar. He'd spent three summers seeing it day in and day out adorning the head of Stinky Bateman.

Drifting about a foot or two from the lake's edge,

the cap was too far for him to reach. He glanced around, searching for a long stick. Finding one laying along the opposite side of the path, he scrambled over to grab it.

"Dammit!"

The shout was followed by a loud crash of branches and underbrush. It came from somewhere behind him. So preoccupied with the ball cap, Neil had forgotten that Patrick had been following him. He dropped the stick. "Patrick?"

He waited for a reply but received none. "Patrick! You okay?"

Still no reply. He glanced back at the ball cap. *There's no chance of winning the race now*, he decided. *Might as well go back and check on Patrick.*

As Neil dropped down into one of the gullies, he heard someone thrashing about in the underbrush just ahead. Coming up the other side, he found Patrick ensnared in the brambles along the path's edge. His arms were tangled in the thickets, and Patrick struggled to get back to his feet. Neil laughed, being reminded of a turtle laying on its back trying to right itself.

Patrick's arms and legs flailed in the air. "Stop laughing and help me outta here!"

A few moments later, Patrick stood beside Neil, brushing dirt from his legs. His arms were marred with tiny scratches, and a trickle of blood flowed from his right cheek.

Neil gave his friend a quick appraisal. "What happened?"

"Tripped. Must have caught my foot on a root or something." He gave Neil a playful shove in the shoulder. "I was trying to keep up with you, you bastard."

"You all right?"

Patrick shrugged. "I'll live."

"Good. Come on."

Jogging back down the path, Neil was certain that he'd lost the race. There was no getting back the time he'd lost. The stick he'd held earlier was still laying in the path as he approached. Pausing, he glanced out across the lake, his eyes searching the water's surface.

Patrick glanced over his shoulder. "Whatcha looking at?"

He didn't want to tell his friend what he'd seen earlier. Like the t-shirt, the figure in the forest, and the voices, this would just be another thing he couldn't prove existed. Just another figment of his imagination. Just another reason for his friend to wonder about his state of mind. But he knew Patrick wouldn't let it drop without an answer. Neil shrugged. "There was . . ."

"What?"

He shook his head, and then turned to face Patrick. "I could've sworn . . . I was certain . . ."

Patrick smiled. "Come on, Brewster. What is it?"

"Remember that damn red cap—the one Stinky Bateman always wore?"

Patrick's eyes narrow for just a moment, followed by a brief flinch of anger around the corners of his mouth. Then it was gone. "Yeah. Bright red, wasn't it?"

Neil nodded and gestured over his shoulder. "I saw one floating in the lake just a minute ago."

"Really?" Patrick pushed forward as if trying to get a better look. "Where?"

"It's not there now."

Patrick folded his arms, giving him a long stare. "Then where is it?"

Neil shrugged his shoulders again. "I don't know. Must have sank? I saw it just before you fell." He leaned down and picked up the stick, showing it to Patrick. "I was going to drag it to shore with this."

Patrick was quiet for a moment, and then frowned. "It's not there now."

"I can see that." The irritation in his voice must have been evident.

Patrick raised an eyebrow. "Look, Brewster, it's understandable if you're a little bothered by Chris Bateman's suicide."

"What? You think I imagined it?"

Patrick shrugged. "You thought you heard his voice earlier—"

"Get this through your thick skull. I do not give a damn about Stinky. I'm not bothered in the least by the fact that the miserable little bastard hung himself." He turned to walk away, then looked back at Patrick. "There was a goddamn cap out there. It sank."

With that he strode off down the path, leaving Patrick in his wake.

CHAPTER EIGHTEEN

Neil sat next to Jeremy on the porch of Sequoia Lodge, watching Steve empty a bag of charcoal into the grill by the picnic table. The grill was nothing more than a black bowl standing on three wobbly aluminum legs, threatening to tip over on the sandy ground. The black rocks clanged into the bowl, kicking up a faint cloud of gray dust. When Steve tossed the empty bag on the ground, Neil watched his friend reach for the bottle of charcoal lighter fluid, flip open the red cap, and then squeeze hard, spewing fluid onto the black briquettes.

"Aren't they self-lighting?" asked Jeremy.

Steve nodded his head, continuing to saturate the charcoal. "That's what it says on the bag. Never works though."

Rob, sitting on the edge of the picnic table, laughed. "You planning to send our steaks to the moon?"

Steve stopped spraying the clear fluid into the grill for a moment. Neil saw the irritation in his friend's eyes. Steve had never been good at accepting criticism, no matter how lighthearted it seemed to be.

"Who's cooking tonight? I am." Steve said, and then resumed pouring the lighter fluid onto the charcoal. "Now shut up and let me get on with it."

Lowering himself into one of the chairs around the campfire, Patrick locked his hands behind his head and leaned back to stare into the sky. "He's gonna set fire to half the goddamn camp."

Neil elbowed Jeremy in the ribs as the pungent fumes reached the porch of the cabin. "This ought to be good."

When Steve had emptied the bottle, he tossed it on the ground by his feet. Knowing what was about to come, Neil was unable to contain himself any longer. He started to laugh.

"What's so funny?" snapped Steve.

Neil said, "Nothing."

Placing the grate on the grill, Steve grabbed a box of matches. Sliding the box open, he pulled out a small wooden match. He struck it against the side of the box and tossed it into the grill.

Neil raised his arms to protect his face from the momentary blast of heat. The fireball roared up into the tree branches overhead. Black smoke trailed behind the fireball, lingering in the air long after the flames had dissipated.

Rob cursed as he leapt from his place on the picnic table. Neil and Jeremy howled as Steve lifted himself up off the ground. Seeing him brushing pine needles and sand from his clothing sent them into more fits of laughter. As the flames in the grill died down, Steve touched his eyebrows, checking to see if they were still there, which only caused the others to laugh even harder.

"Lucky that wasn't Rob. His whole head would've

caught fire," said Jeremy.

Rob reached behind his head and ran his fingers through his shoulder-length hair. "Hence the ponytail."

Patrick, looking up into the trees once again, added, "Enough talking, more cooking. I'm hungry."

NEIL thought the steaks, although delicious, had a mild hint of a lighter-fluid-induced aftertaste. On further reflection, he was certain that mild wasn't the right word to use. When Jeremy pulled out a box of Cuban cigars, Neil was the first to point out the safety concerns. "Are you insane? After those steaks, one belch could turn any of us into a walking flamethrower." Steve seemed to take the teasing all in stride, but Neil knew his old friend wasn't happy.

"None of you could've done any better," Steve was quick to declare.

As the sun began to set, the orange glow cast fiery streaks across the sky, throwing shadows into the tree limbs and the forest below. Nocturnal insects began their serenade. With a crackling campfire before him and a third beer in his hand, Neil glanced at his watch, counting the hours until he would have to make excuses and slip away for his rendezvous with Sammy. Despite the activity earlier in the day, she had never been far from his thoughts. With two more hours to go, the thought of once again touching her supple skin sent his mind into a frenzy of distraction. The memories of their one night together seemed as clear to him as if they had made love just yesterday. He remembered the perspiration glistening on her body as their arms and legs intertwined and the way she bit her bottom lip as they climaxed together . . .

"Brewster!" Rob shouted.

"What?"

"I asked you a question."

Glancing at his friends, Neil struggled to recall what Rob had asked. It was no use. He'd completely blanked out for the past few minutes. He stared back, bewildered, across the fire at his friend.

Rob leaned forward, peering back at him. "I asked what your fiancée was like."

Still a little lost in his thoughts of Sammy, Neil struggled, for a moment, to comprehend the question. "My fiancée?"

"Yeah. I'm assuming you have one," said Rob. "Since you said you're engaged."

"Right! Yes," he said. "Sorry, I was miles away."

"Must have been a woman," said Jeremy.

Steve laughed. "Probably not his fiancée."

Neil gave him the finger and said, "Her name's Sheila Waldstein."

Steve smiled. "Wait a minute! Waldstein? I know that name. She wouldn't be related to one of the senior partners in your firm, would she?"

He grinned. "Well . . ."

"Brewster's dipping his pen in the old company ink," Jeremy said, laughing. "What's the deal? Is Daddy Waldstein giving you a partnership in exchange for marrying his ugly daughter?"

Rob added, "It's got to be something like that. There's always an angle with Brewster!"

While his friends chuckled, Neil turned his head away and bristled at their comments. He knew they were just joking, but their wisecracks were hitting too close to home. Yet truer words had never been spoken. He never did anything without there being some angle, without there being some benefit for him, even if it was just for his own personal entertainment.

"It's not like that," Neil said. "She's pretty damn hot. You know me—"

Steve interrupted, "Yeah, yeah. Only the best for Brewster."

"Sounds like a lot of bullshit to me," said Rob.

Neil was quick to respond in the only way he knew how—a lie. "Hey, we're in love!"

Jeremy snorted loudly. "Now that really is bullshit."

"This coming from the man whose only goal in life was to part the legs of every cheerleader in high school," Steve said.

Tossing an empty beer bottle into the fire, Patrick said, "What the hell would you know about love?" He smiled when he said it, but Neil picked up a sharp edge to his voice.

Leaning back in his chair, he clasped his hands behind his head. "People change. I've grown up. Matured. My priorities are different. Sheila and I have a good thing going."

"And when do you become a senior partner?" asked Rob.

"Right after the wedding."

Patrick pointed at him across the campfire. "Dammit, I knew it!"

Even Neil couldn't help but join in when his friends laughed. Yeah, they were having a good time at his expense, but what the hell? There was something in the atmosphere that made it okay. Besides, he figured they'd each get theirs before the weekend was over.

"Seriously . . . just to be serious for a second," he said. "We really do love each other." He didn't know why, but Neil felt like he had to justify himself, even if it was with another lie. "Yeah, I'm going to be a senior partner, but I do love Sheila."

Jeremy feigned a southern accent, sounding like someone straight out of *Gone with the Wind*. "Gentlemen, I do declare. I believe our friend is serious. Could it be that Brewster is truly in love?"

"I'll be damned," said Rob.

Patrick was quick to add, "I still don't believe a word of it."

Steve rose from his chair, crossing to the campfire to place another log on the dwindling flames. Glowing fire-flies of hot orange ash shot upward, blinking out of existence as they ascended.

Neil glanced at his watch, calculating that he had time for one more beer. "Pass me another Corona." With a freshly opened bottle in his hand, he looked at Jeremy, asking, "What about you? Tell us about your wife."

"Jamie? She's a competition bodybuilder. Met her five years ago," Jeremy said. "The woman's got six-pack abs like you've never seen." He tapped his stomach as he spoke. "Even better than mine."

"She can probably beat the crap out of you, too," remarked Steve.

Jeremy said, "That she can."

Nursing the ice-cold beer, Neil only half-listened as his friends talked and joked around the campfire. He was more concerned about his upcoming rendezvous. It had been a long time since he'd made the trek from the camp over to the caretaker's cabin. He wondered if he'd be able to find his way. There had once been an open path between the camp and the cabin, but he didn't know if it would still be there. Without Chucky Wilcox running up and down the path in his golf cart each day, it might have become overgrown. He hoped there was at least enough of the trail left to guide him along his way. He'd make it, he was certain of it. Nothing was going to stop him from sleeping with Sammy again.

Tossing the empty bottle into the fire, Neil rose from his seat, drawing the eyes of his friends toward him. Stretching his back for a moment, he took a few steps away from the campfire. He felt their eyes follow him to the picnic table.

"Where the hell are you going?" asked Patrick.

Neil tried to be nonchalant. "Just for a walk."

"In the dark?" asked Rob.

He shrugged his shoulders. "Yeah, what's wrong with that?"

"In case you haven't noticed, we're not in the city." Rob gestured, making a wide arc with his arms. "No streetlights out here."

Rob's remark wasn't lost on Neil. Even the light from a full moon often had trouble penetrating the dense ceiling of interlaced pine and cedar branches hanging above them. Any counselor who had ventured out at night without a flashlight often ended up lost, or worse, in the lake. There had been more than a few late-night rescues from Lake Friendship. One misstep near the spillway sometimes meant getting very wet, as well as very hurt.

"I'll take a flashlight," he said, grabbing one from the picnic table, switching the light on and off to make sure it worked. Then, turning it on again, he shone the beam around the campfire, stopping the circle of light momentarily on each of his friends. Steve was grinning. *He must have figured it out*, Neil thought.

"Have fun, Neil," Steve said, still smiling.

Jeremy looked at Steve, then at Neil, and back at Steve again. "What'd ya mean? Where's he going?"

"I don't know nothing," said Steve. "I'm just hoping he has a good time."

"Don't feel like you have to wait up," Neil said.

Puzzled, Rob said, "Where's he going?"

Jeremy looked toward Steve. "Steve, where the fuck's he going?"

As he walked away into the darkness, Neil heard Steve reply, "He's going for a walk."

SUMMER, 1996

GRIPPING STINKY BATEMAN's arms and legs, Jeremy, Rob, and Steve carried the struggling teenager toward the beach of Lake Friendship. The duct tape over the boy's mouth kept his screams to nothing more than muffled groans. Despite his confidence that no one would hear the young boy's cries, Neil kept himself and his friends to the shadows, maintaining a safe distance between them and the other cabins. Patrick followed behind, capturing everything on video with his HandyCam.

Three canoes rested on the beach, having been commandeered earlier from the camp's dock. Neil directed his friends to drop Bateman, still gagged and bound, into the center of one of the canoes. Then, quickly stepping in themselves, Jeremy grasped Bateman's forearms, and Steve clutched his feet, holding him down against the cold metallic bottom of the canoe. Rob grabbed a paddle, pushed the canoe off from the shore, and leapt into the back. With a couple hard strokes, the boat moved off toward the center of the lake. Neil clambered into one of the remaining canoes while Patrick climbed into the other, following along behind the first, paddling silently through the moonlit waters.

When they'd reached the center of the lake, Neil drifted his canoe alongside the other two, being sure to place the one holding Stinky Bateman between his and Patrick's canoe. The red light on Patrick's HandyCam began to flash. Leaning over just enough to allow Bateman to see him, Neil said, "Listen, you little shit. You're gagged and tied. If we were to roll this canoe, you'd sink to the bottom like a rock. Don't squirm when we let you go, or you'll be sleeping with the fish."

Neil caught the fear in Bateman's eyes. They darted around, looking from him to his friends and back to him. The teenage boy must have taken Neil's meaning because he became docile, remaining still as the firm grip on his arms and legs was released. Rob stepped cautiously into Neil's canoe, followed moments later by Steve. Jeremy paused to snarl at Bateman before he crossed into Patrick's canoe.

Leaning over once more, Neil noticed that Stinky Bateman had begun to cry, the duct tape muffling his sobs. It was the most pathetic sight he'd ever seen. Watching the tears streaming down the boy's face made Neil laugh. "Bon voyage," he said, pushing his canoe away and beginning to paddle back toward shore.

CHAPTER NINETEEN

SAMMY POSITIONED THE last stuffed animal on the bed, placing it in front of all the others. It was a beige teddy bear, one that had been given to her eighteen years ago. She stepped back from the bed, surveying her handiwork. He probably wouldn't notice the detail to which she'd gone to get everything exactly as it had been. If everything went as she'd planned, his mind would be too preoccupied with her to notice much of anything. She'd placed the teddy bear in front more for herself than him. It would act as a reminder why she was going through with this.

Satisfied with how the bedroom looked, she changed out of her clothes into the short nightshirt. She'd specifically chosen it for this night. It clung tightly across her breasts, ending halfway down her thighs. It showed far more leg than she was used to, but she'd just have to deal with it for one night. It had to be enticing.

Making her way downstairs, Sammy moved into the

kitchen, pulling a fresh bottle of Johnnie Walker from the cabinet. She set the bottle on the counter next to two clean tumblers. *He loves his whiskey*, she thought.

A glance at the clock showed that she had another half hour before he was due to arrive. She moved into the living room, taking a seat on the sofa. The hem of her shirt rode up her thighs. Wearing nothing but an over-sized t-shirt made her feel exposed. She tried tugging at it to cover herself, only marginally succeeding. She'd have to ignore her modesty when he arrived. The last thing Sammy wanted was for Neil to think she'd changed. He had to think that she still wanted him, just as she did on their last night together.

It'd been the first Saturday in August, Sammy recalled. Five days past her sixteenth birthday. Her father had planned to go out for the evening, giving her the perfect chance to make her birthday wish come true. It was rare for her father to leave the camp during the summer. He'd always said that he needed to be around in case something happened requiring his attention. To have the cabin all to herself for a few hours was an opportunity she wasn't about to pass up.

The weather that day had been overly hot, one of the hottest Augusts in New Jersey history. She knew where most of the camp counselors would be on such a scorching day—swimming in the lake. She was certain Neil would be with them. Slipping into a pink bikini, Sammy scrawled a brief message on a piece of notepaper, and then, grabbing her towel and flip-flops, traipsed across camp to the lake.

He was splashing around in the lake when she arrived at the narrow beach. Sammy made sure that she caught his eye. Recognizing his beach towel, she placed hers down next to it. She stretched out on the towel, her skin glistening with perspiration. He was watching her, she was certain of it. Sammy could almost feel his stare, imagining his eyes undressing her. Sliding on a pair of sunglasses, she laid her head back on the towel to work on her tan.

When Sammy rose twenty minutes later, she folded up her towel and headed back to her father's cabin. Her hope was that no one had seen her slide the folded note into Neil's towel. It contained a simple message.

Tonight at 9. Come to me. S.

She'd been certain that the intention behind the summons was clear, but she'd have no way to know until later in the evening. Sammy remembered returning to her father's cabin feeling skittish. She'd never been that devious before. There had been no telling how her father would react if he found out.

Thinking of her father drew Sammy back to the present and away from the window. It was better that he wasn't here to see this. He'd never have approved of what she was going to do tonight. He wouldn't have been angry, just disappointed. There would've been no words. Just a look—a look of disapproval.

Sammy checked the clock. He'd be arriving any minute. The thought made her anxious, a feeling that was uncannily similar to how she'd felt while she waited for Neil eighteen years ago. A nervous laugh escaped her lips as the parallels of two nights surfaced in her mind. It only served to increase her anxiety. Crossing back in the kitchen, she needed to fortify her courage. She needed a drink. Filling a tumbler with whiskey, she downed it in one long swallow, cringing as it burned her throat. *Too much, too fast*, she thought.

Sammy wet her hair under the sink faucet, making it appear as if she'd just stepped out of the shower. A freshly showered woman had always worked for her ex-husband. She was hoping it would work with Neil as well.

She wondered if she should've worn a bikini instead of the nightshirt. The bikini had worked eighteen years ago. She laughed at the thought. Who was she kidding? How long had it been since she could wear a bikini? She was trying to get him to sleep with her, not scare him away. Glancing down at her bare legs, she wondered if he'd notice the cellulite beginning to show on her thighs. Best to stick with the nightshirt. A bikini would be a bad idea.

She recalled how his teenage eyes had roamed up and down her body when she'd answered his knock at the door eighteen years ago. Sammy had changed into the bikini ten minutes after her father had left for the evening. She'd spent an hour laying on her bed, fantasizing what it would be like to have Neil make love to her for the first time.

Once he'd arrived, Sammy had wasted no time in leading him up to her bedroom. She'd calculated that they'd only have three hours before her father returned. When she'd slipped out of her bikini and climbed onto the bed, she remembered saying, "I'm sixteen now. I want you to be my first."

She hadn't known what to expect from her first sexual encounter. Sammy gave herself over to Neil's every whim. They'd done things she'd never even imagined. Despite the experience being everything she'd hoped, Sammy remembered crying herself to sleep that night. It was Chris's accusations that had brought the tears to her eyes. He was just jealous, she'd kept telling herself. She wanted to deny everything that he'd said about Neil. But by the end of the night, he'd convinced her of the truth, and she'd gone to bed ashamed.

This time, Sammy knew, would be different. This time she'd be in control, directing the encounter precisely the way she wanted. She wasn't a teenager anymore. With a few tricks up her sleeve, Sammy was certain she could make Neil do and say anything she wanted. She was counting on it.

When she heard the knock at the door, she breathed deeply, trying to calm herself. Glancing at the clock, she saw that he was ten minutes late. Lost in her memories, Sammy hadn't realized how much time had passed. She heard him knock again. He was impatient. That was a good sign. She decided to make him wait a few moments longer. When he knocked a third time, she crossed to the door and pulled it open.

Sammy heard him draw in a breath. She felt his eyes caressing her body from head to toe, and then pausing on her pert breasts. The nightshirt was tight across her chest, showcasing her unsupported bosom. That was why she'd chosen it. It had been a good decision.

He smiled, giving her a strong sense of familiarity. Hadn't he smiled like that back then? His square jaw held a faint shadow of stubble, giving him a rough look that Sammy struggled to resist. She cursed herself for losing control.

"Any trouble getting here?" she asked.

Neil shook his head. "Only made two wrong turns."

She stepped aside, gesturing him into the house. Sammy pushed the door closed behind him, and then crossed to the kitchen, walking away as provocatively as she could. She knew his eyes would be locked on her swaying hips. "Let me get you a drink."

As she poured the whiskey into the tumblers, she tried to regain her composure. As before, she was finding it difficult to focus on the task at hand. Her emotions rode on the razor's edge between hatred and infatuation, both bleeding over into the other.

When she returned from the kitchen with two tumblers, Neil was still standing where she'd left him. Sammy carried the two tumblers to the sofa and lowered herself onto the cushion, pulling her bare legs up underneath her. Feeling the hem of her shirt ride up her legs, Sammy fought the urge to cover herself. She kept reminding herself that the immodesty was all part of the plan. *Show him what you've got. Make him want you even more.*

"Are you going to sit down or just stand there gawking?"

Neil sat down next to her, his eyes fixated on her thighs. He took one of the tumblers from her, swirling it around. The ice cube clanged against the glass. "I hope I didn't keep you waiting too long."

Lifting the tumbler to her lips, Sammy looked at him over the upper edge. "Is eighteen years considered too long?"

His eyes darted up to her face for a moment. *He's interested.* She sipped slowly on her whiskey, being careful not to drink too fast again. He drank from his tumbler, quick and efficient, like an expert whiskey drinker. She twirled her tongue around the lip of her glass, trying to add a layer of sensuality to the action. When his eyes narrowed, she knew she'd succeeded.

"How's the weekend going?" she asked.

He seemed to hesitate before answering. Sammy wondered if he would say anything about the voices on the zipline. Would he be willing to confide in her, or would he remain silent, putting on a brave face?

"Good. Good," he said. "It's great to see the guys again."

His smile echoed his statement, but his eyes told a different story. There was an almost imperceptible flicker of uncertainty in them, but Sammy caught sight of it the moment she'd asked her question. He was scared, or at least a bit shaken. "Having fun?"

He drank what was left of his whiskey. "Yeah, a good time's being had by all."

His reply created the perfect opening for her. The lead-in couldn't have been better. She took his glass from him and set it down on the coffee table along with her own. Rising to her feet, she took his hand. "Not by all, not yet."

She led him up the stairs into the first bedroom—her old bedroom. A smile of recognition crossed his face as they entered. She led him to the bed, turned, and, with her arms wrapped around his neck, kissed him. It was a long, passionate kiss, and Sammy felt herself losing control. Her body wanted nothing more than to open itself to his every wish and whim, to lay itself bare before him to be wantonly ravaged. As his lips moved to her neck, she struggled to control her lustful panting. His hands slid down her back and up her t-shirt to grasp her bare buttocks. She drew in a deep breath. Control, she had to get back control.

Drawing back, she looked up into his eyes and pulled the t-shirt off, allowing it to fall to the floor. As Sammy stood naked before Neil, she watched the salacious grin cross his face, and his eyes were aflame with desire.

"I've waited eighteen years to be with you again," she said. "Don't make me wait any longer." With that, Sammy swept the stuffed animals that she'd so precisely positioned earlier from the bed. It was a ridiculous gesture, she knew, but she wanted to draw on those feelings from the past. She wanted to entice him just as she'd done before. Sammy laid on the bed, watching as Neil began to undress. "Hurry. Don't make me wait." She smiled. She was back in control.

CHAPTER TWENTY

ACCORDING TO HIS watch, it was close to three in the morning when Neil slipped from the bed, leaving Sammy sleeping soundly under the sheets. By the dim light of a sea-shell-shaped night-light, he pulled on his clothes, stopping often to gaze at Sammy. She shifted in the bed, caught in a half-awake half-asleep state. The beige sheet slipped from her body, exposing one of her pert breasts. It invoked a smile as he recalled the reckless abandon with which they'd made love. Sammy's unbridled passion had surprised and thrilled him, leaving him wanting more.

Uninhibited, Sammy had practically driven him mad with her hands, her tongue, with every part of her body. He'd quickly realized that the experience was far better if he relinquished control to her, allowing her to guide their lovemaking. It was far from the young teenage girl he remembered from camp. Sammy had grown up and, in doing so, had learned a lot of tricks, some that he hadn't even known. She'd taken him to the heights of passion again and again, leaving him sweaty and exhausted.

There'd been very little conversation until after they'd finished making love. She'd rested her head on his bare chest, saying, "You may not believe this, but I missed you."

"What, since last night?"

She slapped his arm. "No, dumbass. For the last eighteen years."

She'd been right. He found it hard to believe. "No."

"Yeah. I thought about you a lot after you left camp."

"Seriously?"

"Seriously. It was why my marriage fell apart. My husband couldn't compete with your memory." She nudged herself closer, draping her arm over his chest. "He said I was obsessed. But I liked to think of it more like longing for the one that got away."

He ran his hand through her auburn hair, and then down her smooth bare back. Her hair felt like strands of silk between his fingertips, and her supple skin was warm to the touch. "I've thought about you over the years."

Neil wasn't sure why he felt it necessary to lie to her. Eighteen years ago, she'd been nothing more than a summer fling, a blip on the radar in his life. He was sure she couldn't have expected him to pine for her all these years. He hadn't given Sammy Wilcox a second thought until he arrived at camp the previous night. But, at the moment, the lie seemed like the only appropriate thing to say. "Sometimes I'd wonder where you were, what you were up to . . . and if you ever thought of me."

Sammy giggled and shifted her head to look up into his eyes. "Hold me, Neil."

After she'd fallen asleep in his arms, Neil wondered if he could give up his forthcoming partnership to spend the rest of his life with the auburn-haired angel who slept naked beside him. As they aroused and enthralled each other, he felt as if their souls melded into one in a way that he'd never experienced with Sheila, or with anyone else before. His relationships had always been about what he could get out of them. He wondered if he might be missing something.

With Sammy, there had been an emotional response that was unfamiliar to him. It was a feeling he couldn't easily disregard. It had been drawing his thoughts back to her again and again throughout the weekend. Sammy had gotten under his skin in a way that no other woman had before.

Sliding his t-shirt over his head, Neil decided not to wake her and, picking up his shoes and socks, crept from the room. The hardwood treads of the stairs were cool on his bare feet, and he gingerly made his way down to the living room. He sat on the sofa and slipped his socks and shoes on. His hand was on the front door knob when he decided to leave Sammy a note.

Finding a pen and a yellow legal pad on the kitchen counter, he scrawled a quick message.

Sammy, I had to get back to camp. Thanks for a fantastic night. Maybe I can swing back tonight for another couple whiskeys. Say 11 again? See you then.

Neil paused for a moment, unsure how to end the note. He thought maybe something humorous, but he realized that there were too many inappropriate words that would just cheapen the night they'd shared. There was only one word that kept returning to his head, but the four letters seemed difficult to write. When the tip of the pen touched the paper again, he'd decided that it was the only word that seemed to fit the circumstance.

Love, Neil

He left the notepad on the coffee table in the living room and returned to the kitchen. The bottle of Johnny Walker was still standing on the counter. Filling a tumbler to half, he drank it down in one gulp. Then, he turned out the lights and slipped out the front door into the darkness of the forest beyond.

WHEN she heard the cabin door close, Sammy slipped from beneath the bed sheets. A faint chill hung in the air, causing her naked body to shiver. Her bare feet treading softly on the hardwood floor, she crossed to the window and gazed out on the dark forest. She stood to one side, remaining hidden from outside observation. When she caught sight of the circle of light bobbing away from the cabin, she turned away from the window and surveyed the darkened room. The bed comforter had been tossed on the floor in a heap next to the pile of stuffed animals. The faint aroma of sweat and passion still hung in the air. The scent of sex.

Closing her eyes, the still raw memories of the past few hours emerged, causing her to cringe. She'd done everything she could to keep her emotions in check, but their lovemaking had been too raw, too uninhibited. There were too many times when she'd been swept away in the heat of the moment, leaving her vulnerable to the deep confusing feelings that had plagued her all weekend. In every instance, she'd fought to regain control, bringing her inhibitions back into check, allowing her once again to take command of their lovemaking, coaxing Neil toward the end results she'd been looking for.

Crossing the room, Sammy picked up a beige teddy bear from the pile. Its fur was faded and threadbare. The right eye hung from a single thread that had refused to relinquish its hold. A gift for her sixteenth birthday, the teddy bear was the last thing she'd received from Chris. Gazing into the button eyes, she almost felt him near her again. The black plastic circles held her gaze for a long moment, invoking an overwhelming sadness that would have brought her to tears on any other occasion. But tonight, she resolved not to allow it to affect her. She had other things she needed to do.

Setting the teddy bear back in the pile, she looked at the disheveled bedding. An indentation was still visible in the pillow where Neil's head had lain. This time the memories made her feel nauseated, and she rushed to the bathroom, making it only just in time to vomit in the toilet. She heaved a second time and remained on her knees for five minutes before feeling well enough to stand.

Neil's scent still clung to her, his sweat intermixed with hers on her skin. It made her feel as if something were crawling all over her body. It was all too much for her to ignore any longer. She stepped into the shower, vigorously scrubbing his sweat, scent, and semen from her skin, sending it down the drain along with the tears that fell from her eyes.

After the shower, Sammy stripped the sheets from the bed and stuffed them into a black trash bag to burn later. Eventually she'd learn to live with herself, live with what she'd done, and what she was yet to do. Sammy wondered what her father would say had he known how far she'd been willing to debase herself. *It'll all be worth it in the end*, she told herself. *The ends will justify the means.*

SUMMER, 1996

THE POUNDING ON the cabin door woke Neil with a start. A voice was calling his name. He glanced at his watch. 6:34. He slid from the bunk and crossed the cabin to the door. The bunk normally occupied by Redwood Lodge's co-counselor was empty. Brendon had gone home for the weekend and was expected back later that morning. Neil rubbed his eyes and then reached for the door handle.

William Prescott, a counselor from the next cabin, greeted him with disheveled hair and an excited face. Neil restrained his urge to curse at the boy.

"Come on. They found Chris Bateman floating in the lake," said William.

Recalling the previous night, Neil struggled to keep from laughing aloud. The last thing he'd seen was Stinky Bateman's frightened eyes peeking over the side of the canoe. He and his friends had left the boy in the middle of the lake, paddled back to the beach, stowed the canoes, and were back in their respective cabins before two. He shrugged his shoulders, feigning a look of innocence. "What?"

"He was in a canoe. All tied up. They're pulling him to shore now."

Slipping on shoes, Neil followed William down to the lakeside. A cluster of young counselors had already formed along the water's edge. Two canoes had been beached, and camp supervisors, Harvey Brennan and Gloria Satterfield, were lifting Bateman from one of them. The boy looked pale and was shivering as he sat in the sand. Harvey cut the tape from Bateman's wrists and ankles while Gloria pulled the piece from his mouth. Neil cringed at the sound of the tape's removal and was surprised by the fact that Bateman didn't yelp.

Across the crowd, Neil saw Steve and Rob mingling with the other counselors. Jeremy was near the back, fighting to keep a straight face. He couldn't see Patrick anywhere. It looked as if half the camp counselors were there. Some watched in stunned silence while others whispered among themselves. A few eyes glanced in his direction, only to turn away quickly. Some of them would have their suspicions, but none would speak them out loud. They enjoyed watching Stinky Bateman be harassed as much as Neil enjoyed harassing the boy.

Gloria knelt in front of Bateman, gazing into his eyes. "Chris, are you okay?"

Stinky Bateman remained stoic, only giving his head a slow nod. The answer must not have been enough to satisfy Gloria for she touched his forehead and his cheek with the back of her hand. She said, "Who did this? What happened?"

Bateman shook his head, screwing his eyes closed. He muttered, "I don't know."

Gloria wrapped her arm over his shoulder, but Bateman brushed it off and rose to his feet. "I'll be fine."

Harvey stepped forward, trying to guide Bateman away to the camp office, but Neil was surprised to see Stinky Bateman resist. "No, I'm just . . . just hungry."

Bateman pushed past the two adults, and, with his head hung low, he strode off toward his cabin. Neil glanced across the crowd at Steve, who just shrugged his shoulders. There was no doubt that Stinky Bateman knew who'd bound him up and dropped him in the canoe. Neil had looked straight into the kid's eyes. Why hadn't Bateman turned them in? If he'd been in the kid's shoes, he'd have been naming names before even reaching shore. Perhaps Neil was giving the kid too much credit. Maybe Stinky Bateman was a bigger idiot than he'd thought. A smile crossed his face as Neil wondered how fast he could make Stinky Bateman regret keeping his mouth shut.

CHAPTER TWENTY-ONE

Neil held the flashlight limply in his hand, walking in silence and paying just enough attention to his surroundings to keep him from veering off the trail. The moon ducked behind a curtain of clouds, darkening the forest around him. He'd started humming random tunes and somehow ended up with Billy Joel's *Only the Good Die Young*. It somehow seemed appropriate.

He wondered what was going to happen when he returned to New York. Neil couldn't tell his fiancée about the weekend. Theirs may not be a relationship built on love, but they'd both committed to be faithful to each other. As far as she knew, he'd held up his end of the bargain, mostly. There had been one or two dalliances, but who was counting? He let out a mischievous laugh. What happened at camp, stayed at camp.

His thoughts drifted to Sammy, wondering if they could be happy together. If he walked away from the law firm, from the partnership, from Sheila, would he be happy? Everything that he ever wanted was within his grasp, and all he would have to do is walk down the aisle and say "I do." In a few months' time, he'd have what he'd been striving to achieve for years. He'd take the next step in the "Evolutionary Ladder of Neil Brewster." All his hard work was about to pay off, and he couldn't be happier. All of which made him wonder why he was thinking about throwing it all away over one night of salacious passion? Why was he even considering the idea of tossing everything to the wind just to spend his life with Sammy?

A rustling in the branches above startled Neil. He turned the flashlight upward and scanned the trees but found nothing. He swept the light to and fro, like a spotlight, searching the branches overhead. When an owl's hoot echoed from the darkness, he breathed a sigh of relief. He hadn't realized how skittish he'd become. His imagination was getting the better of him. He laughed aloud and scolded the owl. "You scared me, you bastard!" He focused the flashlight again at his feet and moved on.

Neil thought about the note. Why did he write "love" on his note to her? There had been no "love" involved in what happened in Sammy's bedroom. It had been carnal, uninhibited sex . . . and nothing more. Just passion in the most pornographic sense of the word. But the way she held him, kissed him, and looked at him brought something to the surface, confusing and unknown. He didn't for a moment believe it was love. He'd always considered love to be a useless emotion that only compromised one's sensibilities. Never once in his life could he recall saying "I love you" to any woman, not even to get them to sleep with him. Even Sheila had never heard those words uttered from his lips. But tonight . . .

Another rustle in the foliage nearby caused Neil to jump and flick the flashlight around to his right, shining it into the underbrush. The brambles were thick, making it difficult to see much beyond the trail. Nothing stirred as he scanned the immediate area with the light. The owl hooted again, and he smiled. "Stop that, you goddamn rodent!"

Giving the forest one final sweep with the flashlight, Neil moved on along the path. He'd only taken a few steps when he paused to listen. No crickets. No sound. He'd grown so accustomed to their chirping accompaniment that he almost didn't notice that they'd stopped. The silence that came in the wake of their absence seemed to pierce his eardrums now that he'd noticed it. If not for the sound of his own breathing, he'd have sworn that he'd gone deaf. Living in New York, he'd become numb to the constant noise of sirens wailing and horns honking to the point of not noticing it was even there. But when there's no noise at all—when nothing can be heard—the silence seemed louder than all the sounds of the city combined.

To reassure himself, Neil stomped his foot in the sand, just to hear the sound of the impact. The inky blackness of the forest to his right and left was almost impenetrable. The beam of the flashlight was the only way that he saw beyond a few feet. He found himself wishing for the return of the owl.

His best option, he decided, was to return to Sequoia Lodge without further hesitation. He was tired. That had to be all it was, right? The crickets probably went to sleep. As did the owl. All he needed was a good night's sleep. The sooner he got back to the lodge, the sooner he could curl up in his sleeping bag. There was nothing to worry about, he told himself. But he only half-believed it. As his pace quickened, he swung the flashlight to and fro, watching the path ahead as well as the sandy edges of the trail to his left and right. The only sound came from his feet as they sank into the shallow sand with each step.

Because of the overwhelming silence, the snap of the stick resounded like a gunshot. Neil froze, inhaled deeply, and held his breath. The only warning he had was the creaking of an overhead branch, and the soft whoosh of air behind him. Spinning around, he had only a moment to catch a glimpse of the pale gray skin and hollow eyes in the beam of the flashlight before he was knocked backward hard onto the sand.

CHAPTER TWENTY-TWO

THE FORCE OF the blow knocked Neil onto his back, ripping the air out of his lungs. The flashlight slipped from his hand and went out when it hit the ground. He'd only caught a momentary glimpse of what had bowled him over. The face had been horrifying—at least he thought it was a face. He remembered a pair of eyes, open and staring. Harsh pale skin with an icy-gray hue. It must have been a trick of the light.

Everything around him was enveloped in total blackness. Only the faintest of silhouettes was visible above him. He pushed backward, trying to put some distance between himself and whoever, whatever it was. His first thought was that it might be a bear, but he had no way of telling in the gloom. He rattled through his brain, hoping to find some small remnant of information telling him how to deal with bears. Playing dead was the only thing that came to mind.

But then he heard it, faintly at first, only an echo

drifting through the trees on a silent breeze. "Leave me alone, Neil!"

Daring not to move, he remained kneeling in the sand, his eyes darting from left to right, peering aimlessly into the darkness. The silhouette before him was still and lifeless, and the forest had gone silent once again. His ears strained to pick up any sound, anything at all. Then it came again, like a distant echo.

"Stop it, Neil!"

He slowly lifted himself up off the sandy trail, cautiously looking around as he did. He figured he could run for it, if he could just get to his feet. Whatever was happening, he needed to get away from it as fast as he could. As Neil inched his way up, his eyes kept returning to the shadowy figure. It never moved. For a moment, he had an insane urge to reach out and touch it, to find out once and for all what it was. But he brushed the urge aside, choosing instead to follow the more sensible desire for self-preservation.

Once Neil was standing fully erect, he remained still for a moment, not wanting to make too many sudden movements. His leg muscles tightened, ready to spring the moment his brain gave the command. That's when the world exploded.

The forest around Neil lit up with a thousand flashes of white light. His hands flew to his face, shielding his eyes from the intensity. The glare seared through the twilight like bursting white stars, and he spun around and around, desperate for even a second's reprieve from disorientating brilliance. The distorted voice roared through the trees, erupting in his ears.

"Neil, stop it!"

"Leave me alone, Neil!"

Over and over the voice thundered all around him,

slamming his eardrums almost to the breaking point. Shielding his eyes and covering his ears, Neil fell to the ground in a huddled mass.

"Stop!" he screamed, gripping his head tightly between his forearms.

The crushing distortion and chaotic flashes of hellish bright light left him convulsing in the sand, legs flailing, hands and arms wrapped tightly around his head, and his eyes locked shut. Like before, the voices echoed over and over, seeming to merge into one long horrifying sentence. They intermingled until Neil no longer heard individual words.

Even through his closed eyelids, he saw intense flashes of white. Neil twisted and rolled in the sand. He felt its grittiness on his lips and face. How long could he lie there? How long would this go on? He opened his mouth and screamed, but he heard nothing but the resounding voices repeating the same thing ceaselessly.

"Stop it, Neil!"

"Leave me alone, Neil!"

"Neil, stop it!"

That voice, he thought. *Why that damn voice?* It had been nothing more than a high-pitched whine eighteen years ago, but now it was a malignant cancer attacking his mind, his very soul. It was distorted . . . twisted . . . perverted into something evil and callous. The tone seemed accusatory, or was that just his imagination? He couldn't tell. The ruthless cascade of light and sound caused him to lose all sense of where he was and what was around him. He was being blinded and deafened, leaving him feeling helpless and afraid. It was an experience that, until very recently, was wholly foreign to him. It was a feeling that only served to make his plight even more terrifying. He had to do something, and fast. He opened his eyes.

The glaring lights exploded around Neil, forcing him to squint just to keep from being overwhelmed. The forest to the right and left was ablaze, and his vision was speckled with swirling orbs left by the bright flashes. Blurred and disoriented, he tried to glance around, hoping to get enough of his bearings to make an escape. The trees seemed to dance and sway in the pulsating lights, and he struggled to tell which way was which.

The white Converse high-top sneakers hovering over him caught Neil's eye. The laces were untied and the canvas worn and stained. A distant memory pressed its way to the forefront of his mind. He knew where he'd seen them before. They seemed to float in the air above him, gently turning this way and that. After that first glimpse, everything around him seemed to fade into the background. A kind of horrifying tunnel vision set in, focusing on one thing only. His eyes drifted up the bare legs, the skin appeared icy gray. Continuing upward, his gaze fell on the beige shorts, followed by the pale blue t-shirt, the Camp Tenskwatawa logo emblazoned on the front. The arms dangled on either side, drawn down straight by gravity. As the voices continued to batter his eardrums and the lights dazzle his eyes, he felt his stomach knot up in fear.

Next, he saw the coarse rope encircling the neck. The same rope used to tie up the canoes by the lake. Tan and rough. He'd remembered getting more than his share of rope burns from it in his youth. The thick strands were digging deep into the pale gray skin of the neck. The head, tilting listlessly to the right, seemed to twitch and convulse, almost as if it were still alive. With its pale complexion spotted with dark bruising, the young face seemed to dance with the shadows caused by the colorless kaleidoscope around him. The open eyes were blank and dark, with a horrifying gaze that seemed to look straight through him. Up from behind the head, Neil saw the hangman's knot, with the rope leading up into the trees. Resting atop the head of blond hair was the red Snap-on hat. The lifeless body dangled from the rope, rocking gently back and forth, a dead pendulum of human bone and flesh.

And then, just as suddenly as it began, everything went dark, and silence fell upon the forest. Neil felt crippled by his own terror, unable to think, speak, or move. *Is it over?* he kept asking himself. His body trembled, and he took a few deep breaths, trying to calm himself. His heart was still racing, and his ears were ringing. Neil shook his head, hoping to clear away the disorientation and get a grip on himself.

He tried to sit up, feeling nauseous for a few moments. Another deep breath dislodged a few grains of the sand from his caked lips, sending them down his throat, causing him to gag and cough. Then, out of the darkness, he heard the voice again, faint this time, echoing through the trees.

"Leave me alone, Neil!"

As the echoing voice faded, a glaring single light shone into Neil's face, like a brilliant spotlight. Silhouetted within its circle of brilliance was the dark form he'd seen earlier. The outline of the hangman's knot, the shape of the body, and the gently lifeless movement all formed a black mass within the blinding glare.

The fear that had paralyzed him finally relinquished control, and the urge for flight overwhelmed everything else. As he scrambled to his feet, Neil charged off in the opposite direction, running hard, running fast, and running scared. No sooner had he moved when the bright light went dark, leaving him blind once more. But it didn't stop him. If anything, it just made him run faster.

CHAPTER TWENTY-THREE

STUMBLING THROUGH THE dark forest, Neil wasn't sure which direction he was headed, toward Sequoia Lodge or back to the caretaker's cabin. At the moment, he didn't care which. More than once, his foot caught on something—perhaps a rock or a tree root—sending him sprawling to the ground. He felt the sting of low-hanging branches that thrashed over and over at his face. His shins were gouged by indignant brambles that ripped and tore at his flesh.

Although the trail was straight, in his panicked state, he veered off again and again, stumbling though the underbrush until he found his way back to the sandy path. The taste of blood mixed with sandy grit in his mouth told him that he must have cut his lip. He didn't stop to check. Running hard, Neil's lungs were searing as he gasped for air. Despite being an avid runner, he found it hard to keep up the pace but charged on nonetheless. He needed to put as much distance between himself and the thing hanging from the trees.

When Neil broke out from under the canopy of over-hanging branches into the sandy open area of the parking lot, he breathed a sigh of relief. The moon, although partly obscured by clouds, cast ample enough light for him to make out the silhouettes of five vehicles parked at the opposite side. Sequoia Lodge wasn't far away. Stopping for a moment, he leaned forward, placing his hands on his knees to rest. Taking a few deep breaths, he tried to calm his frayed nerves. But his legs gave out moments later. He dropped to his knees, his hands falling forward, sinking deep into the soft sand. Fighting to catch his breath, Neil lost all control and began to cry.

The voice still echoed in the shadows of his mind. Closing his eyes meant seeing that gray face again, releasing another wave of fear through his soul. The memory was vivid and raw, and would probably haunt him for life. The tears flowing down his face stung the scratches and open wounds on his cheeks.

Neil pounded his fists into the sand. "Why? Why? Why? Why's this happening?"

Clenching his hands in frustration, he squeezed handfuls of sand until the individual grains oozed from between his fingers. He brushed away the tears from his cheeks, only to scrape gritty sand across the raw skin.

Still on his knees, Neil tried to rationalize what had happened. His memories were still a jumble, but there had to be some logical explanation for everything that had occurred throughout the weekend. Never one to believe in the paranormal, he refused to accept that he was being haunted by Bateman's ghost. Even if Neil did believe in ghouls and goblins, he figured Bateman would never have enough gumption to return from the afterlife. No, this wasn't a haunting.

Rising to his feet, Neil paced in tight circles around the sandy parking lot. A guilt-induced hallucination? He laughed at the thought. What did he have to feel guilty about? So he had teased the poor kid. It didn't mean he was responsible for Bateman's death. He had mocked people throughout his entire childhood—into college even. None of them had killed themselves . . . as far as he knew. It took eighteen years for him to find out what had happened to Bateman. Could there be others that he didn't know about? What about now? How many lives had he ruined to discredit witness testimony? He'd never been one to shy away from airing people's dirty laundry in public if it helped him win a case. Affairs. Criminal records. Professional misconduct. All of it, and more, was fair game in his book. How many marriages had been ended? How many careers crushed? How many lives had been destroyed?

Neil kicked at the sand, sending a cloud of particles into the air. "No! No! No!" he said. "It wasn't my fault! It's got to be a hoax!"

Continuing to pace, he tried to apply reason to his unreasonable situation. The lights. The voices. The body. It had to be a prank. A sick, elaborate prank. Who would do this to him? Steve? Rob? Jeremy? He refused to believe that. Why would anyone go to all this trouble?

Why? That was the question that Neil kept coming back to. Why? To get back at him for teasing Stinky Bateman all those years ago? His friends had been involved with harassing Bateman at one time or another, so they should be just as guilty as him. He refused to believe that any of his friends were involved. Well, most of them.

He stopped pacing, noticing the rut he'd created in the sand. Gazing at the sky, he watched the moon creep out from behind the clouds, taking the edge off the darkness. Neil sighed, realizing that he should have listened to his first instinct and not come this weekend. Then, turning abruptly, he trekked off toward Sequoia Lodge.

AS he pushed open the cabin door, Neil tried to make as little noise as possible. Despite his best efforts, the hinges creaked, and the handle rapped loudly against the door. Hearing the shifting of a sleeping bag, he saw a dark silhouette rise from one of the lower bunks.

"About time you got back," Steve whispered. "Come on. Don't want to wake the others." He took Neil's arm and led him back out onto the porch.

With the door closed, Neil leaned against the porch railing as Steve, in a t-shirt and boxers, sat down on one of the chairs. Steve opened his mouth to say something, then seemed to change his mind when he got a better look at Neil. "You okay? You look like you've been through the wringer."

Neil figured that his face must have looked like hell. It still stung from the scratches he'd received during his flight. He moved back into the shadows, turning his gaze away from his friend. "I, uh . . . it's nothing."

He breathed deeply, the relative safety of the cabin gave him a sense of relief and comfort. The cool night air filled his battered lungs, soothing the still burning bronchioles. He was beginning to feel like himself again.

"How was she?" Steve asked.

Neil shook his head, feigning denial. "How was who?"

"Oh, don't give me that crap. I know you went to see her."

"Yeah, I did."

"And?"

Neil laughed. "I can't believe you'd ask me that."

"It must have been good." Steve glanced at his watch. "You've been gone almost five hours."

"Were you timing me?"

Steve simply smiled in return.

"Did you know she was going to be here this weekend?" Neil asked.

"Nope. Not 'til I saw her car at the cabin."

"She mentioned you stopped in."

Steve folded his arms across his chest. "I got to know her Dad a year or two back—came down a lot during the sales negotiation. He wasn't all that bad of a guy to be honest. I kinda liked him."

"That's how you got to know her?" Neil felt a slight twinge of jealousy returning.

"Yeah. She was down here a couple times," Steve explained. "She'd always ask about you, wanting to know if I'd heard from you. She had a thing for you. Still does, probably. Well, obviously she does."

"How are you so sure?"

"What else would you have been doing all night? Roaming the forest? Communing with nature? The only nature you were communing with was between Sammy's legs."

Neil snorted aloud at his friend's comment, and then leaned back against the wall of the lodge. In the distance, he heard crickets chirping and the occasional hoot of an owl. The cool predawn air had relaxed him, almost pushing aside any thoughts of his earlier ordeal. "It's so peaceful here."

Steve sighed. "Not for much longer. We start demolition next month."

"At least we got to see the old place one more time."

Steve turned his head. "I thought you weren't the

nostalgic type."

Shrugging his shoulders, Neil said, "I'm not. But . . . you know . . ."

"Yeah, I do."

His mind drifted back to Sammy. He figured she was probably still asleep. She'd told Neil that she thought of him often over the past eighteen years. He'd had no idea how she felt about him and wasn't sure what to think about it all. The only thing he was certain of was that he had to see her again.

"Neil, I know this weekend might not be turning out the way you'd hoped. Please don't think of our concern as a slight against you."

Neil bit at his lip, the quick urge to anger surfaced first in his mind. But drawing in a lungful of cool predawn air, he let the anger fade. "I know. It's just . . . this sort of thing doesn't happen to me. I don't see and hear things that aren't there."

"I've known you since grade school. This isn't like you."

"We haven't seen each other in eighteen years. I could've changed."

Steve laughed. "Not you. You've always been laser-focused. Granted, you were always laser-focused on yourself, but we all were to a point. You couldn't have gotten to where you are today if that had changed."

Neil smiled. "Are you saying I'm narcissistic?"

"In a way, I guess. But you always were. What I'm really trying to say is that everything that's happened . . . it's just not you. That's why I'm concerned."

Letting Steve's words sink in for a moment, he gazed out across the dark forest. If his friend was concerned about him now, he couldn't imagine what Steve would be thinking once he learned about what happened an hour earlier in the forest.

Steve continued, "Not to beat a dead horse, but you seemed fine until you heard about Bateman's suicide."

At the mention of that name, Neil turned abruptly toward his friend. "What are you saying?"

"It just seems like a helluva coincidence. You were fine when you arrived. You heard about Bateman's death, and now you're seeing and hearing things the rest of us aren't. I'm not trying to piss you off. I'm looking for answers just like you."

Looking down at his feet, Neil considered Steve's words carefully. It was only logical that his friend should be worried about him. He wanted to make a snide remark and disregard Steve's worry as unnecessary, but his words came out half-hearted and unconvincing. "I've got nothing to be guilty about. He killed himself."

"I never said you had." Steve paused, and then asked, "What happened? I called dozens of times after you left camp. Not just to tell you about Bateman, but to see how you were doing. You were my best friend. But you never returned my calls. Why?"

Neil shook his head. "I don't know." His voice faltered for a moment as he realized that there was no answer he could give that wouldn't sound egotistical and self-absorbed. "I . . . I just got caught up in things."

Steve chuckled. "I figured as much. With you, it was always onward and upward and to hell with everything else."

The crunch of dried leaves and twigs caught Neil's attention. His nerves still being a bit frayed, he jumped at the sound, peering into the darkness. "What's that?"

Steve didn't move. "Don't know."

Out of the darkness, Patrick emerged, hands in the pockets of his jeans. His shoulders were slouched forward, and his head was down. He stepped onto the porch and seemed startled to find Steve and Neil flanking the lodge door. "What're you two doing out here?"

With a sudden, swift movement, Neil grasped the front of Patrick's t-shirt, swung his friend around, and slammed him into the wall of the lodge. Steve shot out of his chair and gaped. Neil thrust his face within inches of Patrick's. In the gloom, he saw the shocked expression on Patrick's face and felt him exhale. The door to the cabin swung open, and Jeremy stepped out, followed immediately by Rob.

"What the—" Jeremy said.

Pressing his face closer to Patrick's, Neil said, "Why'd you do it? Huh? Why? What did I do to you?"

"What?" Patrick replied.

His fists winding the fabric of Patrick's t-shirt tighter, Neil shoved his friend back into the wall again. "You think it was funny? Trying to scare me? Sounds hilarious, don't it? Did you notice I'm not laughing?"

"Neil!" said Steve, stepping forward to pull him away from Patrick.

"Stay out of this, Steve! All of you! This is between Patrick and me," Neil growled, shoving Patrick against the wall again. "Tell me, you bastard! What're you trying to pull?"

"I don't know what you're talking about!" Patrick said.

"How did you do it? Strobe lights?" Neil said. "And the body? Was it a mannequin? I can't imagine you'd be sick enough to use a real body!" Neil leaned closer, his face an inch from Patrick's. "Or maybe you are! What'd you do, sneak into a goddamn morgue and steal a corpse?"

Patrick tried to push away. "Neil! Get off me!"

Neil's grip remained firm. "Tell me why! Just tell me why! What's Stinky's death got to do with you, huh? What's your game?"

"I had to take a shit!"

Neil glared at him for a moment, then his grip began to falter. "What?"

"I was in the bathroom! I had to take a shit!"

"He was!" said Steve. "I heard him go out about five minutes before you came in."

"But . . . you weren't . . . the bathroom?" His hands loosened their hold on Patrick's shirt. Neil took a few steps back. "That can't be right. I was . . . was so . . ."

Jeremy moved toward him. "Brewster, what's going on?"

Neil's eyes darted around, pausing on each of his friends for a moment. "No one else left the lodge?"

Steve shook his head but said nothing. Neil felt confused. He was certain that he'd figured it out. When he saw Patrick walk up out of the dark, he was confident that his suspicions were confirmed. Patrick had to be responsible for the terrifying light and sound show. He was the obvious choice. But now . . .

"What's wrong with you?" Patrick shouted, running his hands down his t-shirt to flatten out the wrinkles.

Neil didn't know how to answer. To tell them what had happened would be to invite more questions and more concerned looks. He'd had enough of those earlier when he'd seen the red ball cap. More speculation about how he might be experiencing remorse over Stinky Bateman's death was the last thing he wanted to hear. He didn't want to hear it anymore.

But his four friends were standing before him, expecting an explanation for his sudden hostile outburst. Neil didn't have much choice but to tell them what had happened. They listened as he described the voices, the flashing lights, and the hanging body. He caught the darting glances passing between them as he unfolded each detail. When he'd finished his tale, all was silent, no one making any comment.

After several moments, Steve said, "When it gets light, we'll go back and see what we can find."

Neil said, "No, let's go back now."

Patrick folded his arms, glaring at Neil. "Screw that. I'm not chasing imaginary ghosts at four in the morning."

His friend's disbelief was evident by the look on his face. It was a look that Neil found on all their faces as he glanced between them. "We've got to go back now."

"Why, Neil? Whatever we find now, we'll find in a few hours," said Rob.

Jeremy muttered, "If there's anything to find."

"It's too dark," said Steve. "We'll go after sunrise. Let's all get a couple hours of sleep."

SUMMER, 1997

Stinky Bateman had his back against a tall pine tree on a Saturday afternoon when Neil and Patrick entered the secluded clearing. They'd been lounging on the front porch of Neil's cabin when they saw Bateman wander off immediately after lunch with a thick book under his arm. With nothing else planned, they'd decided to tail him. Following Bateman around the lake, they crossed the spillway and passed the girls' cabins. On the far side of the lake, Bateman had vanished up a narrow path branching off the main trail.

Neil, with Patrick in tow, crept along the path a few minutes after Bateman and caught sight of the him in the small clearing ahead. The boy had his knees pulled up against his chest, and the book was balanced on top. Bateman looked far too content in his little world of solitude, and Neil felt compelled to disturb it.

With long strides, he walked into the clearing and dropped down beside Bateman, folding his legs underneath him. Patrick, carrying his Sony HandyCam, hit the record button and began filming. Leaning in toward Bateman, Neil said, "Nice place you got here, Stinky."

Bateman pulled away, glaring. "Leave me alone, Neil."

"Whatcha got there?" He reached for the book, snapping it from Bateman's hands. Flipping over the cover, he glanced at the title. "Anna Karenina?" Holding the book up to Patrick's camera, he said, "Stinky's reading Tolstoy." He tossed the book back at Bateman's chest, being sure to lose his page in the process. "I'm impressed. I never took you for an intellectual. Didn't think there was much up in that old noggin of yours." Neil tapped on the side of Bateman's head with his knuckles, as if knocking on a door.

The boy turned his head away. "Neil, stop it!"

Patrick, still recording with his HandyCam, said, "Doesn't sound like he likes you."

"Yeah. I'm feeling very unwelcome right now." He pushed on Bateman's shoulder, knocking the book from the boy's grasp. Neil was met with a long stare, more pleading than angry.

"Stop it, Neil!" he said, picking up the book and brushing the sand from the cover.

"You know, Stinky, babes aren't impressed by intellectuals." Neil gestured toward the book. "You keep reading crap like that, you goddamn dork, and you'll never get laid." Neil paused, and then peered at Bateman. "You do know what it means to get laid, don't you?"

Climbing to his feet, Neil looked down at Bateman, smiled, and, with his foot, kicked sand in the boy's direction. The gritty white particles covered the book and Bateman's face. Turning to Patrick, he said, "Let's go. I'm bored."

CHAPTER TWENTY-FOUR

NEIL'S FRIENDS FELL asleep almost immediately, but slumber eluded him. He couldn't shake the faint voices echoing in his mind. They were barely audible—almost like distant whispers—just the same three phrases playing over and over. Screwing his eyes closed, he tried to shut out the far-off shadows of his past. Never in his wildest dreams did Neil think that he'd ever hear Bateman's name, let alone his voice, again. But staring at the bottom of the bunk above him, he struggled to clear his mind of the boy's voice. After tossing and turning for a half hour, he slipped from his bunk.

Outside, Neil sat on the porch, listening to the quiet sounds of nature all around him. Everything seemed so peaceful, making it difficult to believe that all of this could've been disturbed by anything other than the rising sun. Yet, not more than an hour ago, the quiet forest had exploded in a dissonance of light and sound, and he'd been caught in the middle. How could anyone have created such utter bedlam in this tranquil setting? Did anyone create it? Could it all have been part of his imagination?

He'd seen the looks his friends gave him when he told them what had happened. Disbelief. Concern. Pity. All the things that Neil would've thought upon hearing such an absurd tale himself. It was the pity that frustrated him more than anything else. He didn't need their pity. He didn't want their pity. He wanted answers. It was down-right farcical to think that Stinky Bateman had come back to haunt him from the grave. There had to be a logical, reason for what was happening.

As the early-morning light broke through the trees, he watched Lake Friendship in the distance; a layer of thick mist hovered low across the water. The white vapor churned in slow undulating swirls, as if it were dancing along the surface of the lake. His watch said it was five in the morning. His friends would rise in a couple of hours, and then he'd lead them back to the path, trying to find the exact location where all hell had broken loose. He already knew what they'd find. Nothing. They'd find nothing. Then his friends would all look at him with the same look of pity he'd seen earlier, probably wondering how close he was to plunging into insanity.

As Neil continued to gaze out across the lake, a faint silhouette became visible in the fog. Between the distance and the dimness of the light, it was hard to distinguish any details, but it looked as if someone was drifting in a canoe. Leaning forward in his chair, Neil moved in for a closer look. The canoe moved slowly among the mist, passing in and out of the swirling clouds of white. The figure seated in the center of the canoe was unmoving, sitting erect as if oblivious to the world around it. Although he couldn't see the face in detail, there was one thing that screamed out to him, one thing that chilled his blood. The red ball cap. Even in the thick fog, the crimson hue stood out like a beacon. Whoever was in the canoe was wearing a bright red cap, just like Stinky Bateman.

He couldn't remember rising from his chair, but he must have because Neil found himself standing on the edge of the porch, his fists clenched and his eyes open wide. The figure wasn't paddling, yet the canoe continued to drift on the calm water, an unseen force propelling it. Sometimes it would float into the dense fog, the red cap being barely visible. Then it would move back into view, wafting along the lake's surface, obscured just enough for him to never fully see the figure's face.

Conflicting desires swelled within him. Neil wanted to wake his friends so that they could see it with their own eyes and know that he wasn't suffering from hallucinations. But he didn't want to turn away for fear that the apparition would vanish, leaving him with yet another unexplainable poltergeist.

As his eyes tracked the boat, it began to drift into the dense mist, gradually fading from his sight amidst the white haze. Neil scanned the water's surface, waiting with bated breath for it to reappear. The seconds dragged by. Maybe it had run ashore on the other side of the lake. It wouldn't be long before the morning sun burned off the fog, clearing the lake of its ethereal covering, making it possible to see straight across the water's surface.

AN hour later, Neil stood on the beach of Lake Friendship when Steve approached. The fog had lifted, and the sky was blue and cloudless. The warmth of the sun pierced through the tree branches and sliced through the chilly morning air, taking the edge off what had been a cold spring night. Although Neil heard the footsteps in the sand, he didn't turn to see who it was. His gaze remained locked on the lake.

Steve placed his hand on Neil's shoulder. "You been out here all morning?"

Neil nodded. "Couldn't sleep."

Steve sighed. "Neil, are you sure you're okay? We're all—"

"You see that canoe out there?" Neil pointed toward the narrow gray boat resting on the water in the middle of the lake.

Steve's gaze followed his pointing finger. "Yeah, what about it?"

"Someone was in it earlier this morning. I've been watching it for a couple hours."

"No one's there now."

Neil refused to take his eyes off the canoe. He felt sickeningly mesmerized by it. "It was drifting in and out of the mist all morning. Are you sure that we're the only ones in the camp?"

"As far as I know."

Neil folded his arms and glanced at Steve. "Someone else is out there. I've seen him. He was in the canoe earlier."

Steve's eyes held him in a skeptical gaze. "Where'd he go? Did he fall in the lake?"

"I don't know. The mist was too thick to see it all the time. He must have jumped out at some point."

Steve turned away from the lake, looking back up to Sequoia Lodge. "What makes you think it's a 'he'?"

"I'm just guessing."

"Someone could have hiked in through the forest— the camp isn't fenced in. I don't think there's any new cars in the parking lot," Steve said. "Maybe someone was doing a little early-morning fishing."

Neil shook his head. "No. He was here for me."

"What?"

"He was wearing a red ball cap."

"What're you saying?"

"Whatever . . . whoever was out there was trying to convince me that Stinky Bateman was in that canoe."

Steve sighed, turned back to gaze out across the lake, and then directed his gaze downward at his feet. Neil heard shuffling in the sand beside him. He knew the reason for the awkward silence. "You don't believe me."

Steve didn't reply at first, only sighing as if it were the only response needed. "Do you blame me?"

"I'd hope you'd give me the benefit of the doubt."

"I want to," Steve said, folding his arms. "But you don't make it easy. Voices in the forest. Corpses hanging from trees."

"I saw what I saw."

They stood silently for a few minutes, both staring out across the lake. The canoe drifted aimlessly on the water, in no apparent hurry to arrive anywhere in particular. Without even looking, Neil knew what Steve's expression would be—a sad, concerned look with a touch of pity. His friend's eyes would be partially closed, his eyebrows furrowed with worry, and Steve would be biting his bottom lip. It was a classic "Steve is worried" look that he remembered all too well.

He'd pondered many thoughts during his solitary vigil at the lake's edge. But one, which surfaced again and again, had lingered in the forefront of his mind. Could it be true that he'd driven Bateman to suicide? Was all that he'd seen and heard the result of his own guilty conscious? He wanted another opinion. Another perspective on the question of his own guilt. Of his four friends, Steve was the one Neil trusted the most to be honest. But what would his friend think? Would Steve take his question as a sign of weakness? It would be what Neil would think if he were Steve. There was nothing to convince him that his friend would think any different. He opened his mouth to speak, but pride trumped everything and the words remained unspoken.

Neil felt the continuing silence between them grow unbearable. "You went to her father's funeral?"

Steve folded his arms. "No. Not the funeral. I couldn't make it to that. But she had a little ceremony—on this beach as a matter of fact. Her father wanted his ashes scattered in the lake. There were only a few people here for it."

"You see her a lot?"

"No. Just once or twice. I saw her father more than her."

"Good."

Steve turned and smiled. "Are you jealous?"

"Nah," Neil said, shaking his head. Then, smiling, he added, "Maybe just a little."

Steve laughed. "Don't worry. She's all yours." His hand touched Neil's shoulder. "Come on, let's get the guys up, have breakfast, and then try to find this corpse of yours."

AFTER breakfast, Neil led his friends along the trail heading back toward the caretaker's cabin. Leading the way, he kept a wary eye on the trail and surrounding forest, searching for any evidence to prove his story from the previous night. The white sand was undisturbed and clean of any indication that anyone had traveled along the path within the past day. He scanned the tree limbs and the underbrush, hoping—desperately—to find something, anything to assure his friends, as well as himself, of his sanity. Behind him, his four friends politely refrained from comment as they followed along.

They'd walked the length of the trail, and as they stepped into the clearing behind the caretaker's cabin, Neil halted and turned to face his friends. Their expressions barely disguised their disbelief.

"Where's this body of yours?" Patrick said, his arms folded across his chest. "Did I miss it?"

Neil caught the quick glance that Jeremy shot toward Patrick. A silent chastisement to which Patrick simply shrugged in silent reply. Rob kicked at the white sand beneath his feet, sending the tiny granules into the air. "I was asking myself the same question."

"Okay, okay," Neil admitted. "There's nothing here."

CHAPTER TWENTY-FIVE

FOLDING THE LID of the cardboard box closed, Sammy stretched a piece of packing tape across the seam. She sat cross-legged on the floor of her bedroom. With a black marker, she scrawled "Stuffed Animals" across the side of the box. Her elbows rested on the box top, her chin dropping into the cup formed by her hands. She allowed her eyes to close for a few moments and felt her head bob forward.

Realizing how exhausted she was, Sammy tried to remember when she'd last slept. It must have been Wednesday when she'd last had a full night's sleep. Ever since, she'd been constantly on the move, making sure that everything fell into place for the weekend. There had been time for a couple quick naps here and there, but it was well over seventy-two hours since she'd really slept.

When she stood, Sammy lifted the cardboard box then carried it out of the room and down the stairs. She added it to the stack of boxes by the front door. A stray hair fell in front of her eye, and she brushed it aside before climbing the stairs once again. With another empty box on the bed, she opened the dresser drawers, removing clothing from each. There wasn't much left for her to pack. Just a few items were left to make the cabin look lived in. Everything else had been moved out a week ago. She only had to clear out the remainder of her personal items, and then the stage would be set for the final act of the drama that she'd been playing out. It had taken almost a year to get to this point. A year of research, of planning, of manipulation. All fueled by her staggering desire for revenge. With the finale drawing near, there was only one question left to be answered. Would she have the strength to follow through with what she had planned?

Sammy stared at the clothing in the box, realizing that this weekend was a culmination of a lifetime of hatred and anger. She'd expected this to be more satisfying, to have a more climatic feeling. But she instead felt confused, sad, and lonely. There'd been no gratification from her actions thus far. She was beginning to wonder if her inclination toward revenge would have the desired result she'd been hoping for. Maybe she'd been wrong. Perhaps there was no way to get closure, no way to get reprieve from her grief.

Her therapist had once said that everyone deals with their grief in different ways, and Sammy needed to find what worked best for her. How did he put it? "If you didn't learn to cry, you'd never heal." He encouraged her to experiment with a variety of activities to find one that brought relief. Journaling. Meditation. Support groups. She'd tried it all, never finding relief until she started planning for this weekend. If her therapist only knew how she was planning to deal with her grief. She was sure he'd not only disapprove, he'd also try to stop her.

Carrying the sealed box downstairs, Sammy

approached the front door, balanced the box against her knee, and struggled to turn the doorknob. Outside, she crossed the porch and stepped down the stairs. She set the box on the ground beside her Ford Focus, lifted the hatch-back, and placed the box inside. Returning to the house, she lifted another box from the floor and headed back outside.

"Let me get that," she heard Neil say as he grasped the box, pulling it from her yielding hands.

Sammy remained still, watching as he walked down the porch stairs and placed the box into the back of the car. She hadn't been expecting him to show up. Not now, and not in this way. What was he doing here? She wasn't ready to face him. It was too soon.

Sammy followed him down the stairs, her pulse racing as she scrutinized his every move. Did she leave out anything incriminating in the cabin? She couldn't remember what state the bedroom was in. The living room might be safe but certainly not the bedrooms. She was sure of it.

"I didn't expect to see you this early," she said.

He smiled. "I can't stay away from you."

She stared at his face for a long moment. The dark shadows beneath his bloodshot eyes told her that Neil hadn't gotten much sleep since they had last seen each other. The fresh scratches and cuts looked red and painful. Events from the early morning must have been worse than she'd anticipated. She reached up, softly touching his cheek. "Are you okay?"

He shrugged. "Yeah, why?"

Sammy tilted her head and frowned. "I don't know. Your face . . . It's all cut up. You look . . . tired. A little pale."

"Someone kept me up late last night."

He smiled, but she could tell that it was forced. "That doesn't explain the cuts," she said.

"I tripped in the dark last night." He turned his face away from her to stare into the forest. He was chewing on his bottom lip. He seemed edgy, nervous, and distracted. She glanced at his hand. It hung by his side, trembling. It was a faint tremble, but just enough for her to notice.

He gestured to the boxes in the back of the car. "Packing up?"

She nodded. "Taking some of Dad's old stuff to Goodwill. I'm sure someone can make use of it."

Neil leaned back against the Ford, glancing aimlessly toward the forest again. Eventually, his eyes came back to rest on her. "Is there anyone else out here?"

Sammy knew why he was asking, but she tried to put on her best puzzled look. "Huh?"

"Here in camp. Do you know if anyone else is here?"

"Other than you and the other guys?" She shook her head. "I doubt it. Why?"

When his response was delayed, she wondered if he would be honest with her. He hadn't been up to this point, she knew that. He'd lied about his fiancée. He'd probably lied when he said that he loved her. Would he tell her the truth now?

His eyes shifted back toward the forest. "There's been . . ." He paused. "I'm just wondering. An abandoned place like this probably attracts a lot of undesirables."

He turned his eyes toward the ground and shuffled his feet in the sand. Studying him closely, Sammy noted how much he'd changed since arriving at the camp two days ago. His confidence seemed rattled, and there was an air of despondency hanging over him. The weekend was taking its toll. She wondered if she was taking this too far. Was she doing the right thing? "Neil, we're so far out in the sticks that we have to have our sticks shipped in. I doubt most people even remember the camp is here."

An awkward silence fell between them. Maybe she should invite him in for a whiskey. Maybe he'd understand if she made a clean breast of it all.

"Do you remember Stinky Bateman?" he asked suddenly.

The nickname was a punch to the stomach. A sharp momentary anger burned within her like flash paper in a magician's hand. She wanted to scream at him. To curse him. To accuse him. To spew a litany of the most hateful words she could imagine. But to do so would ruin everything. She drew in a slow breath and feigned ignorance. "I'm . . . I'm not sure."

"Chris. His name was Chris Bateman."

She paused for a second, trying to make it appear as if it were a struggle to remember. "Yeah. How could I forget? He hung himself here at the camp. Why?"

His eyes darted between her and the forest. The smile had vanished from his face, and she thought, for a moment, that he might be on the brink of crying. But, regaining his composure, he shook his head. "It's nothing. The guys mentioned the little faggot's suicide. I wasn't sure if they were telling the truth," he said.

Her hand moved to her throat, touching the St. Christopher medal around her neck. It felt bitter cold between her fingers. Sammy's jaw tightened, and she struggled to remain calm. She wanted to hurt him. She wanted to kill him. *Not yet*, she thought. *Not yet.*

"I'd better get these boxes loaded," she said, her voice soft, almost a whisper.

"I can help."

She placed her hand on Neil's shoulder. "No. Go back to the guys. Enjoy the weekend." She leaned forward and kissed him. "Are you coming back tonight?" she asked.

He smiled, nodded, and then walked slowly away, heading back toward Sequoia Lodge.

Through narrowed eyes, Sammy watched him walk into the forest. There was no longer any doubt. She knew what she must do.

SUMMER, 1997

THE HEAT ON the last Saturday of July was oppressive, even at night. Despite the sultry conditions, Neil had managed to convince the red-headed Brenda St. James to meet him late that evening down by the rope bridge. Like him, it was her last year as a counselor at Camp Tenskwatawa. She'd been a bit resistant to his earlier advances, so he was feeling pleased with himself when Brenda had finally agreed to their late-night liaison. He'd smuggled a bottle of Jack Daniels into camp a few weeks prior, and he was hoping to use it as leverage to get his hands on Brenda's pert breasts and tight ass.

He'd taken a blanket, which they'd draped across the white sand of a secluded clearing near the rope bridge. Half a bottle later, he found himself entangled in Brenda's arms, his hands expertly undressing her. With naked flesh pressed against naked flesh, Neil felt confident that he was going to score. But the muggy night air left their bodies sticky with sweat, and a torn condom brought a premature end to the evening.

Walking back to Redwood Lodge, the half empty bottle of Jack Daniels concealed within the balled-up blanket, Neil was feeling far from satisfied. Brenda had been adamant that she wasn't going any further without a condom, and since he didn't have another one handy, that had been the end of it. Now he returned to his cabin—an ache in his balls and a scowl on his face.

When Neil entered Redwood Lodge, he was surprised to find his cabinmate not in his bunk. Since having been reassigned as the co-counselor of Redwood Lodge three weeks ago, Stinky Bateman had spent as much time away from the cabin as possible. Probably in an effort, Neil figured, to avoid him. During the week, Bateman had little to fear from Neil because of the kids being in camp, but come the weekends . . .

Neil stared at Bateman's empty bunk for a long moment, wondering where the boy could be. It was well past midnight, and it was unusual for Bateman to be out this late. He'd learned long ago that he could set his watch to Bateman's routines. Up at the same time. In bed at the same time. For Bateman to not be around was odd. Maybe he was out with one of the girl counselors? Neil disregarded that thought as soon as it passed through his mind. There wasn't a snowball's chance in hell that Bateman would be dipping his stinger into anyone's honey. Neil figured he stood a better chance of getting Brenda to do him without a condom than Bateman ever stood with any of the girls in camp.

Not wanting to waste Bateman's conspicuous absence, Neil decided that it would be a good time to do a little digging. Earlier in the week, he'd walked in on Bateman with pen in hand and an open leather-bound book. His curiosity was piqued when Bateman made an expeditious attempt to hide the book. Probably a diary, Neil had figured. At the time, he acted as if he didn't notice, but now, with Bateman out of the way, it was as good a time as any to take a little peek. If nothing else, the little brown book might make for an interesting read.

Reaching under Bateman's bunk, Neil dragged a pale blue American Tourist suitcase out until it rested in the middle of the floor. Popping the latches, he opened the suitcase and stared at its contents. He'd never seen the inside of Bateman's suitcase before, and what he found came as no surprise. The kid's clothes were neatly folded and stacked, with everything arranged with perfect organization. The pale blue Camp Tenskwatawa t-shirts looked freshly laundered. The tan shorts—five pairs in all—were tucked in an orderly pile next to the shirts. Even socks and underwear were precisely arranged within the suitcase, right next to the toiletry bag.

No book. Neil closed the lid and, before sliding the luggage back under the bunk, examined the space between the bottom of the bunk and the floor. Next, he picked up the pillow and rifled through the sleeping bag on the bunk. Still nothing. Yanking the mattress off the bunk revealed nothing either.

As frustration began to set in, Neil replaced everything on the bunk, and then sat down on the edge to think. It was possible that Bateman had taken the book with him. If that was the case, then he was smarter than Neil had given him credit for. There were no other places that he could think of where Bateman could hide the book. Neil was beginning to think that he was destined to lose this round.

Leaning back, he stretched his hands out behind him, resting the palms on the mattress. When his right hand came to rest on something hard beneath the mattress cover, he spun around and smiled. Neil felt the rectangular shape with his fingers and could hardly believe his luck. Bateman had hidden the book inside the mattress cover.

He yanked the mattress from the bunk, unzipped the cover, and reached his arm between the vinyl cover and the foam cushion. Grasping the book, he was quick to pull it out and put the mattress back in its place. Within a minute of finding the book, he was sitting on the edge of his own bunk staring at the cracked leather cover. He felt as if he were holding a gold mine between his fingertips.

Neil wanted to open the book and pore over its pages. Violating Bateman's deepest secrets was a temptation almost too hard for him to resist. But Bateman could return at any minute. There was plenty of time to read it the next day, he figured.

Crossing to the far corner, he dropped to his knees, prying at the loose wall board near the floor. The small compartment had come in handy for hiding his dirty magazines. Now it would conceal his greatest treasure yet. He slipped the book into the darkened space and secured the wall board back in place. Dropping onto his bunk, Neil drifted off to sleep.

CHAPTER TWENTY-SIX

LUNCH WAS A somber affair; the conversation was subdued and sparse. The humor and fun had been drained from the weekend, leaving Neil to feel as if he was responsible for its collapse. His friends, although still congenial, were distant and serious. The jocularity of the first night had held so much promise for the remaining weekend. But forty-eight hours later, he was wishing that he'd never made the trip down from New York. Neil wouldn't be surprised if his friends felt the same way.

He remained near the cold ashes of the previous evening's campfire, watching Rob busy himself by the grill, preparing lunch. His other friends were seated around the picnic table, talking quietly amongst themselves. He wanted to join his friends, but an awkward uneasiness hung over him. It was an odd sensation, being so isolated while sitting mere feet from his friends. Accustomed to being the center of attention, it was a new experience for him, one that he found to be detestable. Leaning back in his chair, Neil seethed, more at himself than his friends. After all, they weren't hearing voices and seeing ghosts. It was all on him. He eyeballed Patrick for a moment, still wondering if there would have been any way that his friend could have been responsible for the previous night. Steve was adamant that Patrick hadn't left the cabin except to use the bathroom. Besides, Patrick didn't know that Sammy was in her father's cabin. How could he possibly plan for such an elaborate hoax on the fly?

Bringing a plate of Bison burgers to the picnic table, Rob announced that lunch was ready. Neil stopped at the cooler to grab a Corona, and then crossed to the table, taking a seat across from Jeremy.

Steve reached into the cooler. "Patrick, what do ya wanna drink?"

"Gimme a Dr. Pepper."

"Grab me a Coke," said Jeremy.

Steve passed the drinks around the table. "What're we doing this afternoon?"

"Wouldn't mind giving the zipline another go, but I'm not sure Brewster is up to it," said Patrick.

"Patrick," said Steve sharply.

"I was just joking for Christ's sake."

"What about the archery range?" said Jeremy. "We haven't done that yet."

Rob nodded. "Now that sounds like a plan."

Steve glanced at Neil. "You up for that?"

Returning Steve's gaze with a hard stare, Neil found a warm enough smile on his friend's face, but he couldn't shake the feeling that something seemed to be hiding behind the brown eyes. "Don't patronize me."

"The archery range it is then."

THE equipment shed, located behind the archery range, was secured with a rusted latch and an equally rusted Masterlock. Steve had explained that there wasn't a key and produced a claw hammer from the gray rucksack he'd brought with him from Sequoia Lodge. Taking the hammer from his friend, Neil delivered four hard blows before the hinged strap separated from the rotting door. The twisted metal was ripped from the wood, leaving splintered screw holes, and clattered to the ground. Yanking the door open, Neil peered into the darkened interior. Thick cobwebs stretched from floor to ceiling and wall to wall. Leaning against the wall to the right were a dozen canoe paddles, their blades vanishing into the darkness of an old wooden crate on the floor. A pile of faded orange life jackets rested on the floor behind the paddles. Neil smiled, recalling how uncomfortable and awkward the flotation devices were to wear with their bulky collar, single nylon strap, and foam-filled side chambers.

Rob pushed his way past Neil, stepping across the threshold. "Outta my way."

Crossing to the shed's back corner, Rob pulled open the doors of a tall metal cabinet, revealing six plastic longbows hanging from a row of hooks. Six nylon quivers filled with arrows stood inside the cabinet.

Lifting one of the longbows from its hook, Rob said, "These bring back memories." Wrapping his fingers around the nocking point, he drew back on the string, watching the upper and lower limb bend under the pressure. When the string was released, it twanged loudly. "I haven't shot one of these in years."

Neil reached for an arrow. The fletching had deteriorated with time, and there were gaps between the faux feathers. He fingered the bullet tip, trying to wipe away the faint layer of rust with little success. "These have seen better days."

"They'll do," said Jeremy. "I doubt any of us are good enough to notice."

SAMMY crept forward through the underbrush, positioning herself within view of Camp Tenskwatawa's archery range. Concealed among the brambles, she waited quietly for them to arrive. She knew it wouldn't be long.

After Neil had left her father's cabin, she'd returned to the kitchen. His note from the previous night rested on the kitchen table where she picked it up and carried it to the sink. She had read the note once more, her eyes hovering on the last three words. Love. What did that bastard know about love? She lit the bottom corner of the letter with a match from a nearby drawer. As the flames raced up the paper, she took joy in watching the words blacken and burn to ash.

The sound of Neil and his friends approaching the archery range drew Sammy back to the present. The silence between them was instantly apparent. Where she'd observed a tight camaraderie between them earlier, a distinct distance now existed. From her vantage point, she saw the six circular targets attached to a tall, moss-covered log wall. The white vinyl covering for a few of the targets was torn or missing, but a couple were still intact enough to see the outer blue ring and the red circle of the bull's-eye. Her father hadn't seen much reason to replace the covers after the camp had closed. "What's the point?" he had once asked her. At the near end of the range, each lane was marked by a waist-high log post rising from the ground.

"You're up first, Brewster," she heard Patrick say.

Neil stepped forward, resting the quiver of arrows

against a nearby post. "If I remember, I was a damn good shot back then. I doubt that I've lost my touch."

Steve laughed. "Arrogant as ever. Show us what you've got."

Sammy watched Neil pull an arrow from the quiver, placing the shaft on the arrow rest just above the handle. With the bowstring in the nock of the arrow, he drew back and sighted his target. When he released the bowstring, the arrow flipped up into the air above him. Neil yelped, dropped the longbow, and rubbed his forearm. She clamped her hand over her mouth, stifling her laugh.

"Dammit!" Neil shouted.

His friends burst into laughter, and their jibes about Neil's archery abilities echoed through the forest. Sammy studied his face, noticing his narrowed eyes and furrowed brow. He must be trying to accept their ridicule in good humor, but she knew he must be fuming inside.

Neil picked up the longbow and arrow. "I've got it this time."

"Everyone stand back," said Patrick. "Brewster's going to have another go!" They erupted in laughter. Neil didn't appear to be amused at all by their jesting. She wondered if any of them had noticed his rising irritation.

As Neil emptied the quiver of the nine remaining arrows, his next attempts managed to find the bull's-eye twice, the blue ring five times, and the outer white of the target twice, and only missed the target once.

Not too bad, Sammy thought. *I could've done better.*

"You've redeemed yourself," said Rob.

"Let's see if any of you can do better," Neil said.

Jeremy gestured toward the target. "Go grab your arrows, I'll give it a try."

Sammy watched Neil walk toward the target. His shoulders were held high. She figured he was feeling pretty good about himself at the moment. If only he knew . . .

As she watched him pull his arrows from the target, Sammy closed her eyes and listened to the forest around her. The voice drifted across the breeze, like an echo from the past. She couldn't stop the tears from forming in her eyes.

"Leave me alone, Neil!"

She was startled when the loud crack roared through the trees. Opening her eyes, she saw part of the log wall behind the targets erupt into splinters. Neil fell backward, his hands raised to protect his face from the flying shrapnel. The arrows he was holding scattered across the ground. Scrambling to his feet, his eyes were wide and his mouth gaping. She followed his gaze to the other end of the archery range. Rob, with his arm outstretched, was holding a long-barreled revolver. Jeremy and Steve, arms folded and smiling, stood next to Rob. Patrick was behind them, holding a small voice recorder in the air. Wiping a tear away from her cheek, Sammy closed her eyes again as the voice looped the same four words over and over.

"You like the voice?" Rob said. His question startled her, and she opened her eyes to make sure it hadn't been directed at her.

Patrick was glaring at Neil. "It's his, you know. Came off one of those old videos I shot. I never imagined that those old VHS tapes would come in handy someday."

Neil glanced back at the target behind him, and then at his friends. His face was red with fury. "What the hell are you doing? You could've killed me!"

"Perhaps that's the point," said Steve.

Neil's eyes narrowed. "What's that mean?"

"Time to make amends, Neil," said Jeremy.

Sammy drew in a deep breath. Jeremy's words cut

her deep. Making amends, isn't that what she'd always wanted? For Neil to make amends for what he'd done? To take responsibility and face the consequences of his actions? Her life had been driven for so long by the desire to see Neil suffer. She'd always hoped that she'd be the one to say those words to him, but, to her disappointment, it wasn't to be.

She watched Neil begin to move up the archery range toward his friends, but Rob twitched the revolver. "Stay right where you are."

Neil held out his hands, his narrowed eyes glaring back at his friends. From where she was hidden, Sammy could only see Patrick's face. The glint in his eyes held a dark, foreboding sense of evil, causing a chill to race down her spine. A malicious sneer crossed his lips.

Neil shrugged his shoulders. "Amends?"

"It's time you paid for what you did eighteen years ago," replied Rob.

There was confusion in Neil's face. She knew he wasn't lying when he said, "I don't have a damn clue what you're talking about."

"You've got blood on your hands, and we're here to make sure you pay for your crime," Steve said.

"Quit with the cryptic bullshit, and just tell me what this is all about!"

As Sammy watched, Patrick stepped forward, taking the revolver from Rob. He inched forward, keeping the firearm trained on Neil's chest. "The four of us have judged you to be responsible for the death of Chris Bateman." His slow strides seemed almost lackadaisical, but his lifted chin and the tightness around his eyes showed his contempt. "As such, we've taken it upon ourselves to ensure that you're held accountable for your actions."

Neil's mouth dropped open, then snapped shut, and his face turned ashen. When Sammy heard him finally reply, his voice was raspy, fluttering with fear. "You said he committed suicide! I wasn't even in camp when it happened! How am I responsible for that?"

Rob stepped up beside Patrick. "It was your actions the last few weeks that lead to his suicide—all the things you did to him, all the things you said. It all contributed to his death."

Steve, who had circled to Neil's left, added, "Especially what you did that last night. That announcement you made over the PA. It was the last straw. He was never the same those last few days between your departure and his death."

With his arms waving wildly, Neil said, "All this . . . this whole weekend was to get me back for Bateman's death? All that stuff that I heard and saw . . . it was all you?"

Jeremy, now standing to Neil's right, replied, "It's amazing what you can do with a fog machine, some speakers, and lots of strobe lights. Rob's a whiz with technology and special effects. He even hooked us up with that corpse." He laughed. "It wasn't real, in case you were wondering."

Sammy's leg began to cramp, but she didn't dare shift her position for fear that they would spot her. Gritting her teeth, she stifled a low moan of anguish and continued to observe the confrontation. She noticed a slight fidgeting in Neil's movements—erratic like a trapped animal. His eyes twitched rapidly, never seeming to stay on any of his friends long enough to focus for more than a moment. She realized that this was probably a new experience for him—being cornered like prey. For once, he wasn't the predator.

"This is bullshit! Every one of you was just as responsible! You were all involved!" Neil said.

"And we've each suffered because of it," said Steve.

"You can't blame me for his death," said Neil. "I wasn't even here."

"You didn't have to be, Brewster," said Jeremy, inching closer to Neil. "You'd done more than enough damage when you were here."

Steve said, "After you left, Chris refused to leave his cabin. Claimed he was ill. The owners told him to go home until he felt better. So that's where he went, locking himself away in his room for three days. He didn't speak to anyone, not even his stepfather. None of us saw him again until he was found hanging from a tree down by the lake."

"Patrick found him the following Tuesday morning," added Jeremy, his fingers clenched into white-knuckled fists. "They figured Chris must have returned to camp in the middle of the night. He'd been dead four or five hours. They called Charlie Wilcox, but he was too broken up to do anything. The camp staff were in no shape to go near the body. We were the oldest counselors in the camp, so they asked us to cut him down, and cover him up—the camp owners didn't want the campers to see it."

Rob folded his arms across his chest. "You were the lucky one. You missed out on having to see those eyes—blank and staring into nothing—and his face, his gray, dead face. I can't sleep at night without medication for fear of seeing it in my nightmares."

"And you didn't have to touch his cold skin. You were lucky," said Patrick, holding the revolver with a steady grip. "I'd close my eyes and see him hanging from that tree. Five years of therapy and a dozen broken relationships. That's what I've endured because of his death, because of what you did."

"Alcoholism and two failed marriages for me," Jeremy said. "I'd wake up screaming at night. Still do. Neither of my wives could take it anymore."

"We've all been haunted by his death," said Steve, moving closer to Neil. "I can't see my two boys without supervision because of anger issues that stem from that night. Ten years of therapy, and I still hear his voice on quiet nights, calling from somewhere in the back of my mind. We've all paid the price for what we've done. All except you."

"You walked out of this camp and went off to follow your dreams while the rest of us picked up the pieces you left behind," Rob said. "While you were becoming a big-shot city lawyer, our lives were crumbling around us. Each grappling with our overwhelming guilt over Chris's death while you stood in your high tower acting like a god."

"You've never carried your share of the guilt," Steve said. "We've paid for our sins. Now it's your turn."

The movement was so quick that Sammy barely saw it happen. Jeremy and Steve lunged forward, grasping Neil's arms, yanking them behind his back. Neil struggled against their grip but couldn't pull himself free. Rob, stepping forward, drove his fist into Neil's stomach. She turned her head away as Neil's legs buckled beneath him. She heard the additional thuds and moans but refused to watch. As much as she wanted Neil to suffer, she couldn't bring herself to turn her eyes back in the direction of the archery range. She flinched at the sound of every punch, hearing the agony behind every bellow that Neil made. She never wanted this, never wanted senseless violence. This wasn't the suffering she had in mind.

When the sounds died down, she turned back toward

the archery range. Neil was laying on the ground, a motionless huddled mass. His four friends stood over him, looking as if they were deliberating over what they should do next. Sammy decided that she couldn't watch any more. She had her own plan to execute. Trying to cautiously slip from the brambles, Sammy glanced once more back toward the archery range. While the others were still glaring down at Neil, Steve was gazing through the forest at her. Their eyes met for a moment, leaving no doubt that he'd seen her. He gave an almost imperceptible nod of his head in her direction, and then shifted his gaze back down onto Neil. She cursed under her breath. Her intention had been to slip away unnoticed. Sammy watched for a moment more, and then pushed her way through the forest toward her father's cabin. There were still a few preparations to be made, and she didn't have much time.

CHAPTER TWENTY-SEVEN

Rob's blows left Neil doubled over in the sand of the archery range, his ribs bruised and his abdomen on fire. He'd never taken a beating like that before. He remained motionless while they stood around him, talking amongst themselves.

"Not feeling well, Brewster?" said Jeremy.

"Poor Neil," said Steve. "Bet you never expected your sins to catch up with you."

"Pick him up. I want a go at him," said Patrick.

A firm grip clamped onto each of Neil's arms, lifting him to his feet. His legs felt weak, refusing to bear any weight without some form of protest. He opened his eyes to find Steve and Jeremy on either side, holding him tightly between them. With what strength he could muster, Neil shrugged his arms, trying to wrangle out of their grasp. With a swift movement, he raked his heel down Steve's shin. A quick twist to his right enabled him to break free from Steve's grasp. He threw a wild punch at Jeremy's jaw. His fist missed its target and left him off balance. Jeremy's grip tightened on his arm until Neil was forced to grimace with pain. Within moments, Steve had regained his hold on Neil. It had been a lame attempt to escape, but he knew he had to at least try. Now, another opportunity would need to be sought.

Jeremy and Steve dragged him back against the archery range's rear berm, pressing his back into the hard surface with ferocity. The uneven wood surface dug into his spine, seeming to hit every pressure point for maximum discomfort. Thoughts raced through his mind, wondering what they had planned for him. How would one make amends for driving someone to suicide? Was it to be a beating, each of them taking their punches? Or was it to be something worse?

Patrick stepped forward, leaned in close, and came within inches of Neil's face. "Are you ready, Neil?"

The punches were ferocious, with a fiery anger fueling each blow. Hard knuckles plunged into his chest and stomach, pushing him toward a crescendo of pain before becoming numb to it all. Unable to do anything else, he allowed his body to go limp, dangling from the grasp of Jeremy and Steve. Each blow became nothing more than a punctuation on a sentence of pain.

Neil dropped to the ground when released, huddled once again in the sand. Coughing, he spat blood from his mouth and wheezed as he tried to take a deep breath. He heard his friends speaking, but their voices seemed faint and incomprehensible. His face fell forward into the sand, tiny particles of grit grinding into his cheek. Five minutes. He just needed five minutes to gather his strength. He could take another round if he had just five minutes. Then, everything went black.

When he opened his eyes, Neil thought he was alone.

No voices. No noise. As his eyes tried to focus, he rolled onto his back, a move which sent waves of pain up his left ribs. He screwed his eyes closed, biting his lip until the pain subsided to a blunt throbbing.

"Don't worry. It'll all be over soon."

Looking up, Neil had found Rob standing nearby, the revolver hanging limply from his hand. No one else seemed to be around. Maybe this was his chance. He'd have to disarm Rob and make an escape before the others returned, but it'd be far from easy. He was in no condition to wrestle Rob to the ground in a fight over the gun. Probably never even get close enough to make a grab for it. There wasn't much hope. He'd need a small miracle.

"They've gone for some rope," explained Rob.

"Why? To string me up?"

Rob laughed. "We've got plans for you."

Neil tried to sit up, but a momentary wave of nausea sent him falling back into the sand. Turning his head from right to left, he surveyed the area as best he could. His glance paused only for a second—just long enough to observe the feathers on the end of a buried arrow shaft. It must've been buried after he'd dropped it earlier. He returned his gaze to Rob.

"Why don't you just put a bullet through my head and get it done and over with?" said Neil. He added a slur to his words. "I'm tired of the games."

Rob took a step forward. "That's what Patrick wants to do. A bullet through the temple, and a deep grave in the forest."

"What's stopping him?"

"The rest of us want to see you suffer. A bullet is too easy."

"Well, you've got me. I've got no more . . ." He allowed his words to fade. Neil outstretched his arms, allowing them to fall lazily onto the sand. He groaned, breathed deep, and rolled his head back and forth on a limp neck. *Got to draw Rob closer,* he thought. *Can I make this look convincing?* His eyes closed, and he muttered a short string of unintelligible words.

"What was that?" said Rob.

Got to get him closer. "I'm not feeling . . . I'm . . ."

Rob stepped closer. "Neil. You still there?"

Keeping his eyes closed, Neil mumbled once more, his voice soft and faint. His fingers burrowed into the sand. He opened his eyes just enough to see through his eye lashes, just enough to catch the blurred image of Rob leaning closer, the revolver held firm in his hand. Just a little more. Letting out a long breath, he allowed his head to fall to one side. Through fluttering eyelids, he saw Rob lean in closer. Neil had no idea when the others would return. It was now or never.

His right hand jerked toward Rob's face, flinging a fistful of sand upward. His other hand reached for his only hope. His fingers found the half-buried arrow shaft, encircling it in an iron grip. He saw Rob's hands clawing at his eyes, desperate to wipe away the grit which had momentarily blinded him. With all the strength he could garner, Neil drove the arrow into Rob's thigh.

The sound of the arrow entering Rob's flesh was dull, seeming almost anti-climactic. For the briefest of moments, Neil thought he might have missed. Then, he heard Rob's roar of pain and felt a warmth trickle down over his fingers. Rob's leg buckled, and he fell to the ground. Wasting no time, Neil scrambled to his feet, letting out a yelp of his own as pain raked down his ribs. A flash of silver made him glance back behind him. Rob grasped the arrow shaft with one hand, while the other waved the revolver, unsteadily trying to take aim at Neil.

Scrambling out of the archery range, he ducked his shoulders at the crack of the gunshot. A tree branch to his right shattered, sending a deluge of splinters and bark raining down on him as he ran off.

GRIPPING his aching ribs, Neil stumbled across the sandy parking lot and threw furtive glances to his right and left. Deep breaths caused sharp pains in his chest. Maybe a cracked rib. His vision was blurred by the sweat that trickled down into his eyes. Running and hiding in the forest had left his arms and legs torn and bloody. Angry brambles and thickets had thrashed at his skin and clothing, tearing them both to shreds.

His feet were unsteady as he made his way across the clearing toward the cars parked at the opposite side. Neil fumbled in his pocket, pulling out his keys with a trembling hand. The furtive glances over his shoulder were no more reassuring than the flash of the Mercedes's brake lights when he pushed the button of the key fob to unlock the car. But when his hand touched the car door handle, he felt a mild sense of relief, knowing that escape was within his grasp. Pulling the door open, his eyes ran along the side of the car, more an unconscious action than a movement with intent and purpose. His hand fell away from the handle as he felt escape slip from his grasp. The rear tire had been flattened, a long gaping gash evident on the sidewall. His gaze moved forward, finding the same result on the front tire.

Undeterred, Neil dropped into the driver's seat. Flat tires or not, he was getting out of here. He could always replace the tires and rims. He only needed to drive ten or fifteen miles up the road. Just to the nearest phone. As he slid the key in the ignition, he smiled. But the smile faded quickly when the engine failed to start.

Resting his hands on the car roof, his head bowed forward, heavy with a sense of defeat. He'd fought so hard to get free, only to find his escape cut off. It felt less like a setback and more like utter failure. The aching in his ribs served as a reminder of what he'd just escaped from, and what Neil would face if he didn't get away.

Leaning his head on the car, he wondered if he could walk out of camp. Perhaps he could make it to the nearest house and call for help. A deep breath and a sharp pain in his ribs told him he'd be hard pressed to outdistance his pursuers. And who knew how far the nearest house was? Or even in what direction? He could wander for hours on the back roads and never come any closer to civilization than he was at that very moment. He slammed his fist down on the roof of the Mercedes.

Opening the car door, he reached into the compartment beneath the armrest, grabbing his mobile phone. A quick glance at the screen told him all he needed to know. No signal. Jeremy had said that there was no signal out here, but Neil had hoped that he'd been exaggerating. No such luck. He decided to try anyway, dialing 9-1-1. Seconds later, he threw the phone back into the car and slammed the door closed. "Damn it!"

Leaning back against the Mercedes, Neil felt helpless, a feeling that frightened him. He grasped his hands together, hoping to stop them from trembling, but to no avail. Closing his eyes, he tried to slow his breathing, to calm his already overwrought mind. His racing thoughts had sent him into a mental paralysis. Indecision would be the death of him. If he wanted to get out of this alive, he'd have to start thinking straight.

Neil jerked his head around as a voice echoed from the forest. It was Patrick. It was difficult to tell from which direction the voice came. He peered around the clearing, scanning for any sign of movement, but saw none. It wouldn't be long before they made their way into the clearing. Glancing down the line of vehicles, he knew it would be a long shot, but it was one he had to investigate. He tried the Ford F150 first—locked. He ran to the Lexus only to be disappointed again. Another shout from the forest pressed him on with a new sense of urgency. They were getting closer.

After finding the other two cars locked, Neil returned to the Mercedes, kneeling between it and the truck. He knew that to remain by the cars would be a bad idea. They'd come looking soon enough. But running aimlessly through the forest wasn't an option either. Concealment was what he needed now. Concealment until he came up with a better strategy.

He heard Steve's voice echo somewhere in the nearby forest. "Let's try over by the cars!"

It was now or never. Neil needed to think fast. He needed to hide. Rising to his feet, he glanced into the Ford's truck bed, finding it empty except for a canvas tarp balled up near the truck cab. With no other option immediately to hand, he clambered over the side into the truck bed, balling himself up as tight as he could, pulling the tarp on top of him. The canvas was damp and smelled of gasoline. The thick odor attacked his nostrils, making him nauseous.

Remaining as still as possible, he listened for any sound. Less than a minute later, Neil heard someone pushing through the nearby underbrush. He drew in a breath and held it, afraid that his own breathing might give him away. The footfalls in the sand were soft, and he strained to hear them. Someone was walking between the truck and the Mercedes. The footsteps paced back and forth for a moment, paused, and then all went silent. He wanted to peek out from under the tarp to see what was happening, but he didn't dare move. At any moment, he expected the tarp to be ripped from over him, leaving him at the mercy of his pursuers.

The silence stretched from a moment to eternity, and Neil fought to keep himself from making any sound or movement. But he couldn't stop his body from trembling. He was certain someone was still standing beside the truck. He hadn't heard them walk away. All he could do was remain where he was and be still, very still.

Neil didn't know how long he lay there. His left arm was pinned beneath his body, making it impossible to check his watch. It must have been five minutes, maybe ten, by his estimation. He began to wonder if he may have been wrong. Should he try to peek out from under the tarp? The slightest move would give away his hiding place to anyone standing nearby. But if no one was there, he was wasting valuable time underneath this tarp that could be used to put as much distance between himself and his pursuers.

With his eyes closed, Neil focused all his concentration on listening for the faintest sound, the smallest hint of someone standing nearby. The silence was thick and heavy, so much so that he thought he heard his own heartbeat roaring from out of his chest. In a moment of fancy, he panicked, thinking that anyone standing even ten feet from the truck could hear the rhythmic pounding, but the moment faded almost as soon as it started.

The sound of distant footsteps in the sand reached his ears, and, as they drew closer, Neil heard a shuffle in the sand beside the truck, almost to his immediate right. He caught a thud as something brushed the side of the truck, rocking it slightly. As the footsteps approached, he heard someone shout, "You see him?" It was Steve.

"Nah! But he's been here," came the reply. It was Patrick's voice.

"He was bound to come by here," Steve said. "The fastest way out of here is his car. Neil won't wander around the forest too long."

There was movement near the side of the truck. It swayed as someone leaned against its side.

"Look at this piece of shit. Ostentatious as always," Patrick said. "He probably keeps this thing locked up in a private garage. Do you know how much that would cost in New York?"

Steve's only reply was an affirmative grunt. Neil answered Patrick's question in his mind. *Six hundred a month.*

"Never liked Mercs," said Steve.

"Me neither," replied Patrick.

Neil heard a sharp click, and then a thunderous crack ripped through the forest, causing him to shudder involuntarily. The gunshot was followed by the tinkle of shattered glass. He fought to keep from trembling as the dull ringing in his ears quickly faded to be replaced by the laughter of his two pursuers.

"That'll teach the bastard," said Patrick.

Steve asked, "Whatcha do that for?"

"Something to do while we wait for the others. Come on. Let's sit down."

He heard them move toward the back of the truck. When he heard the truck tailgate drop open, Neil froze, not daring to even breathe. When the truck rocked, he figured they must have both sat down on the edge of the tailgate. Only a few feet away, he knew that even the slightest movement would give him away. He felt exposed, vulnerable, and most of all, terrified. He knew enough about ballistics to understand that one shot from a .357 Magnum could rip him to pieces. What if they knew he was there? What if this was all just a game to throw him off his guard? What if Patrick was taking aim right now? Imagining a bullet ripping through the flimsy tarp caused him to shudder.

"I still think we should kill him," said Patrick abruptly.

"No. No. We're sticking to plan. You know what we must do. We all agreed."

"It just seems like we're letting him off easy."

"Trust me, it'll be better this way—far more humiliating," said Steve.

Hearing Steve's words left Neil to wonder what had caused his childhood best friend to turn on him. Steve and his other friends had been just as eager to abuse Bateman as he had been back then. They'd always acted as one entity. "All for one and one for all," had been their motto. They'd all taken their shots at Bateman, often all at once. The hypocrisy would be laughable if he hadn't been so frightened for his own life.

He heard Steve say, "Look! Over there! Is that him?"

"Nah, looks like Jeremy," came Patrick's reply.

"Looks like Rob's with him."

Closing his eyes, Neil realized that things couldn't get any worse. He was trapped. All four of them would be within feet of him. He wondered if throwing himself at their mercy would help. Perhaps if he begged for forgiveness. Maybe they'd let him go. The thought of begging repulsed him, but what else could he do?

He heard footsteps approach, slow steady strides in the sand. "Damn, you've got a bad limp. How's the leg?" he heard Patrick ask.

"It'll heal," Rob said.

"You sure?" asked Steve. "That bandage is soaked in

blood."

Rob said, "I'm fine. We've got to find him. I've got a score to settle. Any luck?"

The response must have been non-verbal because Rob added, "Which way do you think he'll go?"

"Probably out to the main road," Steve said. "He's got nowhere else to run."

"It's miles from the nearest town. He'd be walking for hours," said Patrick.

"Neil's got no other options," Steve said. "He can't drive out of here. That cell phone blocker we installed is working, so he can't call for help. He'd be an idiot to remain in camp. Where else can he go?"

"He'll tackle the road back toward Tabernacle," said Jeremy.

"Makes sense," said Rob.

"I don't know. What if he's still out in the forest?" said Patrick. "We could waste a lot of time searching for him on the road, and, for all we know, he could be laying low right here in camp."

Rob replied, "He's got a point. There's plenty of places to hide around here. He's got to be hurting. It's a long hike. He might not think he can make it."

Neil only half-listened as they debated the best way to track him down. Everything they said was right. He had very few options available to him. His ribs still ached from the beating they'd given him. The pain alone would slow him down. Worse yet, he had no idea which way to go. It'd been eighteen years since he'd been in this area. He couldn't remember much beyond the camp.

His hands trembled as a wave of hopelessness swept over him. What would they do if they caught him? Another beating? Or worse? Was this where he was going to die? Far in the forest where no one knew who Neil

Brewster was? No grand epithets. No long funeral procession. Just a shallow hole in the sandy ground.

The truck suddenly rocked, snapping his attention back to the conversation going on just a few feet away. Steve and Patrick had been sitting on the tailgate. Neil figured that one of them must have stood up.

Steve said, "Rob, you and Patrick continue to search the camp. Jeremy and I will walk out toward Tabernacle. If he's out along the road, we should catch him. But in case he's still hiding in the camp, you can work on flushing him out."

The truck shook once more. Patrick said, "He won't last long out here. The city's made that bastard soft."

"Let's meet back here in two hours," said Steve.

Their footsteps faded into the distance. The silence that followed their departure seemed unreal, almost too silent. Neil wondered if they had known that he was there the entire time. Maybe this was all just a game to lull him into a false sense of security, to make him give away his hiding place. What if they were standing around the truck right now, waiting for him to emerge from under the tarp? He decided to wait. If nothing else, he needed a moment to rest, to think.

Maintaining a vigilant ear for any sound, Neil's thoughts turned inward for a moment. He knew there was no denying that he was exactly what he'd been accused of—a cold-hearted bastard. In fact, he'd be the first to admit it. His contemptuous attitude toward his fellow human beings had been his *modus operandi* for most of his life. Almost as if it were ingrained in his DNA. But did that make him responsible for Chris Bateman's death?

Considering things from a legal point of view was what he knew best. Neil scoured his memory for some legal precedent that may have been set by other cases.

There was little chance that he'd ever be held criminally responsible for Bateman's death. But what about a civil case? Wasn't there a Maryland appeals court case in 1991 that held a county school liable for not preventing a girl's suicide? He recalled reading of a 2015 case in Connecticut as well. But those were both focused on the defendant's inaction to stop the suicide. He was being accused of directly contributing to Bateman's death through his own actions.

How would he have approached the case? Neil knew that the difficulty for any attorney would be proving that the suicide was directly caused by his actions. Just because he treated Chris Bateman harshly wasn't proof enough that Neil was the cause of the boy's suicide. Any judge or jury would see that, wouldn't they? The prosecution would have to prove the direct relationship between his actions and Chris Bateman's death. Even as brilliant as he was, Neil would've avoided taking on a case like this. It would be near to impossible to win.

He continued to wait—it felt like it must have been an hour or more but he could be mistaken—until he finally convinced himself that they were really gone. There had been no noise, no footsteps, no voices, nothing. What did he have to lose?

Gently, Neil pulled the tarp back, just enough to peer down the length of the truck bed. The tailgate was still down, but no one was in sight. He paused to listen for any sign that someone was nearby, but he heard nothing. Sliding the tarp off, he sat up, cautious and slow. Peeking over the side of the truck, he saw the shadows of evening begin to fall over the clearing. It wouldn't be long before the forest was covered in darkness. He had no flash-light, matches, or anything with which to light his way. Wandering through the black forest was the last thing that he wanted to do.

Neil figured that he had about an hour, maybe an hour and a half, before they returned. He needed to move fast. The sooner he got away the better. He thought about the cars again. His car was disabled, but maybe if he broke a window . . . He shook the idea away. He didn't know enough about cars to try and hotwire one of the other vehicles. Whatever he did, it had to be on foot. All he needed was a safe place with a phone. Just contact the police and hide until they arrive. There was only one place where he could go.

Neil climbed out of the truck and crept quickly across the sandy parking lot. He threw furtive glances in all directions, watching for any movement, listening for any sound. His legs felt weak and unstable, his breathing labored and painful. If they found him, he wasn't sure how long he could continue to run. He knew he was fighting a losing battle.

As he reached the edge of the clearing, Neil heard a branch snap somewhere to his left. He froze, afraid to move. There was a rustle of branches nearby, and an arrow buried itself into the sand inches from his feet. Without a second thought, he charged into the forest.

A shout echoed through the forest behind. "Run, Brewster! Run!"

The sinister laugh that punctuated the shout impelled Neil to run faster.

SUMMER, 1997

THE LIGHT FROM the full moon was blocked by the tree tops, shrouding the camp in darkness as Neil crept along the back of the cabins, remaining in the shadows as he went. He picked his way cautiously through the underbrush, trying to remain as quiet as possible. A small penlight was shoved in his back pocket, but Neil didn't dare turn it on until he reached his destination. Pausing behind Sequoia Lodge, he glanced at his watch. Twenty-five past one. If they were on time, his friends would be arriving any moment. Crouching down beside the cabin wall, he waited, listening to the incessant chirping of crickets in the dark.

Neil had packed his bag earlier that evening, shortly after the kids had been handed back to the care of their parents. In the morning, his father would be arriving to pick him up, ending his final summer at Camp Tenskwatawa. He'd be skipping out on his duties as a camp counselor two weeks early, but there hadn't been any objections from camp management. With three weeks left before he would be heading off to Harvard, Neil's parents surprised him with a two-week whirlwind tour of Europe, the best part being that they weren't going. They'd planned a full itinerary, which Neil had no intention of following, and were filling his pockets with plenty of cash for the trip.

With this being his last night in camp, Neil decided to go out in style. One more opportunity to lambaste Stinky Bateman was a temptation he couldn't pass up. He saw it as his final curtain call, and he wanted it to be a good one. The discovery of Bateman's diary earlier in the week provided Neil with everything he needed to make his last hurrah one that no one would soon forget.

A rustling in the underbrush behind him announced the arrival of Jeremy, followed moments later by Steve and Rob. Pressing his back to the rough wood of the cabin wall, Jeremy remained standing, looking down at Neil.

"Where's Patrick?" Neil asked.

"Said he had something to else to do," said Rob.

"You wanna let us in on why you got us out here in the middle of the night?" Jeremy whispered.

Placing his finger to his lips, Neil gestured for them to follow him. After peeking around the corner of the cabin to ensure that no one was around, he made his way down the sandy path leading to the large clearing that served as a parking lot. Bright floodlights, poised high upon posts erected around the clearing, shone with intensity over the sand but cast the forest into deep shadows. Skirting along the edge of the clearing, he kept to the shadows, leading his friends toward the recreation hall on the opposite side.

All the lights were out in the hall, and only a single floodlight over the main entrance provided any illumination to the area. Neil and his friends worked their way to the back wall, stopping below a high dark window.

"Here's the plan," he whispered to his companions. "Boost me up to that window. I'll pry it open, and you help me climb in."

"That's the camp office." Steve said.

Neil nodded. "Stinky Bateman's getting a little farewell gift from me."

Jeremy snickered. "What're you gonna do to the little shit this time?"

Neil smiled, but he didn't know if they saw it in the dark. "I'm gonna let the whole camp in on a little secret."

It didn't take much to pry the window open, and Neil was inside the camp office in no time. He leaned out the window and said, "Okay, I'm good."

"Whatcha gonna do?" asked Rob.

He laughed. "I've got the announcement to end all announcements. Get back to your cabins, I've got it from here."

He watched them scurry off into the darkness, remaining near the window for a few moments. The cool evening breeze wafted into the dim office, rustling papers that must have been laying loose on the desk. Pulling the thin penlight from his pocket, Neil shone the beam around the room, picking out the lay of the land before making his move. An old utilitarian type desk sat before him, stacks of paper in neat piles occupied three wire baskets. A Macintosh computer stood in the center of the desk—its pale beige body and dark monochrome screen standing erect, as if guarding the office from intruders. The curled cable extended from the back around to the keyboard sitting before the monolithic box.

To his right, three file cabinets lined the wall. Camp records, probably about every kid that had ever stayed at the camp. He was tempted to search for Bateman's file, but it'd take too much time. Besides, he was there for another purpose. That purpose he found on the opposite wall.

The owners of the camp had planned for almost every situation, including the need to broadcast announcements throughout the entire camp. Hanging from a light post near every cluster of cabins was a cone-shaped loudspeaker. The amplifier and microphone sat across from Neil on a table against the opposite wall. Making his way to it, he shone the penlight across the McGhohan amplifier. It was old, looking like something from the seventies. The gray metallic case was dented and scratched, and the large dials, four for microphones and one each for treble and bass, were marked with faded numbers from zero to ten. A silver toggle switch labeled "Power" was to the left of the dials and sat beside a small round light.

Flipping the switch, Neil heard the hum of the amp as it powered on. The red light glowed brightly, bathing the room in shades of crimson. The old gray Shure microphone sat on the table beside the amplifier, its round screened head rested atop the long neck and square base. He'd already worked out what he was planning to say and stood gazing down at the microphone.

Neil felt a tingle, not unlike what he often felt before pulling a prank on someone. It was a kind of rush, a physical manifestation of pleasure to which he'd become addicted. The euphoric sense of excitement could be overwhelming, and he closed his eyes for a moment, drawing a long deep breath. "This is going to be good."

Pressing down the button on the base of the microphone, he said, "Attention Camp Tenskwatawa counselors, I'd like to let you all in on a little secret about our very own Chris Bateman."

CHAPTER TWENTY-EIGHT

NEIL WAS BREATHLESS when he reached the caretaker's cabin. He stumbled onto the porch and pounded on the door with his fist. He'd been running for more than an hour, darting down narrow trails, or sometimes crashing blindly through the underbrush with no thought for where he was headed. A quick glance over his shoulder reassured him that they hadn't followed, at least that's what he was hoping. He saw no one. He pounded again on the door, praying that Sammy would answer. The Ford Focus was still parked beside the cabin, so he figured she must be around somewhere. A quick jerk on the door knob told him the door was locked. Leaning his shoulder against the door jamb, he rapped on the wood door until his knuckles hurt.

It seemed liked hours before he heard Sammy yell from within the cabin, "I'm coming! I'm coming!"

She yanked the door open, her narrowed eyes and deep frown revealed her irritation. Her eyes opened and the frown vanished, to be replaced with a smile.

"Neil." She glanced down at his mud-covered shirt, torn shorts, and bloodied arms and legs. "What happened to you?"

He pushed past her into the cabin and shoved the door closed behind him. Leaning back against the wall, he took a long, deep breath. He was safe, at least for the moment. He still had to figure out how to get the hell out of there. But at least he had reached some sanctuary. He could rest while thinking through his strategy.

Sammy took hold of his hand, led him to the sofa, and sat down next to him. Resting her hand on his knee, she said, "Tell me. What's going on?"

Neil rubbed his temples with his fingers and closed his eyes for a few moments. When he opened them again, she was staring at him, eyes overflowing with concern. She rubbed his knee with a loving touch and leaned forward to kiss him. As their lips parted, he took another deep breath and fell back into the cushions of the sofa.

"They're trying to kill me," he said.

Her eyes opened wide. "Who?"

"Spent the past couple hours—maybe longer—running from them through the forest," he said. "They've been chasing me. With bows and arrows, and a gun . . . Patrick has a gun."

"A gun!"

He balled his trembling hands together, nodding his reply.

"Let me get you something to drink."

She rose from the sofa and crossed to the kitchen. Neil heard the familiar sound of the whiskey bottle opening and a tumbler being filled. He felt safe. They might still be out there somewhere, but he was in here with her. As long as he was with her, he would be safe.

When Sammy returned, she handed him the glass. Neil gulped it down in one swallow. His hands still trembled, making the ice bang against the side of the glass. The adrenaline that fueled his flight had burned off long ago. He felt the moisture welling up in his eyes. Sammy took the empty glass from him and set it on the coffee table.

Sammy said, "Why are they chasing you? I thought you were friends!"

Neil looked away from her, ashamed of the tear that had worked its way out of his eye. "Bateman . . ." He paused to wipe the tear off his cheek. "It's about Chris Bateman."

Her face was blank, no sign of comprehension. She shook her head. "I don't understand. What've you got to do with—"

Neil turned abruptly toward her, cutting her off in mid-sentence. "They're holding me responsible for his death."

She touched his cheek, wiping away another tear that surfaced. "Why? You weren't even here when he killed himself."

Neil rose from the sofa and moved toward the window. Glancing out, he scanned the area in front of the house, seeing nothing out of the ordinary. The sun was setting, but there was still enough light for him to see clearly around the immediate area. When he turned back around, Sammy was gazing up at him, her hazel eyes bright as ever, seeming to watch his every move with tenderness and concern.

Neil paced back and forth in front of the sofa. "For three years . . . I was his worst nightmare. I teased him. Mocked him. Played the cruelest pranks on him that I could think of. Hell, I'm the one who gave him his goddamn nickname! There wasn't a week where I didn't embarrass him in front of the camp—kids and counselors alike." He felt another tear roll down his cheek, but this time Neil just let it fall. "They think I drove him to kill himself."

Sammy shook her head in disbelief. "How can they think that? It's not like you put the noose around his neck."

"That what I said! I told them that, but they wouldn't listen! They . . . they said it was time to make amends. A life for a life."

Neil wanted to break down. He wanted to fall to his knees and cry like a baby until he could cry no more. "Look at me," he said, holding out his trembling hands. "Top of my class at Harvard. The greatest defense attorney New York City has ever seen. I'm months away from a goddamn senior partnership." He paused to wipe his eyes with the heels of his palms. "I'm scared. Frightened. Exhausted. What've I done, Sammy? What've I done?"

"Neil, calm down. We'll figure this out."

He continued to pace back and forth, flailing his arms frantically. "Do you know what I did to him? On my last night in camp? Do you know?" He laughed. The kind of nervous, babbling laugh that one makes just before they snap. "I thought it'd be funny. You see, I'd found his diary. I knew his secrets. I told the whole camp. Breaking into the camp office was a cinch—the back window had never latched right. It was easy enough to disguise my voice. Then I announced over the camp PA that he was gay. I can't remember exactly what I said, but it certainly wasn't that polite."

Halting in front of the sofa, Neil screwed his eyes closed, fighting to hold back tears. He wasn't sure if it was the exhaustion or the fear that was driving his emotions to the breaking point.

Sammy said, "I remember that night. The camp owners were really upset about it. You know, I don't think they ever figured out who did it. I had my suspicions, but you were gone the next day. I never had the chance to ask."

"It was all just a game to me." As the tears began to flow freely down his cheeks, Neil returned to his place on the sofa. "Just a little bit of fun. I didn't know . . . I didn't realize how much he was suffering. It wasn't supposed to be like this."

Sammy placed her arm around his shoulder, pulling Neil closer. Her gentle touch was soothing. As she ran her hand through his hair, his head fell onto her shoulder. Unable to control his sobs any longer, he cried, the tears soaking into the cotton of her pale blue t-shirt. With her arms encircling him, she rocked gently, holding him tight.

"Neil," she said suddenly. "Did you read his whole diary?"

The diary. That damn diary. If he hadn't found it, maybe this could have all been avoided. "No, just the last few entries." His sobs were beginning to subside. Being close to Sammy had a way of relieving his fears, comforting his tortured soul. "He had a crush on one of the other boy counselors. He never said who it was. But in the last entry, he said they'd kissed the night before."

"Why'd you do it?"

He sighed, trying to think back through the years. "I don't know. Maybe I thought I was better than him." As the tears dried up, Neil lifted his head, looking into her eyes. "I thought it'd be funny."

There was sadness in the hazel eyes that stared back at him. She looked almost heartbroken. Neil held her gaze for a moment before she turned her eyes away. He looked down, glancing at her smooth thighs clad in beige shorts. He couldn't shake the thought that he'd seen those shorts before. Perhaps when he'd been here earlier in the day? His eyes drifted back up to her face, but he struggled to focus. His body ached, his mind was clouded. Sleep. He just needed sleep. He'd see things differently after a good sleep.

Neil wasn't sure how long they'd remained on the sofa, but he remembered hearing her speak through the increasing fog that filled his mind. "Come on, let's go upstairs and get you cleaned up."

Feeling dazed, he rose from the sofa, his legs feeling a little unsteady. It must be the exhaustion finally catching up with him. He gazed down at the sofa, but it seemed so far away. If he could lay down for just a few minutes. Sammy leaned in close to kiss him. It felt different somehow, lacking the passion from the previous night. He felt her pull him toward the stairs.

Every step seemed to become a challenge. His feet felt heavy, and Neil half-walked, half-shuffled across the floor. Sammy began to climb the stairs, leading him up each step with soft encouragement. He kept his head down, keeping a close eye on his feet. He felt as if he could no longer trust himself to walk without sharp scrutiny of each step. Catching sight of Sammy's feet, he smiled when he saw the blue star within a circle on the back of her Converse high-top sneakers. Someone he knew had a pair just like that, but he couldn't put his finger on the name.

When they reached the top of the stairs, Neil felt utterly exhausted. The sleepless night. The chase through the forest. It all must have taken its toll on him. If Sammy hadn't been there, he'd probably have collapsed right there on the landing. But her compassionate urging kept him moving forward. The bedroom had a bed. He could lay down in there. His feet dragged along the hardwood floor as he followed her across the threshold.

The bedroom somehow looked different. It had changed. And the figures in the corners. He couldn't quite make them out. Sammy turned to face him, her mouth speaking but no sound seemed to be coming out. The door swung closed behind him, the hinges screamed for lubrication. Then another familiar sound. No, not a sound. A voice.

"Hey, Brewster. Now you're truly fucked!"

Neil turned, catching sight of Jeremy's fist as it raced toward his chin. He barely felt the pain of the impact. His head snapped back and everything went dark.

CHAPTER TWENTY-NINE

THE FIRST THING Neil remembered was the shooting pain somewhere behind his eyes. It was a dull ache, until he tried to open his eyes. Then it became a sharp burning along the back of his head, just below the scalp. As his eyelids parted, he was startled to find Jeremy's face inches from his own. The icy-blue eyes peered at him with a keen, hard stare.

"He's waking up," said Jeremy.

Neil said, "Do you mind getting out of my face?"

Jeremy laughed and then stepped back. Head still sore and spinning, Neil glanced around, trying to pull together some semblance of where he was and what was happening. He was slouched in a hardback chair. Possibly one from the kitchen. His hands were bound behind his back. The cord was rough on his wrists, reminding him of the old rope from the dock by the lake. Neil gave his hands a quick twist but found that it did nothing more than cause him pain. The room wasn't one he recognized. The walls were pine paneling, like that in Sammy's bedroom. The knotty pine floor was the same as well. It wasn't a stretch for him to assume that he was still in the caretaker's cabin. But the rest of the room was unfamiliar.

A twin bed stood along the wall to his right, the navy-blue comforter smooth and neat. Movie posters from *Men in Black* and *Star Trek: First Contact* were tacked to the wall above the head of the bed, the silver thumb tacks caught his eye as they shone in the light of the overhead ceiling fan. Sammy, with her back turned to him, was staring out of the room's only window into the bright sunshine.

"How long have I been out?" Neil asked.

"About thirteen hours." Steve's voice came from somewhere behind Neil. "It's about six-thirty."

Thirteen hours. Neil felt a rush of panic rise within him. Those thirteen hours were a blank. What'd happened? What'd they been doing with him for thirteen hours? He tried to remain calm, but the darting of his eyes was involuntary. He shifted his still sore jaw and said, "Didn't think Jeremy's punches packed that much wallop."

Without turning away from the window, Sammy said, "I spiked your whiskey."

Neil felt a jolt as someone smacked the back of the chair. "It's good stuff," Patrick said. "The same stuff we used on you the first night."

Neil tried to turn his body to glance at Patrick, but he was only able to catch a glimpse of him in the corner of his eye. "You drugged me."

"How do you think we got you out in the middle of the forest?"

Neil laughed nervously. "Clever. The t-shirt in the tree was a nice touch."

"Adding the word 'killer' was my idea," said Patrick.

Neil glanced to his left, finding Rob leaning against a tall six-drawer dresser. There was a bandage around his thigh; a large crimson stain colored the white cloth. A small framed photograph and a clock were the only things on the dresser. It was an old-fashioned alarm clock with a round face and two silver bells on top, reminding him of Mickey Mouse. "How'd you know I'd come here?"

"We made you come here. It was all about making you think this was your only safe option," Steve said. "We knew you were in the back of Rob's truck. Did you really think hiding under that tarp would fool us? It was just a matter of making you think all other escapes were cut off."

"Face it, Neil. We've been fucking with you all weekend," Jeremy said. "There hasn't been a moment this weekend where you weren't watched by at least one of us. We knew where you were and what you were doing the entire time. We just needed to nudge you in the direction we wanted you to go."

Neil shifted in his chair. The hard seat was uncomfortable. His shoulders burned from being pulled behind his back. He looked toward Sammy who still stood before the window, staring out. She was still wearing the beige shorts and pale blue t-shirt from earlier. Something crept out from the deepest recesses of his memory. A recurring image that finally answered a question that he'd been asking himself throughout the weekend.

"It was you!" he exclaimed. "You were the one in the forest wearing the red ball cap. And the canoe! It was you in the canoe, wasn't it?"

No one said a word. Glances passed between Patrick and Jeremy. Jeremy simply raised his eyebrows and shrugged his shoulders. Sammy didn't move or speak, only continued to stare out the window.

Neil shook his head, as much in disgust as in understanding. The movement renewed the painful ache in his scalp. He gave the cords around his wrists another tug. They were snug, with no give at all. "You guys going to untie me now?"

A hand fell on his shoulder, and he felt Steve lean over from behind. Turning his head, Neil saw the smiling face. "No, Neil," Steve said. "We're not done with you yet."

At the menacing edge in Steve's words, Neil felt his chest tighten. After all that had happened, the thought of what else they might have in mind frightened him. He understood how his friends might find amusement in some of what they'd done early on, but they'd crossed that line, going from harmless diversion to alarming malice. He wondered if he'd ever crossed that line. Had his actions ever been just as alarmingly malicious? "This isn't funny anymore. You've had your fun. I think it's time you let me go."

Jeremy crossed to the bed, sitting down on the edge, the comforter rumpling beneath him. "Our fun's just beginning."

"Look, I'm sorry for what I did. And sorry you guys were here when Stinky killed himself," Neil said. "I can't help that you all lived with that for eighteen years. That was out of my control."

Stepping out from behind the chair, Patrick turned to face him. "You still don't get it, do you? You honestly don't get it."

Neil was forced to admit that the statement was true. He couldn't understand why they'd gone to this much trouble just to get even with him. It had been eighteen years and, to him, Camp Tenskwatawa had been ancient history. Had his friends clung to their anger and hatred all this time? He simply didn't understand why.

"That last night. That announcement you made. You

thought you were just pulling another prank on Chris," Patrick said. "But did you ever stop to think about the other counselor? About what your little prank did to him? What it did to me?"

Neil's eyes opened wide as Patrick's words sank in. "You?"

"Chris and I, we were a godsend to each other. We understood each other's struggles, knew what the other was going through," Patrick explained. "We never meant for things to get intimate, but they did. Then you had to come along and read his diary."

"You're gay?"

"Bravo, Sherlock!" Patrick said, raising his voice. "You've finally put all the pieces together." Patrick paced the small space before Neil while the others watched on in silence. "Yes, I'm gay. Or, as you always used to say, a flaming faggot. You laughed at me because you thought I was 'saving myself for marriage.'" He stopped pacing and leaned down into Neil's face. "I didn't know who I was . . . or what I wanted. And the only person who understood what I was going through was taken away from me . . . by you."

The dark malevolence in Patrick's eyes gripped Neil's soul, seeming to strangle it with fear. There was no mercy behind the cold stare, no sign that a reprieve would be forthcoming. He struggled against his bindings, squirming and pulling on the cords.

Steve leaned over Neil's shoulder. "Unlike you, we didn't abandon each other after camp. If anything, sticking together was the only way we each survived."

Jeremy said, "Cinco Amigos became Cuatro Amigos."

"We didn't know how to reach you at Harvard," said Rob. "We left dozens of messages with your parents, but you never called any of us back."

Neil bowed his head. His parents had passed on every message. He had simply thrown them in the trash.

"Patrick was a mess for years," Steve said. "We rallied around him, helped him get through it. That's what friends do." He paused for a moment, and then added, "I guess you wouldn't know about that."

Neil shook his head. "I'm sorry. How was I to know Stinky was suicidal?"

Patrick turned on him and, in a blur of rage, plowed his fist into Neil's chin. The pain at the back of his skull went from a being a dull throb to a fiery burning in an instant. "His name was Chris!" he yelled.

Neil tasted blood, realizing that the punch had split his lip. He tried to remain calm. It was futile to make any further attempt to get any of the guys to release him, Neil decided. They were hell-bent on revenge. That left him with only one other place to turn for help, one other person who might show him sympathy. "Sammy, how can you just stand there and let this happen?"

Sammy remained silent, gazing out the window. She hadn't said much during the whole exchange, and she had never turned to face him.

"Come on, Sammy. After the other night? I thought we had something special."

"The other night? You have no idea. It took every fiber of my being to keep from vomiting the moment you touched me."

The spiteful words seemed extrinsic coming from her, leaving Neil struggling to believe that she'd just spoken them. "I don't understand."

"I needed to get you to have sex with me to make our plan work," she said. "So, I took one for the team. I'll admit it wasn't all that difficult of a task. At least *you* hadn't changed in that regard."

"But why? What did all this have to do with you?" Neil asked.

Sammy turned from the window and faced him. Her eyes were cold, emotionless. She wore no makeup, and her skin was pale. There was an apathetic expression on her face, like she was beyond caring. She seemed to have aged ten years in the past twenty-four hours. Neil was shocked at how prevalent the frown lines at the sides of her mouth had become. He didn't remember seeing them before. A few rogue strands of Sammy's auburn hair had come unraveled from her ponytail and fell across her left eye. She didn't push it back, didn't even seem to notice. Her frosty eyes locked on him, and she said, "Chris Bateman was my half brother."

CHAPTER THIRTY

Sammy remained silent while her words sank in. Neil's gaping mouth and wide eyes told her that he hadn't been prepared for her revelation. To her surprise, she found pleasure in his shock, a sadistic pleasure, but pleasure nonetheless. She decided to hold the silence for a few moments longer just for effect.

"A little confused?" she said. "My father married Sylvia Bateman. She already had a one-year-old son named Chris. I was a honeymoon baby, as my father used to say." She crossed to the bed, sitting down next to Jeremy. She paused, feeling a somber nostalgia that bordered on heartbreaking. She'd not planned on telling her life story, but the words flowed without thought or consideration. "Mom died when I was seven—breast cancer—they didn't catch it in time. It hit Dad hard. Less than a year later, he was laid off from the refinery. Those two things alone nearly killed him."

She fell silent. Her gaze drifted to the floor. She

couldn't bear to look at Neil. She'd imagined this moment so many times, rehearsing the words that she would say. Her speech was going to be full of vindictive fury. Cold and emotionless. But she became lost in the past, recalling memories too painful to remember but too precious to forget. Jeremy placed his arm around her shoulders, drawing her close and giving her a gentle squeeze. His embrace brought her back to the present, providing the momentary comfort she needed to continue.

"When they offered my father the caretaker job, he wasn't going to take it. The pay wasn't all that great. But it was Chris who convinced him otherwise," she explained. "The three of us needed a fresh start, away from everything that reminded us of Mom. Yeah, there wasn't much money in it, but the job came with this cabin." She paused for a moment, and then added, "We were happy here."

"I had no idea . . ." Neil began to say. She heard his voice crack, and his words seemed to get stuck in his throat.

"That's how Chris wanted it. It was his idea not to tell anyone that Dad was his stepfather. He was afraid the other counselors wouldn't accept him, that he wouldn't fit in," she said. "He never even told me he was gay. I didn't find that out until your announcement, like everyone else."

The room fell silent for a moment; the only sound she heard came from the clock sitting on the dresser. It seemed so loud, louder than Sammy had ever noticed before. How many times had she sat in that room? How could she have never noticed how loud the clock was? She counted off the seconds with each tick, being reminded that each one passed so quickly—how lonely each one made her feel. There had never been so many people in this room before, yet it seemed so empty, so lonely. How many seconds had passed since Chris had died? Millions?

Billions? Could she have sat here and counted them all?

Sammy rose from the bed, crossing back to the window, and gazed out into the sunny morning.

"I came back in 2003 to tell Charlie how sorry I was. The guilt had been tearing me apart for years," Steve said. "I needed to clear my conscience, to somehow feel absolved from my part in his death. I don't expect you to understand, but I know what you . . . what we did over those three summers was partly to blame."

She fingered the St. Christopher medal around her neck. Chris had been wearing it the night he died. It had become a token of her anger. Reminding her that she had unfinished business.

Jeremy said, "I returned in 2004 for the same reason."

"We all came back," Rob said. "Except the celebrated Neil Brewster."

"Every one of us took responsibility for our part in Chris's death," said Patrick. "Except you."

Sammy turned around, leaning back against the window frame. She remained silent while the others passed judgment upon Neil. This was their time. Hers would come later.

"How could I?" Neil said. "I didn't even know he was dead."

Patrick leaned forward. "You wouldn't have come back even if you had known." His words spilled out like venom. "It's only ever about you, only ever about Neil Brewster! As long as Neil Brewster gets what he wants, it doesn't matter who gets hurt in the process! Isn't that your philosophy?"

Sammy waited to hear Neil defend himself, waited to see what he'd say. She knew that there was nothing he could say that wouldn't sound trite, that wouldn't sound like a lie. Any denial that he brought forth now would just sound repugnant. But to her surprise, he remained silent. He offered no defense for his actions. She found it curious. Could it be that he finally understood? Finally saw that there was no justifying what he'd done? She studied Neil's face closely. The wide-eyed look of shock she'd seen earlier vanished, to be replaced by a sad look of contemplation. The corners of his frown lost their anger, curving down in mournful realization.

"And the penny drops," said Rob.

"I'm sorry," Neil muttered. "I'm so sorry."

Steve stepped out from behind the chair. "Here's our dilemma, Neil." He gestured to each person in the room. "We all know how much of a manipulative bastard you can be. We don't know if you're truly sorry, or just saying this to get us to untie you."

"I am sorry. I truly am," Neil said.

His words sounded sincere, and Sammy had no doubt that some part of him meant it. But it was too late for apologies, too late for repentance. He'd lied to her before. Besides, she'd come too far to back out now. Too much was at stake, and she'd committed herself to seeing this through to the end.

"Look, I know there's nothing I can say to convince you," said Neil.

She heard his voice faltering. He must have realized how dire his situation was. She wondered if he'd figure out what was coming. Was he still holding on to some shred of hope that he would escape unscathed?

"You have to believe me. I never realized . . ." he said.

"Realized what?" asked Steve. "How much of a prick you are?"

Neil nodded his head. "If that's what you've been trying to get me to realize, you've done it."

"It's about time. It only took eighteen years," said

Steve.

Sammy heard a sigh of relief escape from Neil's lips. Perhaps he thought that it was over. If only he knew.

"Good. Now untie me so I can go home."

Jeremy smiled. "No, no, no. It's not that easy, Brewster."

"We've got plans for you," Patrick said. "You see those?" He gestured toward the ceiling and then to the wall beside Rob. Sammy didn't need to follow their gaze to know what Patrick was talking about. Her recollection of the afternoon that she and her father had installed the metal hooks was still vivid. She felt a momentary pang as she recalled her father's words.

"I don't want any part of this. Chris would never want to be remembered in this way," he had said.

At the time, she'd felt betrayed, felt as if he was abandoning her. She'd quarreled with him, trying to persuade him to change his mind. But, in the end, he left the cabin, driving himself back to the motel. Left alone, she'd broken down, crying loudly in the empty bedroom. Eventually, she'd pulled herself together, determined to see things through with or without her father.

Jeremy said, "Heavy duty, aren't they? When mounted into a stud, they can hold up to three hundred pounds."

"Neil, how much do you weigh?" said Rob.

Sammy heard Neil gasp and watched his eyes widen in terror. She didn't need to be a psychic to read what was going through his mind. He must have reached the obvious conclusion that the entire weekend was a prelude to a lynching.

"This is it? Lynching *me* isn't going to bring him back," Neil said.

The time had come for Sammy to set the record straight, at least as straight as she could be in present company. She turned her back on him, gazing out the window once again. "Neil, it's not just about Chris. When my half brother killed himself, it broke my father's heart. The man he was died that day, and I spent the rest of my life watching him walk around like a dead man. You destroyed his life, as well as mine." She paused to gather her thoughts. She'd rehearsed this speech so many times, yet it was still hard to find the words. "After news of Chris's death got out, parents pulled their kids out of the camp. Although things got better, the camp never fully recovered. Your actions ultimately destroyed this camp as well." Sammy turned from the window and stared at Neil. "Your friends have carried the responsibility on their shoulders for eighteen years. A responsibility that you should've shared. Unlike you, they've admitted their part and accepted their share of the blame. Now it's time for you to make amends."

Jeremy and Patrick stepped forward, one on each side of Neil. Clamping their hands on his arms, they lifted him from the chair. He struggled to break free, pulling to and fro, but their grip was too strong. Steve pulled the chair away from behind him.

"NO! WAIT!" Neil shouted. "I'M SORRY! I DIDN'T KNOW! I SWEAR!"

Sammy blocked out his pleas. She didn't want to hear his apologies any longer. Even the sound of his voice was beginning to grate on her last nerve. She watched Neil struggle against Jeremy and Patrick's restraint. It appeared that panic had finally overtaken him as he thrashed against their firm grips on his arms. He must have understood that he had few options even if he did escape.

"PLEASE! DON'T DO THIS! I'M BEGGING YOU!" Neil shouted.

His struggle was getting desperate. He kicked out at Jeremy's legs and twisted frantically at his bonds. He'd never get loose. She'd tied the knots herself, making sure they were tight. Neil jerked to the left and right, lurching his body against his captors. Blood trickled down his right forearm where Patrick's fingers had dug deep into his skin. She wondered if Neil had ever had to fight this hard for something before in his life. As he continued to struggle, Sammy watched a form emerge from the shadows by the door. Steve stepped forward, snaking his arms under Neil's armpits and forcing his bound hands above his head, just behind his neck. Neil yelped loudly when Steve wrenched backward on his arms. His face contorted in pain, and his struggling ceased.

"Rob," Sammy said. "Get the rope."

CHAPTER THIRTY-ONE

The hangman's knot had already been tied in the rope when Rob pulled it out of the bedroom's small closet. The rough fibers of the manila hemp formed tightly woven strands, which Neil knew could rip the skin from his neck. He renewed his struggles, but his three captors held firm, their grip never faltering. Rob tossed the rope up through the ceiling hook, and it came to rest in the crook. The noose hung down before Neil, rocking back and forth, ominous and frightening. He gazed through the loop and saw Sammy's face framed by the thick tan fibers. She stared back at him, her eyes vacant and dark. Gone was the beautiful, vibrant woman who he'd slept with the night before. Instead, Neil was staring into the frigid face of a woman he didn't recognize.

"Get the stool," she said.

Rob limped to the closet again, pulling out a small step stool. Setting it down before Neil's feet, he grabbed the other end of the rope and moved back to the wall.

"String him up," said Sammy, her voice absent of any feeling.

"With pleasure," said Patrick, tightening his grip on Neil's arm.

In desperation, Neil kicked at the stool, sending it sliding across the room. Using her foot, Sammy stopped the stool before it hit the far wall. Again, Neil struggled to break free, until Steve wrenched back on his arms, inflicting a grueling pain into his shoulders. He let out an agonized yelp.

"This'll be easier on all of us if you don't fight," Steve said, close to his ear.

"Easier for you maybe."

Sammy moved the stool back into place and held it firm with her foot. Jeremy and Patrick tightened their grip and lifted Neil off his feet, moving him over the stool. When they set him down, his feet landed square in the middle of the stool. Steve released his arms as the noose fell over Neil's head, the coarse fibers jabbing him in the neck. The hangman's knot slid down until it rested against the back of his neck.

"Please. Don't do this."

From the corner of his eye, Neil watched Rob loop the other end of the rope through the hook on the wall. A quick tug caused the harsh cord to rake up his neck until it caught beneath his chin. Rob continued to pull on the rope until Neil was forced to raise himself up on his toes to keep from being strangled. His toes began to tremble almost immediately, either under the pressure or from fear. He wasn't sure which. Tying the rope to the hook in the wall, Rob gave the taut cord a gentle slap, sending vibrations up to the ceiling and down to Neil's neck.

Releasing his arms, Jeremy and Patrick stepped back, leaving Neil to stand precariously on the edge of death.

The sweat on his forehead ran down into his eyes, but he was unable to wipe away the burning moisture. The rope's pressure on his jaw forced Neil to hold his head high, making it a challenge to look at the others.

"What are you waiting for?" Neil asked. It was his attempt to sound brave, but he wasn't even able to convince himself. "Let's get this over with."

Patrick replied, "I think you misunderstand, Neil. We're not going to kill you."

Neil tried to shift his head, but the move only served to constrict his throat. "What? Stop messing around and tell me what you're going to do!"

Steve stepped closer and jabbed him in the stomach. "If you're going to die, you're going to do it yourself."

"Can you see that clock?" Rob asked, gesturing to the alarm clock on the dresser. "Maybe not. We'll move it some place where you can see it. It's closing in on half past seven. We're going to give you twenty-four hours to live or die."

"We're going to leave you here. In twenty-four hours, we'll call the police—anonymously, of course—and tell them where they can find you," said Jeremy. "Whether you're dead when they get here will be up to you. If you can keep from falling asleep and hanging yourself, then you'll get to go home to your fiancée, your partnership, and your perfect life. Of course, if you fall asleep, or give into your guilt . . ."

Patrick interrupted. "That's what I'm hoping for."

"You can't do this to me," Neil said.

Sammy moved closer. "We can, and we will."

Neil tugged at the bonds around his wrists, but the movement caused the noose to draw a little tighter around his neck. "This is ludicrous. I'll just tell the cops who did this. They'll be knocking on your front doors in no time."

"That's where you're wrong, Neil," said Steve. "Do you really think we'd plan all this without protecting ourselves?"

"We made sure we had alibis for this weekend. No one knows we were here," said Jeremy.

Rob smiled. "Besides, you won't tell the cops anything."

Neil tried to twist his neck to glare at Rob without much success. "And why not?"

"Because if you do, you'll lose everything. Your fiancée, your partnership, and maybe even your job," said Steve.

Sammy reached out, gently touching Neil's stomach. She twirled her fingers making figure eights on the fabric of his t-shirt. "I suspect that Mr. Waldstein wouldn't take kindly to knowing that his soon-to-be son-in-law was screwing around behind his daughter's back. My guess is he'd come down pretty hard on you if he ever knew about our little tryst this weekend."

Despite trying to add a defiant edge to his laugh, it came out nervous and unsettling. "It'd be your word against mine. Why should he believe you over me?"

Stepping back, Sammy stared at him through narrowed eyes. "It's amazing what you can do with cameras these days. They're so small, you can hide them practically anywhere."

The bottom dropped out of Neil's stomach, and he suddenly felt ill. "You're lying!"

"Every single second is on video," said Sammy. "Even the moment when you told me you loved me."

He swore under his breath. Neil had forgotten about that. It had been in a moment of recklessness, a moment of climatic ecstasy. He vaguely remembered her legs intertwined with his and their naked bodies thrusting in rhythmic synchronicity. The words had been uttered at the height of passion, spoken more in the moment than out of any emotional meaning. Nothing had been meant by them, she should have known that. But it didn't really matter now. It had been said, and it had been recorded.

Neil knew she was right about all of it. Old Man Waldstein treated him like the son he never had, but one hint of infidelity would bring that to an end in an instant. Waldstein had always been very protective of his daughter, and there was no way that he would ever stand for a scandal. He would be out on his ass without a moment's hesitation. And it wouldn't end there. Waldstein was well connected. He'd ensure that Neil would never work in New York City again. Waldstein was a valuable ally to have on your side, but if crossed, could be a devastatingly powerful enemy. Neil would be lucky if he could get a job as a public defender, a fate worse than death.

Patrick laughed. "I think he finally gets it."

As he glared at Sammy, his sense of betrayal must have been evident in his eyes. "Don't be angry, Neil," she said, her voice feigning pity. "It's not like sex with you was all that good anyway."

"You bitch!" Neil lashed out, struggling to free his hands. The rope around his neck chaffed under the chin, the coarse strands rubbing the skin raw. Every movement he made drew the noose a little tighter, reminding him that struggling only served to lessen his chances of survival. "The cops aren't idiots. Even if I don't tell them anything, they'll know someone hung me up here." He glanced toward Steve. "How long do you think it'll take for them to track this back to you?"

Steve's reply came in the form of a mischievous smile, telling Neil that he was still missing some pieces to the puzzle. "Wrong again," Steve said. "Everything we've told you has been a lie. The company I said I worked for? It doesn't exist. Our careers? Our lives? All lies. You don't know the first thing about any of us."

"The only thing that's true . . ." Sammy paused and closed her eyes for a moment, "is that my father died of a broken heart. Losing Chris destroyed him, and I had to watch Dad slowly go to pieces until there was nothing of him left." She fell silent, and her gaze seemed to drift away for a moment. Her eyes became wistful, not looking at Neil, but through him to another time and place. Then her eyes turned dark and cold once again. "When I found out what you'd done—how you had tormented Chris for three years—I burned for vengeance. But I couldn't do anything, not as long as Dad was alive. But after he passed away . . ."

"This began as a joke. We all came to pay our respects when Sammy scattered her father's ashes in the lake. We were the only ones here. One of us—I don't remember who—said we ought to track you down and give you a good fright," said Rob. "But the more we all talked about it, the more we each realized something drastic had to be done."

The room fell silent. They stood around Neil, each one's eyes conveying a different message. Behind Steve's blue eyes, Neil found a sense of pity. Rob's held indignation, while Jeremy's seemed impatient, glancing at the clock, then at the door, and back to the clock again. Fiery contempt raged behind Patrick's gray eyes, all of it directed at him. And then, there was Sammy, with her dark eyes filled with anguish. She seemed to be swimming in it, almost wallowing in misery. Neil knew it would be too much to hope that her sorrow was over him. Maybe she wasn't as sure about this as she let on. Maybe she was having second thoughts, and she'd change her mind, insisting that the others let him go. He knew the chances were slim, but it didn't hurt to hope.

"It's time we left," Steve said, moving toward the bedroom door.

Patrick stepped closer, looking up at Neil with a sneer. "You're getting off lucky, Brewster," he said. "I still think we should have killed you."

Rob picked the alarm clock up off the dresser and carried it to the bedside table. Positioning it where Neil could see the clock face, Rob glanced at him, and then passed by quietly, avoiding eye contact as he exited the room.

"You're all gonna burn in hell for this," Neil said.

Giving him one final look as he left the room, Jeremy frowned and shook his head. "Don't worry, Neil. We'll follow you down."

CHAPTER THIRTY-TWO

"You can't leave me here like this!" he shouted.

The only reply was a faint grating sound as the branch of a pine tree brushed against the small square window across the room. There must've been a light breeze outside, but all he saw were the pine needles tapping on the smudged panes of glass. He knew that shouting was an exercise in futility. If anything, it just made matters worse. Too much movement just caused the noose to tighten and constrict around his neck. The margins between life and death were too slim to risk any further reduction. He decided to conserve his shouting for a later time when it would be more fruitful. But then . . .

"Help! Get me out of here!"

No one was there to hear him, and even if someone was, he knew they wouldn't help him. Neil was alone. Just him and the alarm clock, counting down the seconds with an incessant ticking.

He'd lost track of how long he'd been shouting.

Perhaps thirty minutes, maybe more. They had to be gone. Even though Neil hadn't heard any cars drive away, the utter silence in the house drove home the fact that he was alone. Despite all that had happened and all that was said, he still clung to the hope that this was all just a prank, and they'd be back any minute to release him. But as the clock continued to mark the passing of time with its irritating regularity, his hope diminished.

As the first few hours passed, Neil remained confident that he'd beat this. He'd recalled many all-nighters from his time at Harvard. Being up for twenty-four hours or more cramming for a big exam had sometimes been the norm for him. He seemed to remember thirty-six hours being his all-time-record . . . without drugs. With drugs? That was a whole other story. Back then, he hadn't been averse to taking a little speed to keep himself going. What he wouldn't give to have some now.

Defiance permeated his every thought through the first hour. He wasn't about to give them the satisfaction of dying. In twenty-four hours, he'd walk out of this cabin with his head held high, knowing that he'd beaten them. He may never be able to avenge himself, but Neil would stand strong in the knowledge that he'd survived.

As the second hour passed and the third began, he felt the first cracks in his own bravado begin to show. His defiant determination began to fade. His stomach churned loudly, reminding him that he hadn't eaten since the previous day. His mouth had long since gone dry, leaving his tongue feeling pasty. He'd moved beyond just being thirsty to being desperate for some water. Like food, Neil hadn't had a drink since the prior evening's whiskey. The thought of that last drink caused him to shudder, remembering how it had gotten him here.

With each passing hour, the physical toll of Neil's

suffering was becoming more and more evident. His lower back ached from having to stand erect for hours. The coarse rope binding his hands scraped at his wrists to the point of bleeding. His arms and shoulders were stretched to their limit and sore. Neil's toes had been numb for hours, and muscle cramps had forced him to alternate from one foot to the other. Making matters worse, the small stool on which he was forced to stand wobbled every time he shifted his weight. More than once, the stool had almost slid out from under his feet, and only with some fancy footwork was Neil able to shift it back into position. As noon approached, he was feeling less certain about his chances of survival.

By one in the afternoon, Neil was forced to wet himself, and would have to deal with the indignity of facing the police with soiled shorts. The smell of urine was strong, acting as a constant reminder of the humiliation he'd face. But there was nothing he could've done. By two, he found himself nodding off, either from lack of food or the interminable boredom. He wasn't sure which. His eyelids were heavy, with each blink holding the potential to become something more. Falling asleep meant facing the grim reaper. Despite his weariness, he'd been lucky enough to catch himself each time, but as the day progressed, he grew more concerned.

Shortly after four, Neil broke down, unable to control his emotions any longer. The tears flowed freely down his cheeks, under his chin, and soaked into the rope around his neck. The physical strain, combined with the very real possibility of his own death, became more than he could handle.

From the window across the room, Neil watched the day pass, and then turn to night, the darkness beyond the glass being absolute. With the sun gone, his only light was the small lamp on the bedside table. The dim bulb burned beneath the white frilly shade, casting shadows throughout the room. He was grateful that they'd left the light on. He wasn't sure if he could have faced the night in utter darkness.

Sometime after eleven, Neil closed his eyes for a second. The second turned to ten seconds, and then to twenty. Just a moment's rest was all he needed. Just a quick moment of sleep. The rope's sudden contraction around his neck jolted him awake. He gasped for oxygen, but the coarse cord crushing his windpipe impeded his attempt. His body spasmed violently, fighting to cling to his last visage of life. *I'm going to die*, he thought.

Cutting deep into his neck, the rope refused to give against the downward pull of his weight. Pain shot down his neck and into his spine. He felt as if, at any moment, his head would be ripped from his body. What would kill him first? Suffocation or decapitation? His feet flailed desperately, searching for something—anything—to use to relieve the pressure on his neck. As he grew more desperate, the spasms grew more violent. While his lungs burned, Neil thought of Chris Bateman. *Is this what he endured in his last moments? Is this how it felt to be hanging from that tree?* The room was growing dim, his vision becoming blurred. *Is this the blackness of death come to swallow me up?*

Ready to give up all hope, Neil prepared to face what he'd come to realize was an inevitability. The spasms were beginning to subside, and his vision had all but gone dark. In another moment, he'd be dead. Then his toe touched something hard. Moments later, Neil was once again standing on the stool, his body trembling as he drew in long deep breaths.

That had been the closest he'd ever come to death. He

must've fallen asleep, just long enough for his legs to relax. The tears streamed down his face. Death had knocked on his door, and Neil had almost answered. His body ached from the ordeal, especially his neck, which felt like it had been ravaged. His thoughts returned to Chris Bateman. *Did he struggle as he hung from that tree?* Neil wondered if Bateman had had a last-minute change of heart but couldn't find a way to save himself. Or did Bateman simply allow the darkness to swallow him up?

How much despair must Chris have been in to reach the point where hanging was his only option? The question that had been swirling around in Neil's head for hours could finally be ignored no longer. Did he drive Chris Bateman to suicide?

He recalled putting the boy through hell for three summers, the final one being the worst. His mockery had been relentless, not giving the poor kid a moment's peace. When he'd reflected, forty-eight hours ago, on the things he'd done to Chris Bateman, he'd laughed. Laughed at his cleverness, at Bateman's humiliation, and at the boy in general. He'd rejoiced in his own sadistic cruelty, in the wretched way that he poured out his scorn upon Bateman. Feeling smug wouldn't begin to describe how Neil had felt. There had been an egotistical self-satisfaction that bordered on the extreme, one that revealed the true depths of his sadism. He'd laughed with amusement at every memory. But he wasn't laughing now.

He could deny it no longer, and to do so, he realized, would just have diluted his soul even further. Unlike in the courtroom, the burden of proof wasn't falling on the prosecution, it fell on him, the defendant, to prove that his actions had no influence on Chris Bateman's decision to take his own life. Neil's soul was on trial, and he was his own judge and jury. His heart became the prosecutor while his mind the defendant. The emotional versus the logical. The case against him was clearly spelled out, his acts of inhumanity paraded before the so-called court. With each, the prosecutor—his own heart—connected the dots one by one, drawing a direct line between his actions and Chris Bateman's death. There was a clear path leading to the inevitable conclusion that he couldn't be more guilty than if he'd placed the noose around Bateman's neck himself.

Neil's mind, unhampered by emotions, launched into diatribe of legal rhetoric, attempting to dismiss each piece of the prosecutor's case against him. It cited precedent after precedent, and challenged the evidence as circumstantial at best. His mind quoted statistics about suicide and worked to build an image of a mentally unstable boy who simply couldn't hack it in life. Could the accused be expected to take the blame for the death of someone who was obviously troubled to begin with?

After the closing arguments and a brief deliberation, the verdict was in. Guilty. Neil's heart, although hard for most of his life, had finally succumbed to the emotions that he'd kept in check for many years. His soul was convicted, and he was forever to be damned. His mind tried to appeal, but he knew the truth. His own actions had contributed to Chris Bateman's suicide. If he had not treated the kid like he had, Bateman might have been alive today. Chris Bateman hadn't deserved Neil's mockery or ridicule. The poor kid had done nothing to deserve the scathing conduct that Neil had so cruelly engaged in at Bateman's expense. There would be no acquittal. Now, Neil was serving out his sentence. Twenty-four hours of his own personal hell.

CHAPTER THIRTY-THREE

AROUND MIDNIGHT, NEIL began to recount out loud the events of the past forty-eight hours to keep himself awake. The details were still fresh in his mind, some still too raw to dwell on. As his solitary narrative unfolded, he wondered how he'd missed all the signs that pointed to the truth. How could he have been so foolish—maybe self-absorbed would be more appropriate—not to see what was coming, not to realize that he was being set up? Neil simply accepted everything his friends had said and gave no thought to any possible deception. He recited as much of the conversations that he could remember, and those that he couldn't, Neil made up with words that he thought seemed appropriate.

Trying to remember every detail in order was challenging. The level of emotional turmoil he'd experienced left the events a bit jumbled in his mind, and it took some effort to get them straight.

As the hours passed, and the sleep deprivation worsened, Neil found it more difficult to focus, often losing track of what he'd been saying. Words, sometimes, were hard to come by, and he found himself repeating the same thing over. His bleary eyes were dry and itchy, but he could do nothing to relieve the discomfort. He'd urinated on himself a second time, filling the room with the nauseating odor of urine. Some had run down his legs and soaked into his socks, adding to his irritation and humiliation. Perhaps that was their aim all along, to humiliate him in the worst way. He'd worked hard to cultivate a reputation for always being in control of every situation. When news of this got out—and it would get out—that reputation would be tarnished. There would certainly be whispers and laughs behind his back, and even a few to his face. Neil would have to endure a humiliation that he was unfamiliar with, but one that he'd too freely been willing to dispatch on others. There was no point in trying to fool himself into thinking that nothing would come of this. Word spreads fast among the attorneys in New York City, and this would spread like wildfire. Neil may survive these hellish twenty-four hours, but this would only be the beginning of a far worse hell that would begin when he returned to the city.

THE hands on the clock said 7:29, telling Neil that his nightmare was almost over. His head was spinning, his back ached, and his legs were numb. He was beyond the point of exhaustion, sliding toward delirium. Hours before he'd considered his best course of action when he was released. He realized that no one could ever know what really happened this weekend. Not Sheila. Not the police. No one. His friends had been right. His forthcoming partnership in the law firm, as well as his career, were too important to throw away simply to punish them for this weekend. For him, it would be a quiet return to New York, trying to forget everything. He'd live with the humiliation, hoping that no one asked too many questions. If he was lucky, it'd all blow over in a few months. Of course, there would be a police inquiry, but he'd just feign ignorance of the identity of the culprits and explain it all away as being a random event by an unknown assailant. Now with his ordeal coming to an end, Neil began to giggle uncontrollably.

As the clock hands reached seven thirty, he tried to calculate how long it would take for the police to arrive, but the numbers all seemed to run together. It can't be too long, he figured. Although exhausted, he was certain he could hang on a little longer. What's an extra few minutes compared to the past twenty-four hours?

Outside the window, all he could see were the thick intertwined tree branches. Neil couldn't see the road, the driveway, or anything else. It'd been all he had to look at for the past twenty-four hours.

He wondered where his friends were. How far away had they gone while he hung there? If everything they'd told him was a lie, there was a good chance that none of them lived anywhere near the camp. One could drive a long way in twenty-four hours. He could hire a private investigator to track them down, but what would that accomplish? Even if he could find each of them, what would he do? Exact his revenge? Neil knew, perhaps better than anyone, that he'd be hard-pressed to prove anything that happened over the weekend. It'd be his word against theirs. Five vs. one weren't good odds. It might be best to just let sleeping dogs lie. He gave the clock another look. 7:33. If they'd made the call at exactly 7:30, the police would be on their way. It was just a matter of waiting. Not long now. He giggled again.

The click seemed extraordinarily loud in the otherwise silent cabin. It was followed by a creak. His senses snapped back from the brink of delirium. Perhaps a door opening somewhere downstairs.

Someone must be in the house, Neil reasoned. That was faster than he'd expected. He couldn't help but breathe a sigh of relief. It would all soon be over. There'd be awkward questions to answer, but he'd had twenty-four hours to come up with a story. It was plausible, if not a bit simple, but Neil figured it would be enough to satisfy any of the country bumpkin cops in these parts.

Anxious to be freed, Neil decided to save his rescuers the time it would take to search the house. "Up here!" His voice was a bit hoarse, but he hoped it was loud enough. "Upstairs! Upstairs!"

He heard footsteps moving around the first floor. Why aren't they coming upstairs? They must not have heard him. "Upstairs!" The noose was making it difficult to shout any louder.

The footsteps stopped. They must have heard him that time. Just to make sure, he shouted one more time. "Upstairs! The back bedroom!"

The footsteps were moving again, sounding like a slow, methodical trek around the first floor. He couldn't tell where in the cabin they were. The kitchen, maybe. But they were down there somewhere. He wondered why they hadn't come upstairs yet. Surely there wasn't the need to search too hard. There weren't that many rooms downstairs, or even in the entire cabin. Neil had shouted as loud as he could. He couldn't believe that they hadn't heard him.

The footsteps grew louder. It sounded like they were headed to the front of the cabin, toward the stairs. Then he heard them mount the stairs. They moved slowly, seeming to take each step with deliberation and care. Neil grew impatient. To be so close to rescue and have to wait was intolerable. Why were they moving so slow? Couldn't they pick up the pace? Didn't they realize that he'd been here for twenty-four hours? Each footstep's deep thud sounded heavy, leading him to believe that his rescuer was wearing boots. One set of footsteps, one person, one cop. It didn't surprise him. Police departments out here didn't usually have many officers. For all he knew, this could be some part-time rookie, barely out of the police academy.

The footsteps reached the top of the stairs. Neil heard them outside the bedroom door but couldn't understand why they'd stopped. "Come in and cut me down!"

Everything went silent. No movement at the door, no footsteps. *What the hell's going on?* "Sometime today! I've only been hanging here for twenty-four hours!"

Still, there was no response. "Did you forget how to open a damn door? Just turn the knob!"

Nothing. Not a sound. Neil was certain someone was standing just outside the door. What were they doing? Waiting for a personal invitation? He didn't know who this cop was, but he'd be sure to report this to his superiors. He gave another glance at the clock. 7:36. "I know you're out there, just come in and cut me down!"

The door knob clicked. Neil tried to twist his head around to look at the door, but the tightness of the noose made it impossible. He heard the door creak open, and a faint draught crossed his shoulders, chilling his neck. "Thank god! Cut me down from this."

The footsteps crossed the room, stopping behind him. Neil sighed. "Thank god you're here. You've no idea what I've been through."

There was no reply. Just silence. Neil heard slow,

rhythmic breathing behind him. He knew someone was there. Why hadn't they spoken? His anger intensified. It was outrageous that he should be left hanging there when a police officer was standing right behind . . .

His thoughts paused as a new realization crept into his conscious. What if that wasn't the police standing behind him? His friends could drive a long way in twenty-four hours, but why? If there was a guarantee that Neil wouldn't finger them for the crime, why would they have to flee? But why come back? Maybe to see if he survived? He wondered if one of them had a change of heart and came back to release him. If so, their timing couldn't be worse. Why couldn't their sense of responsibility have kicked in hours ago? He wondered which one had succumbed to their guilt. He couldn't turn his head to see who it was. But perhaps he could catch their reflection in the window.

At first, he wondered if he was hallucinating. Neil recognized the face, but it was impossible. Older and heavier than he remembered, eighteen years had not been friendly to the man standing behind Neil. "You!"

The reflection continued to stare, first at the back of his head, then at the window so that their eyes met. The man remained stoic and expressionless. Not saying anything, just staring. "You were dead!" said Neil.

Silence. Neil heard the slow, measured breathing behind him, even a faint wheeze during exhales. But no words. "Are you going to just stand there and stare?" said Neil.

Still nothing. The sagging skin hung from the jaws, and the double chin seemed more pronounced than Neil remembered. The head had gone from balding to bald. The arms hung lifelessly at the end of slouched shoulders. The look gazing back at him was hard to describe. Puzzled, perhaps. Or maybe confused, unsure, or contemplative. Maybe deliberating. That's what it looked like. Deliberation. Neil had seen the same look hundreds of times on the faces of jurors and judges. It was deliberation, and Neil knew he was the one being deliberated over.

"I've been dead since the day Chris took his life." Charlie Wilcox's voice fluttered, as if he were anxious or scared. The soft-spoken man sounded older, more fragile than Neil remembered. Neil wanted to turn and face Wilcox, but his legs barely had the strength to keep him standing, let alone spin himself around. He'd have to settle for his reflection. "Was your death just another part of this charade?"

Wilcox remained silent, just staring at him. Neil grew impatient, infuriated. Hadn't he been through enough?

"You might say that it was a charade inside a charade."

Her voice was piercing in the otherwise silent room. Neil hadn't heard her come in. He couldn't see her reflection in the window and assumed she must be by the door. He caught a faint whiff of jasmine. Neil imagined Sammy, with her hair draping over her shoulders, standing within the door frame. Probably had her arms crossed, leaning against the jamb.

Wilcox turned away, walking slowly toward the door. "Where's he going?" asked Neil as he heard Wilcox leave the room.

"He's seen what I brought him here to see," said Sammy.

"You said he was dead."

"He's as good as dead. We'd been planning this a long time, but Dad began having second thoughts, deciding a couple weeks ago that he couldn't go through with it. He's been staying in a nearby motel. I convinced him to come this morning to see how much you'd suffered."

Neil felt the slightest of touches as she moved past him. She stepped between him and the window, turning to face him. He could only imagine what he must look like. His hair was probably wild, he hadn't shaved in days, and he'd pissed his pants. Did she realize how humiliated he was feeling? "Why've you come back?"

A smile formed on Sammy's face, the same one that once teased him in his childhood. But the eyes were different, darker and more malevolent. "To see you one last time."

"End this . . . please. I'm exhausted. I'm filthy. I want to go home." He knew it was probably the truest thing he'd ever said. "Get me down, please."

"Do you remember my father? Not the man you just saw, but the man he was eighteen years ago?"

"Uh, maybe."

"Describe him."

He didn't know what she was playing at. He assumed that he was meant to suffer a little longer. "I don't know. He was . . ." Neil stalled. His head was swimming, probably from a lack of sleep. What should he say? The only thing he recalled was thinking that Wilcox was a moron back then. Just an ignoramus who wobbled around the camp fixing the shit that Neil and his friends broke. He'd never been kind to the old caretaker. Now Sammy wanted him to describe her father. What should he say?

"Handy with tools." Neil was grasping at straws. "Good at fixing stuff. Look, can we talk about this after you get me down?"

"Tell me more."

What did she want him to say? Should Neil tell her how he had made her father change dozens of light-bulbs by destroying them with a BB gun? Or maybe how many times he'd cut the ropes on the rope bridge? "More?

Sammy, I don't know what else to say. Can you just get me—"

"Tell me!" Her voice was like the crack of a whip in the otherwise silent room. The smile was gone, replaced by a steely grimace.

"He was . . . was happy to be here. Happy to be working at the camp." That's all he could say. He didn't really know what else she wanted to hear.

"Happy. That's an interesting choice of words. Very apt. He was very happy . . . until the day Chris died, the day my half brother died. From then on, I've done nothing but watch him spiral downward into a morose shadow of the man he once was." She looked down, examining something on the floor. Neil couldn't tilt his head to see what it was. "When my Mom died, he promised her that he'd take care of Chris, raise him to be a good man. It wasn't easy for him, being a single parent of two kids. But he did the best he could. After Chris died, he felt as if he'd failed." She paused for a moment, and then added, "Dad's got cancer. They'd given him only six months to live. He's had only one regret in life. That he didn't save Chris."

"I'm so sorry. I really am."

Sammy said, "You know why Chris never gave you up to the camp supervisors?"

He shook his head.

She looked away toward the window. "He was desperate to fit in. Always awkward in social settings, that was the Chris I remember. Just wanted people to like him. You and your friends were popular, and he was afraid that he'd be hated if he ratted you out."

She turned back toward him. Her eyes were looking at Neil again. They were dark, so very dark.

Sammy said, "My father and I started planning this when he got his diagnosis. Faking his death wasn't all that hard. We only needed to convince your four friends that he was dead. No one else needed to know." She half-smiled. "No need for fake death certificates and all that. Just a small fake ceremony and an urn full of ash. Easy enough. Even necessary, you could say, to get your friends to cooperate. Sympathy for a grieving daughter sucked them right in."

She'd tricked them. He'd known there had to be a reason they'd betrayed him. "You must be pretty pleased with yourself."

"Oh, they were all a little too eager to join in."

She was trying to shift the blame. Neil knew his friends better than that. They wouldn't have gone along with this if they'd known the whole truth. They just wouldn't, would they? They'd all been tight. They'd been best friends throughout their childhood. Granted, Neil hadn't seen them for eighteen years, but people don't change *that* much. Los Cinco Amigos would always be Los Cinco Amigos, right? They'd all agreed, follow you down. It had been their motto, their creed.

Neil's thoughts began to twist toward an unsettling truth. When he'd left that last year, he'd turned away from them. He'd left them behind . . . and they hadn't followed. They hadn't followed him, not like they always had. And, worse than that, they hadn't waited for him either. Neil came this weekend expecting everything to be the same, expecting them to fall in line behind him like they always had. He assumed that the power he had over them as a teenager would still be there, still reign supreme. He had thought they'd pick up where they left off. But they'd changed . . . and he had not.

Sammy was smiling like she knew what he was thinking. There was still an unanswered question lingering between them.

Neil had to know. "You come back to gloat? I've had all I can take. How many times must I say sorry? I admit it, okay? His death was my fault. Cut me down."

"It's confession time, Neil. You have a mysterious power over me, you know that? I've spent months planning this weekend, and I thought that I'd accounted for every detail." Her smile was gone. "But I didn't account for how I'd feel seeing you again. Eighteen years ago, I fell hard for you. I loved you. That night when you came to the cabin, it was a dream come true. I'd wanted you just as badly as you wanted me. But after you left that night, Chris came to the cabin. He knew you'd been with me." She turned and walked to window. She turned to face him, leaned back against the window frame, and folded her arms. Her eyes looked him up and down, and one corner of her mouth rose into a half-smirk. Her gaze left him feeling ashamed and humiliated.

Sammy continued, "He told me everything you'd done to him. I had no idea and didn't believe him at first. Thought he was just jealous. But . . ." Her voice faded for a moment. Then, she bowed her head. "I hated you after that night. Hated you for what you were doing to Chris. After his death, I spent years despising every fiber of your being. It consumed me, even breaking up my marriage. You destroyed everything in this world that I loved. My half brother. My father. This camp. My marriage." There was another pause. "But when you showed up here Thursday night, you stirred up some deep hidden desire. I had second thoughts about going through with our plan. But when we had sex the other night, it all became clear."

She moved back across the room. Slow and deliberate. So close now that he could feel the heat radiating from her body. Was she going to let him go? Her gentle touch was on his chest, so light and intimate.

"I never told your friends what I really had planned. They'd never have gone through with it if they knew. You asked me why I came back. I guess I owe you that much." She glanced at the floor, and then looked up into his eyes. "I've come back to be your guilty conscience." Her hand touched a small silver medallion around her neck, tugging hard on the chain. Funny, he'd never noticed it before. The chain snapped, and she allowed it to fall to the floor. "Neil, it's time for you to die."

EPILOGUE

THE SUN CREPT up over the trees, shining down on Lake Friendship. Sammy watched the light dance on the water's surface, blazing flames rolling with each ripple and wave. Her hands were buried deep within the pockets of her gray sweatshirt. The color had seemed somehow appropriate when she pulled it on the night before. It matched her mood.

A few wisps of her hair fluttered in the gentle breeze blowing across the lake. The air was crisp and moist, the result of a passing shower in the middle of the night. It hadn't taken long for Sammy to find the loose board where Neil had stashed Chris's diary. The discovery of the small leather book brought with it a compulsion to be read, and read it she did, finishing it around four in the morning. Afterward, she'd sat listening to the sound of the rain pattering against the roof and window of Redwood Lodge, remaining in the cabin until sunrise.

The turning of each page drew a picture of a Chris Bateman Sammy had never known. So much had happened during those last three summers that Chris had never shared with her. She'd always thought they were close, but she had never known how much he was hiding. Depression. Isolation. The suicidal thoughts. The struggles with his sexual identity. She'd never realized how troubled her half brother had been.

He detailed each prank that Neil and his friends had played on him. It pained her to read each account and left her feeling as if she'd betrayed Chris because she'd fallen in love with Neil. But there was something more in the diary that disturbed her. Chris seemed to take a certain perverse pleasure in the abuse. It had become his way of feeling accepted. The pranks had been cruel to the extreme, but to Chris, they'd become an affirmation of approval from Neil and his friends. It was why he never told anyone about the abuse. He'd become a tormented soul, torn between his need for acceptance from his peers and his own humility. The incompatibility of the two had only served to foster the dark depression that had already taken hold, leading him down the path toward self-destruction.

She watched the water caress the beach with a gentle wave, lapping quietly at the sand. The diary hung at her side from limp fingers. How could she not have seen it? How could she not have known? Her infatuation with Neil Brewster had blinded her to everything else for three summers. Sammy cursed herself for allowing a teenage crush to distract her from seeing the truth. If she'd known, she wondered, could she have saved Chris?

As a brisk wind blew in her face, Sammy knew this would be the last time she stood along the edge of Lake Friendship. With too many memories lingering among the trees, she never wanted to see Camp Tenskwatawa again. There was nothing keeping her here. What had once been the best days of her childhood were forever tainted, leaving her with nothing but a mind full of guilt.

Sammy fished into her pocket for a lighter, and then, raising the book in front of her, ignited the corner of the diary. As the pages began to burn, she heard a car pull up somewhere behind her in the distance. She glanced over her shoulder, saw the Lexus stop by the edge of the parking area, and frowned. *Why is he here?* she wondered.

Holding the diary by two fingers, she watched the flames engulf the pages. When Sammy felt the flames nipping at her hand, she let the burning book fall to the sand. It continued to burn, the leather blackening. Footsteps approached, but she didn't turn around.

Patrick said, "Is he gone?"

"Yes."

He halted beside her, his eyes following hers to the burning book at their feet. "Is that—"

"Yes."

"Did you read it?"

Sammy could've told him the truth, but she didn't want him asking questions. It was hard enough for her to comprehend what she'd read in the diary. She wasn't about to burden Patrick with it as well. "No. Better to let his secrets die with him."

Wisps of black smoke drifted up from the smoldering pile of burnt paper and charred leather. Watching the flames dwindle into nothing, Sammy felt an emptiness sweep over her. Everything that she'd lived for was now gone. The smoking remains of the leather book were all that remained of her lifelong pursuit for vengeance, leaving her to wonder what she had to show for all her toil. So much had been lost, and she felt as if nothing had been gained. Her half brother was gone. Her father was gone. The man she once loved was . . .

Patrick said, "You gonna be okay?"

Without turning to look at him, she said, "It was the hardest thing I've ever had to do. Watching him suffer like I did."

"It couldn't have been easy."

"It just went on and on, as if it would never end."

"Are you glad it's over?" he asked.

Sammy turned from the lake. "Not sure I feel anything."

Patrick frowned, folding his arms. "I wonder where Neil is now. Probably back in New York, licking his wounds and cursing our names. Do you think he'll ever change?"

Sammy hesitated for a moment. "He could be at the bottom of the lake for all I care."

Patrick laughed. "We can only wish."

Sammy lips broke into a smile. She found the irony to be almost too funny. "Why'd you come back?"

"Don't know. Maybe to see if he'd survived." Patrick shrugged. "Was going to come back yesterday, but I decided to hold out in case any police were lingering."

She was quick to reply. "He wasn't here when I came back." Then she wondered, had she replied too quickly?

A strong gust of wind blew across the lake into their faces, forcing Sammy to close her eyes and turn away. When she turned back and glanced down, she found that the wind had blown the book's ashen pages across the lake's sandy shore line.

"How's your father doing?" Patrick asked.

She jerked her head toward him in surprise. "You knew?"

Patrick slid his hands into the pockets of his jeans. "Come on. Did you really think I wouldn't?"

"Did the others know?"

He shook his head. "I doubt it. How is he?"

She hesitated, remembering the heartbreak she'd felt when she'd returned to the motel to find that he'd left.

"Gone. He left a note. Said he loved me, but . . ." She paused to draw in a deep, emotional breath. "I'd gone one step too far, and he didn't want to see me anymore. He wants to die alone."

Patrick reached for her, drawing Sammy into an embrace. They stood quietly on the edge of the lake while she cried into his shoulder. When her tears subsided, she pushed away, turned her back to him, and folded her arms.

"He was right. All I've done is throw salt in an open

wound."

"It's over now. Time to move on."

Patrick began to walk back to his parked Lexus. He halted for a moment and turned back toward her. "There's one thing that puzzles me."

She looked at him over her shoulder. "What's that?"

"When we were playing football, Neil saw someone watching us. Wearing one of those red ball caps Chris always wore. And he claimed to see the same thing in a canoe on the lake. Was that you?"

Sammy shrugged. "No. Not me. You sure it wasn't one of the other guys?"

Patrick shook his head. "It wasn't us. Hmmm, maybe Neil was feeling guiltier than he was letting on."

He turned away and walked to his car. Pulling the door open, he looked down at her. "You leaving? I can drive you back to the cabin to get your car. Maybe we can grab dinner?"

Sammy looked at Patrick and smiled. It was time for her to leave. There was no point in remaining any longer. "Yeah, give me one second. I've got something I have to do."

She walked to the water's edge. Fishing in her pocket, she pulled out a small cluster of keys. Gazing at them in her hand, her eyes traced the Mercedes logo on the topmost key. It, along with the rest, would no longer be needed. Sammy drew her arm back and threw them into the air. They spiraled out over the lake and splashed into the water about fifty feet from shore. A smile crossed her lips as she remembered what she said to Patrick just a few minutes earlier. *"He could be at the bottom of the lake for all I care."*

Sammy watched ripples race from the point of impact, forming ever widening circles on the water's surface. She whispered, "Farewell, Neil."

Her gaze drifted up to the opposite side of the lake, freezing on a solitary figure standing among the trees. She couldn't make out any details, but the red cap stood out like a beacon within the foliage. The sight of it made her shudder. Could it really be—?

A horn beeped behind her, making her jump. She glanced over her shoulder. Patrick sat in his Lexus, looking down at his lap, probably checking his phone. When she turned her gaze back to the opposite shore, the figure and its cap had vanished.

With her head bowed and her hands buried deep in her pockets, she turned from the lake and walked toward the waiting car. She slid into the passenger seat and pulled the door closed.

Patrick asked, "What was that all about?"

"Just laying a ghost to rest."

ACKNOWLEDGEMENTS

First and foremost, I want to thank my wife, Diane, for her love and support, and for "tolerating" this little habit called writing. Her patience and understanding of my need for "space" while I write is appreciated. I couldn't ask for a better partner on life's journey.

Thanks also to my editor, Cherrita Lee, without whom this book would be full of every grammatical error known to man. Her ability to add the polish to my work is indispensable. As always, it was a pleasure to work with her.

I'd like to extend my gratitude to the members of my critique group: Sara Badaracco, Michael Clarke, Karin Wandersee, Joan Hill, Ellie Searl, Christine Schulden, the "narrow"-minded Paul Popiel. Their criticism, both good and bad, was invaluable, particularly through some significant revisions.

Thanks also to Blenda Morris, Maggie Collier, Laura Fiorentino, Bill Bochow, and Sonja Bochow for being early readers of a "far from ready for primetime" version of this story. The value of their feedback was inestimable, and critical to the further development of this book.

I'm grateful to Grant Blackwood for his guidance and advice during and after ThrillerFest. He was instrumental in solidifying several key decisions related to the direction of the book.

And finally, thanks to Dayna Anderson and everyone at Amberjack Publishing for being willing to invest in me and my book. It is always gratifying to work with such a great group of people.

ABOUT THE AUTHOR

Born and raised in southern New Jersey, Michael Bradley is an author and software consultant. He has presented at IT conferences in the United States and in Europe, and his frequent travels have connected him with a variety of people in the US and abroad. When he isn't on the road, working, or writing, Michael hits the waterways in his kayak, paddling creeks, streams, and rivers throughout Delaware, Pennsylvania, Maryland, and New Jersey.

Before working in information technology, Michael spent eight years in radio broadcasting. He worked for stations in New Jersey and West Virginia, including the Marconi Award winning WVAQ in Morgantown. He has been up and down the dial, working as an on-air personality, promotions director, and even program director. His time in radio has provided him with a wealth of fond, enduring, and sometimes scandalous memories that he hopes to one day commit to paper.

Michael lives in Delaware with his wife and their three furry four-legged "kids."